A MIX OF MAGICS

ARUCADI, BOOK 3

E. ROSE SABIN

A MIX OF MAGICS

ARUCADI, BOOK 3

E. ROSE SABIN

ARUCADI ENTERPRISES, LLC
2019

A MIX OF MAGICS
E. ROSE SABIN
©2014
Reprinted 2019
ARUCADI ENTERPRISES, LLC

COVER ART BY IGOR DEŠIĆ, ©2018
https://igordesic.artstation.com/

ISBN: **0692295054**

ISBN-13: **978-0692295052 (Arucadi Enterprises)**

PROLOGUE

When he first came to the land, its bounty had satisfied his physical hunger. Heavily laden fruit trees offered tasty fruit the year round. He could gather an abundance of nuts fallen beneath the caronut trees. The fish in the stream were easily trapped. After he learned to make a fire using sticks and dry leaves, he feasted often on baked fish, roasted apples or peaches, and caronuts that burst from their shells when placed on the embers. Later he learned to trap and skin small game such as rabbits and squirrels to vary his diet.

The meadows and hills were fair with wild flowers the year round. They swayed in a gentle breeze sweet with their perfume. White clouds drifted gracefully across a calm blue sky. Birds sang from the trees; butterflies drank nectar from the blossoms.

With the passing of the years, the hot wind of his anger blew across the land, withering the fruit trees, making barren the nut trees, turning the flowering meadows to fields of sharp, sword-like grasses and then to stubble. The stench of decay replaced the fresh scent of blooming trees and plants. A pall of dust choked the air.

Game became scarce and fish avoided his traps. He grew gaunt with hunger But the land proved bountiful in another way. It provided him with plenty of time to practice magical arts, to test his abilities, to experiment and hone his power. And the less it fed his physical hunger, the more the land fed his rage.

Soon, very soon he would have the power to flee this lonely land and return from whence he came.

Then he would hunt down those who exiled him here and he would take his revenge.

CHAPTER ONE
A GOOD IDEA

Veronica slammed into the house and threw her schoolbooks onto a convenient winged-back armchair. She stormed through the sitting room and into the dining room beyond it. "Aunt Kyla," she called. "Aunt Kyla, where are you?"

"In the kitchen," came the answer.

She found Kyla, her guardian and honorary aunt, seated at the kitchen table, staring at a paper.

"Aunt Kyla, I can't stand that school another day! Pleeeease, you have to let me quit. Aunt Abigail and Aunt Leah can teach me like they used to. I learn more from them than I do from the stupid teachers at the stupid school. All the kids hate me. They make fun of my red hair and how short I am and they say I do funny things. If they only knew! But I haven't done anything to them. I swear I haven't. Not since I—"

Kyla had turned toward her halfway through her diatribe, and Veronica finally noticed her red eyes and tear-stained cheeks.

"Aunt Kyla, you're crying! What's wrong? You're not upset with me, are you?"

"No, no. I've just gotten very sad news." She swept her hand across the paper she'd been staring at.

"What is it? What's the news?"

"This letter," Kyla said. "It's from Lisbet's parents. You know the letter I wrote telling them of her death and asking them if they could come here for their grandchild. This is their answer." With thumb and forefinger as though touching something vile, she picked up the single sheet of plain white stationery and read from it. "We want nothing to do with the bastard child. You may drown it in a bucket if you wish. So far as we are concerned, we had no daughter, and most certainly we have no grandchild."

"How awful!" Veronica gasped, her own troubles forgotten. "As sweet as Lisbet was, how can her parents be so mean?"

Kyla shook her head. "It's the prejudice we too often encounter against the gifted," she said.

"But their own daughter! And a granddaughter they don't even want to see. That's so hateful."

"It's more fear than hate, I think," Kyla said. They're afraid of what they don't understand."

"Yes, I guess it's that way with the kids at school. But they aren't that bad. The kids can be mean, but they don't want to kill me or anything. At least, I don't think they do. But will they just get worse as they grow up?"

"They will if they don't learn any different. But they can learn—from you. If they see that there's nothing to fear from you, they may also decide there's no reason to hate you. Let's hope so." Kyla picked up the letter and shook it. "But the question we have to answer right now is what we're going to do about the baby."

"We can raise her, can't we?" Veronica asked eagerly. "Now that you found someone to nurse her, it shouldn't be a problem."

Kyla sighed. "It's a bigger problem than you realize. I have no experience taking care of a baby. Neither do Abigail and Leah, even if they could be persuaded to move back in with us. And Mayzie can't stay here all the time. Her husband wouldn't like that, and her little boy wouldn't either. Bennie needs his mother. Mayzie's only hired to nurse the baby. She will have to spend a lot of time here for a few months, but as the baby gets older and starts sleeping through the night, Mayzie won't have to stay nights and can even go home now and then during the days."

"Well, but we'll be here," Veronica objected.

"You'll be in school most of the day," Kyla reminded her. "And I have the responsibility of guiding the Community and teaching the new members to use their powers. Anyway, a baby needs a mother and a father, not a bunch of aunts."

Veronica subsided into thoughtful silence, brooding over what Kyla had said. Inspiration struck and she looked up, wiggling with excitement. "I have it!" she said. "You can write to Ed and Marta and tell them about the baby. They'd be the perfect parents for her."

Kyla thought in silence a few moments, considering. Then she smiled at Veronica. "You know," she said, "I think you're right. That would give me the reason I need to bring Marta and Ed here to Port-of-Lords." She rubbed her hands together and beamed. "Yes, that would solve several problems. It's a very good idea."

CHAPTER TWO
LETTERS

Marta had only to finish the Janlon baby's white silk naming-day dress and she'd have completed all her current commissions. She gazed pensively at the sewing machine Ed had bought her with his earnings as a hansom driver and smiled, knowing how proud it had made him to purchase it for her. This work, though, was too delicate to be done by machine. She took a seat by the front window and commenced hand-stitching lace to silk by the light of the afternoon sun. As she drew her needle gently through the delicate lace, carefully attaching it to the underlying silk, she thought how wonderful it would be to make a dress like this for an infant of her own. A pang of sorrow accompanied the thought. The only flaw in her marriage to Ed Robbins was her failure to conceive a child.

She and Ed had done well settling here in Sharpness. The town had proved hospitable, its people friendly. They'd found jobs quickly, and their new neighbors welcomed them without prying into their backgrounds. So they'd stayed, and for the first time in her life, Marta felt that she *belonged*. Only the lack of a child kept her happiness from being complete.

The window gave her a clear view of the walkway up to her house. She was intent on her sewing when she heard a cheery whistle and looked up to see Ed's cab and horse by the hitching post and Ed walking briskly toward the house. Quickly she put the silk and lace aside and rose to greet him.

He saluted her with a smile and a tender kiss. "Not much business this afternoon," he said, hanging his cap on the hat rack by the door. "I thought I'd come home and get an early supper. I've promised to drive the Kramers to Essell this evening for a lodge meeting."

"I wish you'd told me," Marta said, breathing in the warm, horsy scent that always clung to him. "I don't have anything ready."

"That's all right. I don't need much. I'll be invited in for a share of the buffet after the lodge meeting. A bit of smoked ham on a slice of the bread you baked yesterday will hold me till then."

She laughed and kissed his cheek. "You're easy to please," she said. "But you'll be home late, then?"

He nodded. "I won't get in until near midnight, and then I'll have to take care of the horses. So don't wait up for me."

She made a face. "I don't like that."

"They'll pay well," he reminded her. "Oh, and this should make you feel better." He reached into his coat pocket and pulled out a brown envelope. "This was waiting for us at the post office today." He handed it to her with a grin.

She glanced at the sender's name and matched his grin with a big smile. "It's from Kyla! I haven't heard from her in months. Why didn't you open it?"

"I wanted to wait and let you have the pleasure."

She tore into the envelope and pulled out the folded letter. A smaller white envelope fell out, and she put that aside to read the letter first.

Ed sat in his easy chair and she plopped down on his lap and read aloud:

"Dear ones,

"Sorry I haven't written in such a long time. I've been coping with Veronica—her schooling, her growing powers, and her volatile nature as she enters her teens. I'm always having to deal with complaints from the school she attends now. Abigail and Leah insist, though, that she needs the socializing with other young people, and I agree. She also needs instruction in subjects outside their areas of expertise. They continue to work with her at home, but at school she is studying advanced courses in science and mathematics. Part of the problem she has is, I fear, due to the instructors' conviction that 'young ladies' ought not to study such subjects and their consequent readiness to find fault with the least little infraction on her part. She does try, but being a high-spirited girl, she lets her back-talk get her into frequent trouble. Too often she speaks before she thinks.

"Well, I don't need to burden you with that, all the more because you may be tempted to say, 'I told you so.' I don't regret taking Veronica under my wing—not at all. She has wondrous talents, which I hope you will have the opportunity to witness soon for yourselves. Which brings me to the purpose of this letter. Not that I need a purpose, when I am so overdue in writing and have, after all, the obligation to keep in touch."

"When is she going to get to the point?" Ed asked impatiently.

"Soon, I think, but you know Kyla and her high-blown style. It probably comes from having a father who was a scribe." Marta went back to the reading.

"As I have told you in previous letters, I have gathered a fine group of people able and, unlike

Abigail, eager to receive power. Here in Port-of-Lords we have not encountered the sort of opposition we faced in Line's End, Dabney, and Carey. I meet with my trainees regularly, and some have become quite skilled at exercising their magical gifts, though none has displayed as much talent as Veronica."

"She's told me all this before," Marta muttered, looking up at Ed. "I'm afraid this is just another plea for us to come out there and work with her."

"Well, hurry and read the rest so I can grab my snack and be off."

"I'll hurry, but there's quite a bit more. Here goes:

"One of the first to receive the power gift and one of the fastest learners was a young woman named Lisbet. I believe I mentioned her in an earlier letter. Now I must tell you that we have lost her under tragic circumstances.

"Lisbet is from a wealthy family, and her parents arranged a marriage to a younger son of one of the lords of the port for whom the Port-of-Lords is named. She did not wish this marriage. She had a lover who was of a lower station. In defiance of her parents she ran away with her lover and wed him. The affronted suitor went after them, found them, and shot her new husband. Her family praised him for this deed, and they and her vengeful fiancé repudiated her. Homeless, she came to me in despair, and I took her in, though it made our small home a bit crowded.

"Lisbet was deeply depressed, and, what was worse, we soon learned she was pregnant. I hoped that having a child to care for would lift her spirits, but she grew even more despondent as the time of birth drew near. The baby, a little girl, arrived after long and hard labor that left poor Lisbet depleted of energy and will. Abigail and Veronica both tried to heal her, but she used her own power to resist them, having no desire to live. Despite all we could do, she faded away and passed from this life three weeks ago, her babe only days old.

"We got in touch with Lisbet's parents to tell them of her death and of the birth of their grandchild, but they wanted nothing to do with what they termed 'the bastard infant,' and left her care to us. I have secured the services of a wet nurse for the babe, but that is a temporary arrangement.

"Marta, I know how you and Ed have wanted a child. I wonder if you would be willing to take on the care of Lisbet's poor little girl. She is a normal and healthy baby, despite the frailty of her poor mother. I do not feel I can or am qualified to raise her. I've had no experience with infants (except for a brief time when Claid—but that's another story, and one you know), and I really have all I can do to see that Veronica is properly raised.

"In the hope that you will want to take and love this little orphan I have enclosed two railway tickets to Port-of-Lords. If your decision is contrary, you may return the tickets by the next post, and I will redeem them for their full value. But I pray that you will not say no to this child who so needs the loving parents that you and Ed would be.

"With the tickets, I have enclosed instructions for finding our house. I hope to see you within two weeks. And if you are grateful to have this beautiful little girl, there may be something you can do for me in return.

"Faithfully yours,

"Kyla"

Marta had read more slowly as she realized what Kyla was proposing. When she finished the letter, she gazed into Ed's face, hardly daring to breathe.

He took from her hand both the letter and the small white envelope that had accompanied it. From the envelope he withdrew two train tickets and a hand-drawn map. He stared at these for a moment, then met Marta's gaze. "Well, do we go?" he asked.

Wetting lips suddenly gone dry, she answered, "Of course we do." Then after a moment's thought, she added, "I can guess what Kyla wants from us in return. She'll try to keep us there in Port-of-Lords. We may have to do some very clever bargaining."

Veronica pounded on the door of the small apartment shared by Abigail Dormer and Leah Wesson. Not waiting for a response, she tried the door. Unlocked!

She burst in, waving a sheet of blue stationery. "Aunt Abigail, Aunt Leah, they're coming! Marta and Ed are coming. They're going to adopt Lisbet's baby."

Abigail hurried out from the kitchen, and Leah carrying a dust mop, came from the apartment's single bedroom.

"How did you get in?" were Abigail's first words.

"The door wasn't locked," Veronica said.

"Oh, Leah. How can you be so careless?" Abigail turned to berate her partner.

"Didn't you hear what I said?" Veronica demanded. "Marta and Ed are coming here. They'll adopt the baby."

"That's wonderful news!" Leah enthused, hurrying to embrace Veronica. "It will be so good to see them, and I know how happy Kyla must be to have found a home for the little one."

"Yes, and they'll name her, and we'll have something better to call her than 'the baby' or 'the little one'," Veronica said, hugging Leah, while Abigail marched past to lock the entrance door.

Abigail returned and pointed to the sheet of stationery clutched in Veronica's hand. "Is that her letter? May I read it?"

"Actually, it's from Ed," Veronica said, handing her the letter. "It's short. Just says they're coming, they want the baby, and it tells what day and time they expect to arrive."

Abigail perused the letter. "Hmm, says they'll be glad to see everyone. It doesn't mention me—or Leah. Ed probably still resents me for not telling him for so long that he's my cousin."

"Oh, Abbie," Leah said, slipping her arm around the older woman's waist. "Ed forgave you for that a long time ago. It's your guilty conscience that makes you read that into something he didn't say. You need to put it behind you. I know Ed has."

"Aren't you glad they're coming, Aunt Abigail?" Veronica asked, wrinkling her forehead in puzzlement.

"Of course she is," Leah answered for her.

"I'm happy for the little one," Abigail said. "I doubt they'll want to stay here in Port-of-Lords, once they have her."

"Aunt Kyla says they'll have to stay until the baby is weaned," Veronica said. "She keeps hoping they'll move here permanently."

"That would be wonderful," Leah said, smiling broadly.

"Well, yes, of course," Abigail said. "Kyla could use their help with the Community, now that it's growing so. But I'll warrant they won't want to do that."

Aunt Abigail always looks at the downside of things, while Aunt Leah looks at the bright side. I wonder how they manage to get along and even love each other.

Aloud Veronica said, "Well, I'm going to hope that everything goes so well that they'll like it here—the city, the Community, and being with us again—and they'll stay."

"Yes, we'll certainly hope that," Leah said.

Abigail handed Ed's letter back to Veronica. "It's been my experience," she said, "that the more you hope for something to go well, the more likely it is to go bad."

CHAPTER THREE
PORT-OF-LORDS

Neither Marta nor Ed had ever seen a city this large. They stood outside the railway station clutching their valises and staring at the tall buildings and teeming traffic. The salty, fishy tang carried on the wind alerted them to the nearness of the ocean, though they could catch no sight of it.

"Mister, for the last time, do you and the lady need a cab?"

Ed jerked into alertness. The man must have been calling out to him for some time.

"Yes, we do," Marta answered before Ed could recover.

The man ignored her. "Sir?" he said.

"Yes," Ed said and handed him the map Kyla had sent. The man took their valises and helped them into the carriage. "Your first visit to Port-of-Lords, sir?"

Ed agreed that it was.

Taking his seat on the front, the driver cracked his whip across the horses' backs, driving them into motion.

Ed frowned. He never found it necessary to beat his horse to make her go. When these horses plodded too slowly for their driver's liking, he applied the whip again, not lightly, but sharply across their flanks.

Guessing that the driver would not take kindly to a stranger's criticizing his methods, Ed forced himself to remain silent. When the driver again sent the lash across the horses' backs, the whip flew back and struck him across the face. His loud outcry was doubtless due more to startlement than pain, but it made Ed smile. The whip's behavior had been no accident. Marta had used her power.

The driver took them a little farther without any more use of the whip, and stopped in front of a neat white house in a somewhat rundown part of town. "This is your address," he announced. Ed jumped out and helped Marta down, since the driver made no move to do so. They picked up their valises, and Ed paid the driver a silver trium. Without an offer to give change or a thank you for the generous payment, he put the coin into his wallet and the wallet into his back pocket. As he climbed up to the driver's seat, the wallet lifted gently from the pocket and flew to Marta's hand. She extracted the silver coin and sent the wallet flying back into the cab, where the driver could find it later—if his next passenger didn't find it first and pocket it.

"He was robbing us," she said in response to Ed's disapproving look. "The way he treats horses and women, he has no right to that coin."

"Better we lose a coin than get arrested for stealing," he said.

She shrugged and marched up to the house. Ed followed more slowly, taking time to observe the crowded buildings and wrinkling his nose at the odors of fried sausage, onions, and garlic that permeated the air. Kyla's house stood out from its neighbors by virtue of its slightly larger size and much neater appearance.

The door opened before Marta could knock. Kyla threw her arms around Marta and drew her into the house. Ed waited, and in a moment Kyla reached out again, pulled him through the door, and enfolded him in a warm embrace. Then she drew away and looked up at him with a big smile. "Ed, you've grown a beard. It looks quite distinguished."

He grinned. "Marta says it makes me look older."

"I mean that in a good way. It makes people take him more seriously. And Kyla, you've cut your hair!" Marta touched the neatly bobbed brown hair that had hung below Kyla's waist when Ed had last seen her.

"Yes, Veronica talked me into it." She laughed. "I should say she shamed me into it. 'Aunt Kyla, long hair is so out of fashion here in Port-of-Lords.'" Kyla imitated a teen-ager's disdainful tone. "'You look like a country bumpkin with your hair hanging way down your back.' I said, 'Well, I *am* a "country bumpkin." I was born and reared in a country town even smaller than Carey, where you come from.' Her answer: 'Well, we live in a big city now, and we should look like it.'" Marta laughed. "After that scene replayed at least three times, I gave in and let Veronica cut and style my hair."

"How is Veronica doing?" Ed put in quickly, before the conversation about beards and hair could go any further. "And where is she?"

"She's at school. She'll be home in about an hour. She can't wait to see you. She begged me to let her stay home from school so she'd be here when you arrived, but I insisted that she go." A worried frown creased Kyla's brow for a moment. "She's doing well, but she's headstrong. When she's determined to do something, there's no dissuading her. Like about the length of my hair."

"Has she learned to control her power?" Marta asked.

"She can control it very well—when she chooses to do so," Kyla said, and quickly added, "That's most of the time. She certainly hasn't forgotten how dangerous it can be. She hasn't harmed anyone, but she has played some unkind tricks, mostly on classmates but occasionally on her teachers. She doesn't try them on me—she knows better."

Ed grinned but Marta shook her head. "She hasn't yet, you mean. She may get more rebellious as she gets older."

Kyla shrugged. "She may also grow wiser and more cautious once she makes the transition from child to woman. At fourteen she's in this in-between time that's hard on all of us—including Veronica herself."

"Maybe while we're here we can help you out with her," Marta said.

"That would be wonderful. I'm so glad you've come," Kyla said. "Four years without seeing you is far too long. Your letters just haven't been enough."

Marta bristled. "Well, considering that I could neither read nor write until Ed taught me, I think I do very well."

"You do indeed," Kyla said quickly. "I think it's wonderful how well you've learned. I was commenting on their frequency, not their content."

"Marta has so much sewing to do, she's busy all the time," Ed put in, remembering too well the heated bickering the two women so easily fell into and wanting to deflect it before they could get started. "We've both had all the work we can handle."

"I'm glad you've done so well," Kyla said, leading them to armchairs in the comfortably furnished front room. "But raising a child takes time. You won't be too busy, will you?"

"Of course not. We'll make time," Marta said emphatically. "We've come because of the child. Where is she?"

"She's in the back room, with Mayzie Tellent, the wet nurse I've hired to care for her. I'll have Mayzie bring her in."

Marta's hands trembled, making Ed suddenly aware of how sweaty his own hands were. He wiped them on his trousers before reaching over to take Marta's hand in his.

Kyla left them and returned in seconds, a tall, buxom young woman at her side. The woman held a blanket-wrapped bundle. Kyla pointed to Marta, and the woman lowered the bundle into Marta's arms and backed away.

From out of the blanket a tiny face peered up into Marta's, the deep blue eyes fastening onto hers. A smile dimpled the soft pink cheeks. A tiny hand reached out and clutched Marta's extended finger. "She's beautiful!" Marta breathed.

Ed could only nod. He reached to touch the tiny girl with one tentative finger, and found that finger clutched in her other wee hand.

"She likes you." Kyla laughed and added, "Both of you."

Could this tiny, adorable little girl truly be theirs? She had to be. Ed read that determination in Marta's face, and he felt it no less than she. He thought he hadn't minded not having a child the way Marta did, but this child awakened in him a protectiveness and love so fierce it rivaled what he felt for Marta.

His daughter. His daughter to be loved and cared for and provided for. To fill a void in his life he had not known was there until now. He lifted her from Marta's arms, held her to his face, and let her tiny fingers play in his beard. She was so soft, so fragile. He breathed deeply of her clean, new-baby smell.

Marta looked up at him, her face radiant. "Our little daughter," she whispered as though afraid to say the words.

"She is our daughter," he said firmly. "She must be."

The child cooed and gurgled in agreement.

"Does she have a name yet?" Marta asked without taking her eyes off the baby.

"No, we've left that to you," Kyla responded with a grin matched by Marta's wider one.

"She's a dream come true," Marta said. "Maybe we should call her Dreama."

"I like that!" Kyla said, clapping her hands. "It's perfect for her. We'll have to have a big Naming-Day celebration and invite the whole Community of the Gifted. I'm eager for you to meet them all."

Ed didn't care for that idea, but not wanting to argue, he just said, "Is the Naming-Day a big custom here? It's only observed occasionally in Sharpness."

"Oh, yes, here it's always done. The rite will establish you officially as the baby's parents," Kyla replied, then added, "It's a part of the state religion, and although we don't follow that, I've found it important to follow local customs when we can so that we blend in. You know all too well how much opposition some people have against the gifted. We try to avoid creating controversy as much as we can."

Marta frowned, but Ed understood all too well. He said, "We'll definitely want to do whatever it takes to make this little girl legally ours." Then he quickly changed the subject, Kyla's "we" having reminded him to ask about their other friends from Carey. "What about Abigail and Leah? I expected to see them here."

"They've moved into a flat of their own. They felt they needed more privacy, and we needed space for Mayzie and the baby. They'll be by when they know you've come."

"They're both well?" Marta asked.

"Oh, yes, though I have to report that Abigail is as cantankerous as ever. She doesn't even want to be part of the Community of the Gifted we've formed here because Leah can't be part of it, not being gifted."

The baby screwed up her tiny face and began to cry. Mayzie stepped forward—Ed had forgotten she was there—and said, "Shall I take her? It's time for her feeding."

With obvious reluctance Marta surrendered the baby into Mayzie's outstretched arms. The woman carried the baby into the back of the house.

Immediately the room where they sat felt empty, the child's absence creating a void. Ed found himself wanting to go after Mayzie, to beg her to return with the baby and feed her here.

"Mayzie is very good with her," Kyla said. "And she has plenty of milk, having just weaned her own child as she started nursing this poor little one. He was ready, and this one needed all her milk. I doubt we could have kept the baby alive if not for Mayzie."

"Oh!" Marta said. "What will we do when we leave? We have a four-day journey by train to reach home. And I can't think of anyone in Sharpness who could nurse the child. I wonder if Mayzie could—"

"No," Kyla said, smiling slyly. "Mayzie would never leave her husband and little boy. If you want the child, you'll have to stay here with me until she's weaned."

Marta stared, unbelieving. "But that will be months!"

"Yes," Kyla said smiling. "It will."

CHAPTER FOUR
PREPARATIONS

Veronica sat on the living room floor and played with the baby. Little Dreama. She liked that name. It fit the tiny girl, with her crystal blue eyes, her pink-cloud softness, and the hide-and-peek dimples in her cheeks. The name wouldn't be officially hers until her Naming-Day, but that didn't matter to Veronica.

"Dreama's really already your name," she told the baby, bouncing her up and down while the child gurgled with laughter. "It's just not official yet, but we don't care about that, do we?" She clapped Dreama's tiny hands together. "And we're going to hold the ceremony right here in our house, Dreama. And the whole Community will come here. Some of them haven't even seen you yet. And you know what? They'll all bring presents for you." She tickled the baby's stomach, inducing more laughter.

The house would be crowded with the whole Community gathered in it. Usually they met either in member Marchion Blandry's house because the wealthy merchant lived in a large house with an elegant living room that they all fit comfortably in, or they met at Petros Birge's home, which was also large. Petros lived with his parents, who were happy to see their crippled son take part in a group that accepted him and ignored his handicap. They generously turned the house over to him and his friends and went out for dinner or to see a play while the Community met. So having the Community come here would be different and exciting even if it wasn't as comfortable as it would have been to have the ceremony at Mr. Blandry's house or Petros Birge's.

Despite all the frantic preparations and all the extra work it meant for her, Veronica couldn't wait for the day to come. Not only, not even especially, because that day would confer on the baby her name and official personhood. Not even because Veronica had been granted the privilege of standing with Ed and Marta on that day and reading the name blessing from the *Breyadon*, though that prospect thrilled her.

She'd expected Aunt Abigail to do that, or Aunt Kyla. Among all those who'd received the gift of power, only she and Aunt Abigail could see as normal Arucadian what appeared to all others as unknown words and odd symbols. Aunt Kyla could sing over it until the words became legible for her, but they had decided that such singing would distract from the naming service. And Aunt Abigail had expressed her usual reluctance to use her power. So the honor had fallen on Veronica, much to her delight.

But the thing that most excited Veronica would come when Dreama's Naming-Day was over. Ed had promised to try to teach her how to travel to other places, other worlds. Maybe even a world of her own making!

Ed had created his own world, his "special place," as a refuge from an abusive father. He'd made it a beautiful world, with woods and hills, meadows full of flowers, and sparkling streams filled with fish. He didn't go there anymore, though. He'd taken an evil man there, a man bent on murder, a man whose gifts of power made him doubly dangerous. Veronica shuddered at the memory of Jerome Esterville and the harm he'd caused before Ed had transported him to that lovely but lonely place and left him there where he could do no more harm. Jerome was as wicked as his mother, the saintly Mother Esterville, was good. Veronica never understood how such a good woman could have such an evil son. It defied explanation.

Just as Ed's ability to create his own world defied explanation. His need had opened the way. Veronica had no such need, but she was certain she could develop the talent with Ed's help. There *was* a need, though it was Aunt Kyla's, not hers. And it was not to create a world but to visit that nexus between worlds where the Power-Giver existed as a mind sealed in a great crystal. Aunt Kyla explained that the Power-Giver, who had once been a mage named Alair, still channeled power to those who could receive it, but he no longer communicated with her through mindspeech. Aunt Kyla was desperate to find a way to reestablish that communication. She felt sure Ed and Veronica together had the power to visit the Place of the Sphere.

"And she's right, Dreama," Veronica said, tickling the baby again. "I know she is. I haven't told anybody but you, but I've practiced using my power to jump from one place to another, and I can do it. Once, I was going to be late to school. I was too far away to make it on time even by running as fast as I could. So I pictured the classroom and my desk and there I was! The teacher was just calling roll, and was she surprised when I answered to my name! She'd seen the empty desk just seconds before. But I pretended I'd been there all along, and since nobody had seen me come in, she couldn't prove I wasn't. It made her real nervous. She thinks, see, that I do things like that to torment her, but I don't."

The baby gurgled and laughed as though sharing the joke.

Mayzie came into the room. "Veronica, Miss Marta wants you to come try on the dress she's making you. And it's time for the baby's feeding."

"Time for Dreama's feeding," Veronica said, not moving. "Call her Dreama, Mayzie."

"It's bad luck to use the name before Naming-Day. I've told you over and over."

Veronica laughed. "That's a silly superstition. Even Aunt Kyla says so. We gifted don't believe in such things."

Mayzie sniffed. "You gifted don't believe in a lot of things us normal folk know to be so."

"You mean like the gods?" Veronica asked, feeling mischievous. Aunt Kyla had warned her not to tease Mayzie, but Aunt Kyla was out shopping. And Veronica did enjoy seeing Mayzie get all flustered.

"Hush, you know what I mean," Mayzie said, rubbing her hands together nervously. "It's not smart to mock the gods, whatever you think, young missy."

Veronica laughed. "Our Power-Giver is stronger than Ondin. His power isn't limited to just this one province. I'll bet he's stronger than all twelve undergods put together."

"I won't listen to such nonsense." Mayzie picked Dreama up and swept out.

Giggling, Veronica got up and went to the small room Marta had appropriated for her sewing. Marta was seated at her table with the lovely green dress spread out in front of her.

"I think this is ready to be hemmed," she said, holding the dress out to Veronica. "It's taken a lot longer than I expected. If I had my sewing machine here, I could have done it in a day."

Veronica smiled. She'd heard this same complaint every time she came in for a fitting. "Aunt Kyla does all her sewing by hand," she said.

"Yes, and your Aunt Kyla could have done this dress, but she knew I'd do a better job, even without the machine."

"She had to make her own dress," Veronica objected. "And Mayzie's, and—"

"I know, I know. And I had to make mine and Dreama's and Abigail's. Thank the gods, Leah will make her own."

"Do you believe in the gods, Marta?" Veronica asked as she stripped off her dress and held the lovely green one up to her.

"I never did until I met Mother Esterville," Marta said. "Put that dress on—but be careful. Don't tear it or get it dirty."

"I'm being careful." Veronica slipped the dress over her head and hunted for the armholes. Marta jumped up to help her, and in a moment her arms were guided carefully to the openings and the dress was eased over her head and settled into place.

"Honestly, I think you've grown since I measured this on you last week."

"I wish I had," Veronica said, sighing. She hated that she was shorter than all the other girls her age. "If Mother Esterville is so good, how did she have a son as bad as Jerome?"

"Those things happen," Marta said and, stuffing pins between her lips, knelt and began to turn up and pin the hem.

"*I* think he might have turned out different if she'd paid more attention to him and less to her gods."

Marta jabbed a pin into the material and glared up at Veronica. In a muffled voice she said, "You think too much."

"I have nightmares about Jerome sometimes," Veronica confided. "I dream that he makes me do awful things."

Marta spat out the pins and hugged Veronica. "He can't do anything to you ever again. Where Ed put him he can't get to us."

"I hope you're right. Just thinking about him scares me." Veronica shuddered and added, giving Marta a pleading look, "I wish you and Ed would come live here. Do you have to go back to Sharpness?"

"We have a house there and a lot of friends. Ed has his carriage and horses, and I have my sewing. Between us we make a good living. I don't know that we could here. And besides, Sharpness will be a good place to bring up a child."

"Dreama's so lucky, getting you and Ed as parents." Veronica sighed. "I wish Aunt Kyla was as easy to talk to as you and Ed are. I wish I could go with you when you leave. I could help you with Dreama."

"And before long you'd want to go back to Kyla," Marta said, shaking her head. "It's always easier to get along with people when you don't live with them."

"But she's so strict with me. And Aunt Abigail's even worse. You wouldn't be like that."

"You don't know what I'd be like," Marta said. "Kyla loves you very much, that I know. She'd be very hurt if you asked to go home with Ed and me. And we couldn't give you the opportunities you have here in Port-of-Lords."

Marta stuck one last pin into the dress, rose to her feet, and surveyed her handiwork. "I think that's even.

Take off the dress, and I'll sew the hem. And let's hear no more talk of you going back to Sharpness with us. Your place is with Kyla. Ed and I have Dreama now, but if you left, Kyla would have no one."

"But Dreama's just a baby. I'm not, and she treats me like one all the time." Veronica struggled out of the dress, tossed it to Marta, and stalked from the room.

CHAPTER FIVE
NAMING-DAY

Marta had thought Naming-Day would never come, and now that it had she thought it would never end.

The number of members in the Gifted Community was much smaller than Marta had expected, only fourteen including Kyla and Abigail, and she'd unintentionally insulted Kyla by expressing her disappointment at that. Now, however, when all the members thronged into Kyla's front room, to Marta they seemed a multitude. The room grew unbearably hot, yet she had to bear it. The candle on the table that would later receive the Naming-Day gifts gave off a sweet, heavy scent that made Marta feel nauseated.

While Kyla played the gracious hostess, Veronica insisted on taking Marta and Ed around to introduce them to each Community member. Marta murmured greetings and meaningless phrases to each one, hardly aware of what she was saying. At first she tried to remember the names of these strangers, but her mind was too preoccupied with the coming ceremony to concentrate. She wanted only to stand or sit next to Ed and take comfort from his presence. She glanced with envy at Abigail and Leah, ensconced on a settee placed against the wall, as much out of the crowd as it was possible to be in the small sitting room and generally being ignored by the rest of the attendees.

Marta did take note of one shy young man about

whom Veronica whispered as they approached him, "Isn't he good-looking? And I love his name—Winter Salas. I wish he were two or three years younger—or that I were two or three years older."

When Veronica informed her that he was an empath, Marta understood both his shyness and the reddening of his face as Veronica spoke to him. He no doubt picked up Veronica's fascination for him and found it terribly embarrassing. Marta guessed he was at least eighteen, possibly a year older.

"He's studying art," Veronica told her. "He's very talented."

The poor young man grew even redder at that and mumbled something about not being all that good. Marta felt bad for him and drew Veronica away to spare him further embarrassment.

Only one other Community member's name stayed with her. She'd been told beforehand about the Honorable Camsen Wellner, a priest of Ondin. That a priest who served the god of Port Province should also belong to the Community of the Gifted, Marta found odd and rather jarring. Wellner, Kyla had told her, had the gift of throwing fire and of creating powerful illusions. "You should see the marvelous dragon he can form from smoke," Veronica gushed when she presented him to Marta. He shook his head at that praise, almost as embarrassed as Winter had been.

Kyla had suggested, and Marta and Ed had agreed, that they should have two celebrants for the Naming Ceremony, rather than the usual one, and that the Honorable Camsen Wellner should perform the customary Naming-Day rituals, with Mayzie, as a native-born citizen of Port Province and the baby's nursemaid, reciting the blessing-prayer.

After meeting the priest, Marta regretted that

decision. It was clear to her in speaking to him that he was conflicted about his dual roles as a priest of Ondin and a member of a Community that honored the Power-Giver rather than the patron-gods of Arucadi's twelve provinces. His awkward attempts to explain how he reconciled the two roles only made her uncomfortable.

Wellner seemed to Marta to take longer than necessary to deliver his remarks to the group and to dedicate the child to Ondin—an aspect of the service that Marta disliked. Dreama grew restless and fussy. Her cries, increasing in volume, drowned out some of the speeches. Just as well. Had the priest of Ondin really needed to rehearse the entire history of Port Province?

After Wellner finally finished, Veronica read the name blessing from the *Breyadon,* and Kyla called on the Power-Giver to protect the child and grant her the gift of power that would make her a part of their community. A young woman named Trille sang a song praising the innocence and beauty of babies. Her voice was lovely and the melody pleasing, but Marta could not follow the words. For Marta the ceremony droned on and on.

Dreama's crying always made Marta nervous. Each time she rushed to comfort the baby, Ed told her she would spoil the child. But he was just as bad. He adored this little girl who had miraculously become their daughter. It pleased Marta to have him standing so proudly beside her for the official Naming, rocking Dreama gently in his arms and beaming, not at all impatient as Marta was. When Dreama fussed and cried, he offered her his finger to suck, and risked the disapproval of the Honored Wellner by whispering to the child to calm her.

At last the ritual was concluded with first the priest and then Kyla addressing Dreama by name. Priest Wellner said, "I greet you, Dreama, daughter of Edwin and Marta Robbins, and I entrust you to Ondin and to the great gods Dor and Dora. May you bring your parents great happiness."

Kyla kissed the babe on the forehead and said, "Dreama, may your life be filled with love and joy, and may the Power-Giver bless you with his gifts."

Following those blessings, each guest walked past Ed and Marta, touched Dreama lightly on the forehead, and placed a gift on the table with the candle.

At last Mayzie could take Dreama into the back of the house and suckle her, while from the kitchen Leah and Abigail brought out trays of little cakes and glasses of a sweet wine punch.

Veronica, in her lovely green dress, circulated among the guests like a seasoned hostess, chatting animatedly, making certain each guest was served and punch cups kept filled.

In contrast, Marta stood woodenly, holding her plate and cup, unable to eat a bite. She itched all over, her stomach felt queasy, and her head throbbed. She wanted desperately to escape to the back of the house, get out of her hot clothes, and be alone with the child who now was truly, officially hers. Instead she nodded and smiled at the guests, not hearing their conversation, not caring about anything but being free to go to Dreama.

"Patience, love," Ed whispered into her ear when for a moment no one was chattering at them. "They'll all go soon."

But the guests seemed determined to linger. Marta bit her tongue to keep from shouting, "Go home, all of you!" Ed slipped his arm around her and she leaned against him. It was wonderful how he sensed her unease and did his best to protect her. He would be a marvelous father to little Dreama. Picturing Ed as a father gave Marta the first moment of peace and contentment she'd had since the ceremony began.

The moment was cut short by a scream from the back of the house.

"Mayzie!" Marta raced from the crowded room, Ed close behind her. "Mayzie!" she called again, looking for the wet nurse first in Mayzie's room, then in the kitchen and the sewing room. They found neither Mayzie nor Dreama.

"Maybe she went to the outhouse and carried Dreama with her. I'll go see." Veronica dashed out the back door. Until she'd spoken, Marta hadn't noticed that she'd followed them. Marta saw nothing but the void left by the baby's terrible absence.

In seconds Veronica returned, her face ashen. "It's empty," she stated, her voice quavering. "I checked all around. No one's out back."

"What could have happened?" Ed asked, looking stunned. "Mayzie wouldn't have taken the baby anywhere, would she?"

"No, especially not on this day of all days," Kyla stated,

Marta's gaze met Veronica's. The sudden horror that surged through her was mirrored on Veronica's face. In unison they said, "Jerome!"

CHAPTER SIX
LOSS

It was Ed who fell apart. He sat on a kitchen chair rocking back and forth, moaning and repeating over and over, "Why did he take her? What will he do to her?"

Marta understood. He was reliving the abuse he had suffered as a child. She dared not give way to her own fear and rage; for Ed's sake she had to hang on. She went to him and held him. "We'll get her back," she said with more conviction than she felt. "He won't get far."

"He could have simply killed her if that was what he wanted," Kyla pointed out. "Why would he have taken Mayzie if he meant to harm Dreama?"

No one questioned that Jerome Esterville was responsible for the abduction. The moment that Marta had spoken his name in unison with Veronica, she knew. Jerome Esterville had caused them untold trouble back in Carey before Ed had transported him to a land that Ed had imagined into existence on a world in another plane. The discomfort Marta had felt throughout the naming ceremony hadn't been because of the heat and the itching hadn't been caused by the stiff new dress. She'd sensed the presence of evil but failed to recognize its once-too-familiar signature. As she recalled it, she remembered as well Jerome's ability to transfer his rage and resentment to others—as he'd done to Veronica, then only nine years old. No wonder Veronica had sensed him when Marta did.

"All our gifted friends are still here," Veronica said. "We'd better put them all to work."

At least someone was still able to think logically.

Marta shook Ed. "You've got to help me," she told him. "Maybe if you picture Dreama in your mind, your power can take us to her."

He looked up, his eyes bleak. "If he's hurt her ..."

"We'll get him before he can. You've got to pull yourself together. Use your power."

He nodded and, standing, put his arm around her waist and held her tight against him. She saw his eyes close in concentration.

With no transition they stood on a desolate, wind-swept plain. Beside them a dry channel marked where a brook had once run, and at intervals along it dead, twisted tree trunks kept guard like grim sentinels.

Ed groaned and sank to the parched ground. "My beautiful land! My special place! What happened to all the fruit trees? The flowers? It's nothing but a desert. He's destroyed it."

"Get up, Ed." Marta tugged at his arm. "You can't face Jerome like that. Where is he?"

Ed resisted her pulling. "I don't know." He scooped up a handful of sand and let it trickle through his fingers.

"Well, you were looking for him and for Dreama, weren't you?"

"Yes, but—" He stopped and peered around. "This is where I always came when I was in trouble. It was my safe place."

"So your mind brought us here now not to find Dreama but to be safe?"

"I didn't mean to." He sounded like a little boy whining to an angry parent. "I left Jerome here. It's where he should still be."

"Ed, get up." Her fingers dug into his arm. "You have to try again. And this time, focus on Jerome, not on a place."

He lumbered to his feet and linked arms with her. His eyes shut tight in concentration, but Marta kept hers open.

Nothing happened. The minutes snailed by, and Ed and Marta went nowhere.

Either Ed's grief was blocking his power, or Jerome hid somewhere nearby, with Dreama and Mayzie. Marta sniffed the air, using her power to search for a scent of Dreama and the wet nurse. She sensed nothing. If they *were* here, their presence was shielded.

She and Ed would have to conduct a physical search. It would probably be a waste of time, but what else could they do? Marta didn't have the ability to transport them anywhere, not even back to Kyla's house.

"It's no use." Ed sank back to the ground. "I'm trying, but when I picture Jerome, all I can think of is what he might do to Dreama, and my power drains away."

"So we're stranded here," Marta said, not adding the obvious fact that if this was not where Jerome had gone, his trail was growing cold and their chances of finding Dreama were fading.

When Ed and Marta disappeared, Veronica gave a whoop of joy. They'd find and rescue Dreama and Mayzie and be back in no time.

But Aunt Kyla looked as worried as ever. "Go

ahead, Veronica, get the rest of the Community in here and let's put them to work."

Veronica didn't want to leave the kitchen, so convinced was she that Marta and Ed would return at any moment. But since recruiting all the gifted had been her own suggestion, she could hardly refuse to go. She hurried back to the sitting room, told the others what had happened, and ushered them into the kitchen.

Ed and Marta did not return.

Abigail busied herself with gathering up the plates and punch cups and set to work washing the dishes. How like her to think of cleaning up at a time like this.

At Kyla's direction all the others formed a circle, even Leah, though she had no gift. Kyla took Veronica's hand and drew her into the circle. "Now," Kyla said, "we'll send our power searching for Mayzie and little Dreama. Since we can all picture them, we should be able to find them more easily than we could find Jerome, whom only Veronica, Leah, Abigail, and I know."

Veronica didn't agree. Jerome's power signature would be strong, but Mayzie was not gifted, and what could an infant do? She thought it senseless to conduct a search for the two who could send no signals. She tried to tell them this, but Aunt Kyla and Aunt Leah both shushed her. They knew how much power she had, yet they insisted on treating her like a child!

If Ed and Marta got back quickly, it wouldn't matter. But time passed, they did not return, and to Veronica her power was being wasted in the circle.

Without saying anything and without breaking her handholds with Kyla and Leah, she pulled out of the joint search and sent her own power hunting for

Jerome. He would be shielded, but she knew his signature all too well. When she was a nine-year-old child, he had sent his anger into her and caused her to do a terrible thing she could never forget.

She caught a faint trace, a familiar evil scent. But it grew no stronger as she searched. Surreptitiously she pulled power from the others in the group to add to her own. They might notice the drain, but they would not guess its cause. Yes, it was wrong to do such a thing, but the situation called for desperate and daring measures. The added power increased her range, and again she picked up the elusive scent. She narrowed her focus and threw all her strength into an attempt to pinpoint its location.

A fuzzy picture swam into her mind. She thought she could make out Mayzie holding the baby and cowering in front of a male figure. That figure had to be Jerome, though it looked nothing like the man she remembered seeing five years ago. Not that the features were at all clear, but the form was tall and menacing and scarcely looked human at all.

She needed their location—Mayzie, the baby, and their captor. Veronica tried to broaden her view to include the surrounding area.

Kyla jerked her hand from Veronica's. "What are you doing?" she demanded.

The vision vanished as every face in the circle turned toward her.

"I almost had them," she said. "Now they're gone."

"Almost had who?" Kyla practically shouted the question.

"Mayzie and the baby. Who else?" Kyla had no reason to be angry with her, and Veronica made no attempt to hide her own anger. "Somebody had to do something."

"Ed and Marta are doing something," Kyla snapped. "You could have interfered with them and even put them in danger—and Mayzie and the baby, too."

"Well, I didn't. I saw Mayzie and the baby, but I couldn't tell where they were. Ed and Marta weren't with them; I'm certain of that."

"Did you see Jerome?"

"I guess so. It didn't look like him, though. He was scary-looking, big, a lot taller than poor Mayzie. Too tall to be human, even."

"How close to them were you?" Kyla asked. "And where were they?"

"I don't know," Veronica confessed. "It was all hazy, like a dream. I just saw them, not anything around them. I wasn't close enough to them to see details. I could see that Mayzie was real scared, but that was all."

Kyla fell silent, looking thoughtful.

Abigail, who'd come back from the kitchen, frowned and said, "Are you certain you really saw them and didn't imagine it? Or maybe it was a vision?"

That was Aunt Abigail, always questioning, always doubting. She still didn't trust magic, even though she was gifted. And that thought led Veronica to say, "I'm certain. But why don't you get the *Breyadon* and try a locating spell. That should settle it."

She thought it was good advice, but Aunt Abigail made no move to follow it. Veronica stamped her foot. "Nobody's doing anything!" she said. "At least I was trying, and if you hadn't interrupted me I might have found out where they were and—"

"That's enough, Veronica," Aunt Kyla cut in, using her soothing voice the way she did when she thought

Veronica might throw fire or something and hurt somebody as she had when she was nine. But then she'd just discovered her powers and hadn't learned to control them. And Jerome had somehow transferred a lot of his anger to her. Now she wasn't a little girl anymore. She glared at Kyla. Why couldn't she see that her adopted niece only wanted to help? And had the power to do it?

Aunt Kyla gave her the look that warned her to be quiet and stay out of adult matters. Well, she'd show her. She'd show them all. They didn't want her to do anything? They wouldn't let her help? Okay, she'd put on her good girl act and not let on, but she *would* try again to find Mayzie and Baby Dreama. She'd just be more careful not to let Kyla and the rest find out what she was doing.

Scowling, she stalked from the room, heading for the kitchen.

Aunt Abigail followed her. "I've washed most of the dishes. You can dry them and put them away," she said. "That will be a big help."

Sure, washing and drying dishes and putting them away would be a real smart use of her talents. She didn't bother to answer, just ignored Abigail and walked on through the kitchen to the back door, went outside, and slammed the door behind her. She stopped a short distance from the back door and waited to make sure Abigail didn't follow her.

Neither Aunt Abigail nor anyone else came to call her back. No doubt they were all too preoccupied with planning what to do—instead of doing it. Well, *she* would show them. She headed out of the yard and toward a small park nearby where a bench in a shady arbor would provide solitude in which to work.

Seeing Abigail follow Veronica into the kitchen, Kyla assumed that Veronica would be under the older woman's supervision. Abigail would certainly understand that the rest of the group could not waste precious minutes dealing with a temperamental teenager in this time of crisis. Ed and Marta hadn't returned, and what that might mean caused Kyla greater worry. It might mean that they'd found Jerome and were dealing with him and would soon be back with Dreama and Mayzie. But she couldn't block the thought of other possibilities. Nor could she risk leaving everything to Ed and Marta if they had found Jerome. After all, by their own choice they'd rarely used their powers in the five years since they'd gone off on their own. Who knew whether their abilities had not weakened from disuse?

The power circle had broken up with Veronica's defection, and the guests milled aimlessly about, talking among themselves or merely standing apart looking lost and confused. Grandmotherly Winnie Calder, a new member of the Community, had her arms around Leah, consoling her, using her newly discovered gift of spreading calm and peacefulness. Kyla suspected that Winnie also had a gift of healing, a gift she hoped they wouldn't need.

"Listen," Kyla addressed the group, "we're all upset, but we have to stay focused and pool our strength. I'm sure Ed and Marta, wherever they are, will do all they can. We have to do what we can from this end. We can't afford to waste time just waiting for them.

"Now, Veronica said she saw Mayzie and the baby. Maybe she did and maybe she didn't. If she did, we ought to be able to see them, too. But we need to be careful not to let their captor know we're spying. I only hope Veronica didn't alert him. She means well, and she has great talent, as you know, but she doesn't think things through before she acts."

She gazed around the room, assessing the talents that were spread among the guests gathered here. Several had gifts that would prove useful if they could discover Jerome's whereabouts. Others might be a hindrance and should be sent away. She disliked hurting anyone's feelings, but this was not the time to tread gently.

Winter, being a powerful empath, was already looking ill. He would be relieved to be sent home. She went to him. "Winter, I'm sure you're picking up on everyone's grief and confusion. Please feel free to leave. There's no need for you to suffer, and there's really nothing you can do here."

He gave her a grateful look and nodded. "I am feeling a bit sick," he said, rubbing his forehead. "Please don't think I'm not willing to help."

She patted his shoulder. "I know you're willing, and if there's anything you can do, we'll send for you. Right now, you're only making yourself miserable by staying."

"Thanks." He turned toward the door, then turned back and whispered, "The fear and anger and feelings of helplessness are horrible enough, but somebody registers as excited and pleased."

He whirled away before she could ask who that somebody was and rushed for the door like a man pursued.

He must not have known who, she thought. *Otherwise he would have said. Unless he's afraid of the person. He's such a timid young man.*

It was hard to believe that someone, a member of the Community, would rejoice at calamity. Excited, he'd said. And pleased. How could anyone feel that way? She had to think—and hope—that whoever it was, the pleasure and excitement were due to the prospect of having the opportunity to show off his or her power by participating in the rescue.

Zauna Raye, an older woman, approached diffidently and tapped her arm. When Kyla turned toward her, she said, "I believe I can help, but I need my crystal ball. I'm sorry I didn't have the foresight to bring it. But I'll toddle along and get it and come right back."

Zauna was not one of those Kyla would have asked to leave. The woman's slovenly dress and unkempt appearance belied a kind and generous nature and a calm acceptance of her lot in life. Kyla found her a steadying influence. But if Zauna needed her crystal ball, she should get it. She might see something helpful in it—maybe even discover where Jerome had taken Dreama and Mayzie. So she thanked the woman and watched her make her way to the door.

"Why are people leaving?" an imperious voice demanded.

Kyla knew without turning to face him who'd spoken. Professor Firstan Morence was highly gifted, but unfortunately he had little regard for the feelings of others, believing himself to be superior to most if not all the other members of the Gifted Community. She didn't need to cope with his arrogance now of all times.

"Professor, there are too many of us here all exercising our power. We'll get in each other's way. I'm suggesting that those whose powers aren't immediately needed leave now but stay on alert to return if we need them later. And that includes you, please."

"You're ordering me out?" He demanded, his eyebrows raised. "My gifts could certainly prove valuable."

"They could indeed, Professor, if we had anyone to use them on. But at the moment, we don't." Professor Morence had the ability to project his thoughts into the minds of others. He also practiced coercion. Both were dangerous gifts, and although he was careful in his use of them, Kyla found it hard to trust him fully. She kept herself well shielded when in his presence, and she knew many of the other gifted did the same. "Surely you can see, Professor, that we have no time to waste bickering."

Trille approached and gave Kyla a kiss on her cheek. "I agree, and I'm going to leave. My abilities really don't fit this situation, and I do have a concert to prepare for."

The renowned singer possessed great power, but she was right, her particular gifts would not be of benefit at this time as they all had to do with manipulating water. Kyla returned her kiss and accompanied her to the door.

"If you should have use for my gifts, send for me and I'll come at once," Trille said and took her leave. Kyla was relieved to see Professor Morence follow her out. She couldn't have endured more argument.

The Honored Camsen Wellner approached her and, not meeting her eyes, said, "I feel I, too, should leave. You have no more need of me, and I am due back at the Temple of Ondin for afternoon devotions."

"Thank you, Honored Camsen, for your blessing," Kyla replied, knowing his reluctance to use his gifts. She would have preferred that he stay. His ability to create illusions and to throw and sculpt fire could well prove useful in a confrontation with Jerome. But could she trust the priest to use those gifts? Having no time to explore that question, she said, "If we should need of your gifts later, I hope we can call on you?"

"Uh, yes ... yes, naturally," he said, reluctance clear in his voice. "And I'll pray to Ondin for all of you." Hurriedly he took his leave. Kyla hoped they would not have to call on him, that his abilities would not be needed. Why was it, she wondered, as she often had about Abigail's similar distaste for using her powers, that so much talent was given to someone who was loath to use it?

Next came Gorvy and Darnell Mack, husband and wife. Kyla could see no need at present for Darnell's ability to shape-shift, and her husband's only ability, so far as they knew, was as a quencher of power. If they caught Jerome, that ability could be useful, but until then neither of them could offer much help.

As they prepared to leave, Petros Birge who had lost his legs in a tragic childhood accident, rolled up to them on the wheeled platform on which he got around. "Gorvy, Darnell, I intend to stay," he said, propelling the wooden platform by turning its two large wheels with his hands. "I hope I can be of use. But would you be so kind as to stop by my house and tell my folks I'll be here as long as I'm needed?"

They not only agreed to notify Petros's parents, they turned to Marchion Blandry and asked whether he was staying and would like them to inform Mrs. Blandry. The wealthy merchant looked questioningly at Kyla.

Kyla nodded. "I don't know whether your gift of seeing auras will be helpful, but we will certainly need your ability to enhance power."

"Then, yes," Marchion answered the Macks. "Please do let my wife know I'll stay here as long as I can be of service. She's not a worrier, but she will fret if I'm gone overnight."

When the Macks departed, those remaining, with one exception, would all be invaluable in the search. Kyla gave the exception, Renni Natches, the newest member of the Gifted Community, a meaningful look, but the young woman failed to take the hint. Could she be the one to whom Winter had been referring, the one whom he'd described as excited and pleased by the tragic turn of events? Kyla reminded herself not to make snap judgments.

"Renni, your gifts may be needed later, but at present it would be best for you to leave and get some rest in case we have to call you back."

The young woman narrowed her eyes. "Oh, no. You aren't getting rid of me. I can find a way to be useful here, and I don't need rest. If nothing else, I can lend power to those whose gifts you will use right away."

Kyla could find no way to insist on her leaving without revealing the mistrust she felt. She didn't want an argument. They needed to get to work right away. "All right," she said, though she saw no way the young woman's gift of altering memories would be of use. "If you agree to let any of us draw on your power when we need it, that will help."

Renni nodded. "I agree to that." Her triumphant grin strengthened Kyla's suspicion that she was the one whose excitement Winter had felt.

Kyla turned to the remaining gifted, reasonably confident that she could rely on all of them to do their parts in the rescue attempt. She could imagine ways in which each one could use his or her gift to rescue Mayzie and Dreama and in a confrontation with Jerome if they faced that.

Lore Kaplek had the ability to transfer to another place and to bring items, but not people, to himself from another place, if he could visualize the location. Young, good-looking, and personable, he might well be the reason Renni had wanted to stay.

Petros Birge possessed the marvelous gift of transferring his consciousness into other minds, from which he could observe events without being observed, an invaluable ability if only they could send someone to wherever Jerome had taken Mayzie and Dreama. But so long as they remained ignorant of that location and had no way to reach it, Petros's gift would be of little help. His acute hearing also could only prove useful if they had someone to listen to. Hoping to discover the whereabouts of the kidnapper and his victims, Kyla welcomed Petros's decision to stay.

Marchion Blandry downplayed his gift of seeing auras and webs of power, but Kyla wished she could ask him privately what Renni's aura looked like and signified. She felt certain they would find other uses for his abilities, but at present his most valued gift was that of enhancing the power of others.

And finally, Winnie Calder's ability to calm others and keep them focused would certainly prove useful. Feeling increasingly worried and tense, Kyla could have used that gift now, but she did not ask Winnie for that comfort, not wanting to give the impression of weakness when they needed her strength.

The time for action had come. She considered calling Abigail and Veronica in from the kitchen, but decided that it would be better to leave them out of this for the time being. Veronica had great power but her lack of control could jeopardize the group effort. If Marta were here, she could help Kyla prevent

Veronica from acting rashly, but without her help the danger was too great. And where *were* Marta and Ed?

As if in answer to her question, Zauna returned, bearing her crystal ball and wearing the gaudy and well-worn garment she habitually wore for fortune telling. She was breathing hard, and her face was flushed. She must have run all the way. Kyla pushed a straight chair up to the table of baby gifts and piled those unceremoniously on the floor along with the extinguished candle. Zauna placed the crystal on the table, and sank down onto the chair Kyla provided.

She said, "Now, please, everybody be very quiet and let me concentrate."

Kyla waved the others back when they would have crowded around. Even if they looked directly into the crystal globe, none of them would see whatever it was that Zauna saw.

Reminded by the crystal of Alair's crystal residence, she sent a mental message to the Power-Giver: *Alair, please, help her locate Dreama and Mayzie. And Marta and Ed.*

She wished for a reply but didn't expect one. He'd been silent for so long. This was not the time to think about that problem.

Zauna stared intently into the crystal while her audience, it seemed to Kyla, held their collective breath. It was almost unbearably quiet. No sound came from the kitchen, and looking around, Kyla saw that Abigail had joined the group and was standing next to Leah, who had remained despite not being gifted.

Where was Veronica?

"Aha!"

Zauna's cry swung Kyla's attention back to her and the globe into which she was peering.

Petros and Lore both moved nearer to Zauna, probably expecting their talents to be needed.

"Oh, no!" Zauna straightened and turned her gaze to Kyla. "I had them. Marta and Ed. They were standing together in what seemed to be a very desolate place. And then, suddenly, Ed disappeared, and Marta is looking all around. She seems distraught."

CHAPTER SEVEN
SEPARATION

"Since we can't go anywhere, we'd better start searching this desolation," Marta said, taking a firm hold on Ed's arm. He nodded, but did not otherwise move. His eyes were pools of despair.

"Ed, we can't just stand here." Marta took a couple of steps and tugged him along after her. "We won't save Dreama this way."

"Jerome's gotten stronger," he said, gazing off into the distance. "Much more powerful. While we've let our powers grow rusty these past five years. He's too strong for us."

"So you're just giving up?" Marta released his arm and stepped in front of him. She put a hand under his chin, tilting his face upward so that his eyes met hers. "You're just going to let him have Dreama?"

"No." He ran his hands through his hair, a nervous gesture she hadn't seen him use in years. "I don't know what to do."

"Then you'd better concentrate on getting us back to Kyla. Maybe she and her friends *will* know what to do."

"When I try to picture them, all I see is Jerome. Hurting Dreama ..." He broke off, choked with sobs.

"Then why aren't we going there—wherever *there* is? Unless we are there. We have to explore further. They may be here somewhere."

Ed's shoulders slumped. "You said you didn't sense them."

"I don't, but this is a big place, isn't it? They may not be near enough to sense. Ed, pull yourself together. We can't just mope around while Jerome does who knows what to Mayzie and Dreama."

"I'm trying, Marta. Trying to find them. Nothing happens."

"Well, draw on my strength if that will help. Take all you need."

Ed closed his eyes, stood perfectly still, and squinched his face in concentration. Marta tried to send power to him but had no sense of any power flowing from her to him. She blinked back tears. She couldn't break down. She had to be strong for Ed. But the tears wanted to come. She turned away from Ed, walked a couple of paces away, studying the ground.

"I think ..." His voice trailed off.

She turned back to face him. He was gone.

Gone! Without her. Why had she left his side? Why hadn't she kept her grip on his arm? Where was he?

She spun around in a circle, looking in every direction, peering off into the distance. Not a sign of him. She was alone and stranded. But no, he'd use his power to call her to him. Surely he would.

But minutes—too many minutes—passed, and she remained in the dry, barren wilderness to which they'd come. Now there was no holding back the tears.

Veronica sat on a bench in a spot shaded by a trio of large and leafy babwood trees. She leaned her head against the back of the bench and closed her eyes. A passerby might assume she'd fallen asleep, but her mind raced along many pathways.

She didn't know how Ed had imagined a place into existence and had gone there, but he had, and she was certain that if he had, she could do it too. He'd said he'd visited it first only in his mind, using mental images of an ideal place to retreat to when his drunken father abused him. He'd been a young child when he'd created his "imaginary" place, but he had only traveled there and found it real after he'd met Kyla and Marta. Had it been real before that time, but he hadn't known it until Marta and Kyla awakened his magic? She tried to recall all he'd told her about the part that he had not imagined, the part that had been a portal to the Dire Realms. He hadn't known about that part until he accidentally took Jerome to his world and couldn't get back to this world. It was when they were exploring beyond the area Ed considered "his" that Ed had discovered the portal inside what seemed to be a ruined building, a building that Jerome had refused to enter.

In discovering the portal, Ed had encountered a friendly Dire Lord, one known to Marta and to Kyla, and had acquired the ability not only to return home but also to transport himself to and from that world more easily. But while Jerome waited outside, he, too, had encountered a Dire Lord, an evil one who had awakened his power and turned it to wickedness.

So why had Ed thought that by returning Jerome to that land and stranding him there, he had disposed of the threat Jerome represented? It seemed obvious to Veronica that Jerome could find a way to reestablish contact with the evil Dire Lord and increase his power to the point of being able to escape and wreak havoc. If Jerome had reached out to the evil Dire Lord, he had most likely transported Mayzie and the baby to that other part of the world Veronica only wondered why it had taken Jerome so long to act. She did not intend to be as foolish as Ed had been.

She'd seen Mayzie and Dreama; she knew she had, whether or not Aunt Kyla believed her. And the person with them had scarcely looked human, though it had Jerome's face. She shuddered. She could never forget that face.

Veronica had no desire to confront Jerome, no desire to visit that world. Her plan was to create a place of her own that she could transport herself to. She would have preferred to transport Mayzie and Dreama back to the house, but even if she had that ability, they wouldn't be safe there. Jerome could easily snatch them again.

She thought about what kind of place she wanted. She didn't intend to inhabit it for a long period of time. She only needed somewhere to use as a kind of way station, a hidden refuge to which she could shift Mayzie and Dreama and Ed and Marta so Jerome could not find them. And then she'd let Ed transport them all back to his and Marta's house, where perhaps Jerome wouldn't think to look.

But no, Jerome was clever enough to look there. So it might be better to create a haven where Mayzie and the baby could hide until Kyla and the others dealt with Jerome. She had to think this through.

Marta and Ed's panic over the loss of Dreama was hampering their powers. They'd have to stay in the safe place, too. But once they had Dreama safe in their arms, they'd calm down enough to use their powers again, and they could help capture Jerome, so probably they wouldn't need to remain in the refuge very long.

Veronica had confidence in Aunt Kyla's and Aunt

Marta's abilities and in the abilities of the friends who worked with them. And Ed's powers were awesome. All of them working together would succeed in locating and subduing Jerome in a short time. She didn't know what they'd do with Jerome, but they'd find a way to prevent him from ever being a danger to them again. Her task, self-appointed, true, but one she believed she could accomplish better than anyone else, was to rescue Dreama and Mayzic.

She concentrated on the sort of place she wanted. Somewhere secure and comforting. A walled garden, the wall high enough to deter intruders. A garden with lots of brightly colored flowers, but nothing with thorns. Lots and lots of butterflies for Dreama to watch and laugh at. A blue sky with puffy white clouds that formed animal shapes. A fountain that sprayed colored bubbles instead of water. A cushioned rocking chair for Mayzie and a cradle for Dreama, set on flagstones near the fountain. Perfect weather—not hot but never cold, just pleasant with a cool, refreshing breeze that blew the fountain's bubbles about.

She could picture it all clearly enough. She tried to put herself in the picture and could do so mentally, but when she opened her eyes she was still on the bench in the shaded arbor. Maybe her imagined place was too complicated for a first attempt.

She took away the bubbling fountain, the chair and cradle, the flagstones. Sadly she dismissed the butterflies. She made the garden smaller, the flowers less flamboyant. When she had the picture firmly in her mind, she tried again. This time before opening her eyes she imagined the feel of the ground, spongy and soft, beneath her feet. She imagined the feel of a light breeze against her arms, let her fingertips mentally caress the velvety petals of a trumpet flower.

Finally, she pictured Ed standing facing her, looking startled, heard his voice saying, "What ... Where's Marta? How did I get here?"

Veronica opened her eyes. Ed stood nearby, gazing around in puzzlement. Brightly colored flowers had indeed sprouted around her. But she was still seated on the bench in the park. She hadn't gone anywhere.

Nor had she meant to bring Ed to her until she'd found and brought Mayzie and Dreama. She never intended to separate Ed and Marta. So when Ed rounded on her, demanding to know what had happened, she didn't know what to say. Except, "Ed, I'm sorry. I was trying to build a place the way you did. A safe place I could transport Mayzie and Dreama to. But, I guess I made a mistake."

"I guess you did. Get Marta. Right now!"

He stood directly in front of her, glaring so fiercely she could not concentrate. Even when she closed her eyes, the heat of his anger rolled against her like waves against the breakers just off the coast. She tried to picture Marta beside Ed, calming him, but it was no use. She sensed too strongly his wrath and beneath it the weight of his despair.

"Ed, I can't do it. If you walk away where I can't see you, I'll try again. Or better yet, *you* do it. You have the power."

He just shook his head and didn't move. She sensed that he *couldn't* move, his grief and fear too great to permit movement or use of power. She rose to her feet. "All right. I'll have to go somewhere else. I can't concentrate with you standing right in front of me. You stay here."

When she tried to circle around him, he grabbed her shoulders. "Find Dreama," he said, his voice breaking. "Bring her here. Marta too."

He released her then and let her slide past him and walk away. But his plea added to the pressure she felt, and she was too tense to do what he asked. Scared now, afraid to face Kyla and the others but knowing she needed their help to do anything, she walked slowly toward home, leaving Ed alone in the park.

CHAPTER EIGHT
DISASTERS

Kyla wanted her to leave. She'd made it fairly obvious. And exactly for that reason, Renni was determined to stay. Her gift might not be needed—probably wouldn't be—but Renni hated doing what people wanted her to. She got enough of that at home. Just because she refused to marry the man they'd chosen for her, her parents insisted on treating her like a five-year-old instead of a twenty-five-year-old. Because that man had money, her parents considered him an acceptable choice. They kept reminding her she wasn't getting any younger and few eligible young men remained. They really meant few *wealthy* young men. They weren't concerned about her happiness; they only wanted to be certain she married well enough to support them in their old age.

She would never marry their choice. She could make her own way in the world. Kyla had. She admired the gifted leader, and intended to emulate her. But to do so, she had to hone her gifts, perhaps discover others besides the ones she knew she had. And how better to do that than to remain here in this time of crisis and, if she couldn't be of any help, observe those who could. How else could she learn?

She joined the group clustered around Zauna and her crystal ball. Being tall, she could peer over the shoulder of others to view the crystal. She thought she saw shadowy figures in it, but she couldn't distinguish them. It could have been no more than her imagination. She had no reason to believe she had the talent of crystal gazing.

At Zauna's sudden cry Renni jumped back, colliding with Lore who'd come to stand directly behind her. "Whoa," he said, placing his hands on her shoulders. She shrugged them off, annoyed by the familiarity in his touch, and stepped away from the group.

Call it intuition, call it presentiment, Renni had a strong feeling, almost a certainty that Veronica was behind Ed's sudden disappearance from the scene Zauna described seeing in her crystal ball.

Renni liked Veronica. The kid had a lot of spunk. A lot of talent, too. When she'd said she'd seen Mayzie and the baby, Renni had believed her and fully understood her frustration when Kyla jumped all over her for interfering. The poor kid! She was really in for it if she'd done something that backfired and made matters worse.

Even as these thoughts raced through Renni's mind, Veronica entered the room through the door from the kitchen. The expression she wore told Renni her intuition hadn't been wrong. Nor had her guess as to what Kyla's reaction would be.

Kyla rounded on the girl and demanded, "Where have you been? What have you been doing?"

"Trying to help," Veronica said softly, as though it hurt to reply. She was blushing furiously, poor girl.

"And?" Kyla demanded, showing not the slightest bit of sympathy.

"And I guess I made things worse," she confessed, her eyes lowered. Good thing Winter had left. Renni didn't need to be an empath to feel the girl's pain.

"I asked you to help me with the dishes, and instead you disappeared," Abigail chimed in. "Where did you go off to?"

Ask her what she did, Renni urged mentally. No one picked up on the thought.

"I just went outside," Veronica mumbled, speaking to the floor. "To a quiet place where I go sometimes."

"So you just wandered off, despite what was happening here, and despite the fact that I'd asked for your help," Abigail continued her accusations.

Leah whispered something to Abigail, probably asking her to ease up. Renni liked Leah. She was kind—and sensible. How she ever got hooked up with Abigail, Renni couldn't understand.

Still no one asked Veronica what she did. *Guess it's up to me.* Renni spoke. "What did you do? Did you find Ed and Marta? Did you do something with Ed?"

Everyone turned and glared at Renni as though she'd sprouted horns. Everyone, that is, except Veronica. Still addressing the floor, she said, "I didn't mean to, but I brought him back here and left Marta stranded, I guess, back in the land that—"

"You did *what?*" Kyla demanded. "You left Marta where Jerome can get to her?"

"Now, Kyla," Winnie Calder soothed, spreading her calming influence over the Community leader.

"Where is Ed then?" Abigail demanded, unaffected by Winnie's gift of tranquility.

Veronica wiped at her face. She must be crying, though she had her head lowered, so Renni couldn't be sure. "He's back in the park. He's mad at me, and he wouldn't move, so I left him there."

"You left him alone? In his state of mind? You little idiot!" Abigail shook off the hand Leah placed on her arm.

"I didn't know what else to do," Veronica said, and Renni heard the catch in her voice. The poor girl was distraught.

Renni couldn't stand it. "Look, let me take Veronica, and we'll go find Ed and bring him back here, while the rest of you see what you can do about finding and fetching Marta."

She didn't expect them to accept her plan, but Kyla nodded. Perhaps under Winnie's influence, she said, "Yes, go ahead. We do have to find Marta. She needs our protection."

"I'll go with you," Lore said, stepping forward with a big smile. "You shouldn't go out by yourselves."

"No," Renni said firmly. "You stay here. You'll be needed here, and I won't." Without giving him the chance to argue, Renni grabbed hold of Veronica's arm and pulled her forward. "Come on, Veronica. We'd better hurry."

Veronica didn't resist. She had to be relieved to get away. She didn't say a word, though.

They left the house, got halfway across the backyard, and Renni asked, "Which way?"

Veronica pointed to the gate that let them out onto the street, and as they passed through it, she finally spoke. "I left him in the park just down the street. What if he's not still there?"

"Let's deal with that if it happens," Renni said, walking faster. The girl's fear was not unwarranted.

They reached the park, and Veronica led the way through it to a secluded arbor. There on a bench sat Ed, raking his hands through his hair. He looked up when Veronica called his name. Tears streaked his cheeks.

"I've tried and tried to go back to Marta, and I can't. I don't know why. And I can't bring her here, either. Did you have any luck?" His gaze was focused on Veronica. Renni doubted that he even noticed her.

Veronica shook her head. "I went back to the house to try to get help, but all they did was yell at me."

"I'd yell at you, too, but I guess it wouldn't help," he said. "What's done is done. We just have to find a way to undo it." He rose to his feet slowly, as though lifting a great weight. "We'd better get back to Kyla's house. We can't do anything here."

He walked away, and Veronica fell into step beside him. "I'm sorry, Ed. I wanted to help. I didn't mean to separate you and Marta. I'm not even sure how it happened."

He shrugged. "Are they making any progress locating the baby?"

"I can't see that they're doing anything at all," Veronica said bitterly. "That's why I tried. I thought somebody had to do something."

"They are trying. I'm sure they are. You just can't see what they're doing."

Ed had to believe that, Renni supposed, but Veronica was right. Nobody was doing anything because nobody could agree on what to do. Oh, Zauna had gazed into her crystal and had seen Marta and Ed, and then Marta alone. And now it was clear why. But nobody had located Dreama and Mayzie. Nobody really seemed to be planning a way to rescue them.

The despair Ed felt was evident with every step, evident in the slump of his shoulders, the droop of his head, his clenched hands. She scarcely knew him, but Renni felt sorry for him. He'd come all this way for a child he could call his own, and now that child had been whisked away, he'd been separated from his wife, and he was left with nothing. Even his gift, his strong talent, seemed to have vanished. The grief was causing that loss, but so long as that grief continued, the talent wasn't likely to return.

But the power he had was still there, all of it, hidden under the miasma of grief. If he could ... forget the grief. Forget its cause. Then he could think calmly. He could bring his wife home. He could help the others find the baby girl that was to be his and Marta's daughter. And even if he didn't remember Dreama, he'd fall in love with her all over again as soon as he saw her. Renni had no doubt about that.

She could use her talent to make him forget. She'd have to choose the moment carefully. Walking behind him and Veronica, she considered. He'd be disoriented if she took his recent memories from before Dreama disappeared. Seeing how hard he'd taken her disappearance and now his separation from Marta, she'd have to take the memories back more than from just before Dreama's abduction. She'd have to take several days' worth of memories. She felt sure that she could do it, although up until now she'd blanked no memories more than a day old. But she saw no reason why she could not remove memories several days or even weeks old. They'd almost reached the house. She'd wait until they entered and do it just as they approached Kyla. That way Kyla and the others could ease the confusion he'd certainly feel.

Kyla gazed around the room, thinking what to do. She had Winnie working to keep everyone calm, and she'd sent Zauna back to her crystal ball. She'd asked Abigail to look through the *Breyadon* for a spell that she could use to find and contact Marta. Once before Abigail had used such a spell from that book to contact Ed when he was in his "special place." It was vital that they find and retrieve Marta. So Abigail had gone for the *Breyadon* and was hunting through it for the spell she had used then.

"Here it is!" Abigail announced.

At that moment, Veronica and Renni walked in, and Ed with them. Progress, at last! She hurried to greet Ed and stretched out her arms to give him a hug.

He backed off, a wild look in his eyes. "How ... I don't understand. Kyla? Where am I?" He gave a frightened glance around the room. "Who are all these people? Where's Marta?"

What was the matter with Ed? This was more than an effect of grief. Had Jerome somehow done something to Ed's mind? Frowning, Kyla glanced at Veronica, who looked equally puzzled and then at Renni, who met her glance with a defiant look that revealed what had happened. Probably to ease Ed's grief Renni had used her power to erase memories.

She'd have plenty to say to Renni about that later. First she had to try to explain things to Ed. She pointed to Veronica. "You know Veronica, but she's grown up a good bit, since you last saw her five years ago. And this," she indicated Renni, scowling at her as she did so, "this is Renni Natches, a new member of our community here in Port-of-Lords, and, I suspect, the reason for your confusion and loss of memory. Her gift is the removing or altering of memories. You apparently don't remember coming here from Sharpness several days ago. What is the last thing you do remember?"

"I'm in Port-of-Lords?" He shook his head as though to clear it. "I came here several days ago?"

"That's right. You don't remember traveling here?" She repeated her previous question. "What is the last thing you remember?"

Tugging on his beard, his brow puckered in thought, he spoke slowly "I took off work to go home and eat lunch. On the way home I stopped by the post, and we'd received a letter from you, Kyla." He gazed at her wonderingly. "I didn't open it; I wanted Marta to have that privilege. I got home, and Marta had been sewing all morning, and she set her work aside. She was thrilled to get the letter and wanted to read it right away, before we had lunch. She opened it and started reading it aloud. And ... and the next thing I know, I'm walking into this room with these two young ladies, and you're coming toward me. And I don't understand."

"Of course you don't. Because this young lady," Kyla pointed an accusing finger at Renni, "used her gift to erase over three weeks' worth of memories from your mind."

"But why? And where's Marta?"

Kyla bit her lip, considering how much she dared tell him. Everyone gathered around her except for Zauna, who stayed at her crystal ball. Kyla wished she'd sent more of her guests away. Especially Renni. She'd known all along the young woman was trouble.

While she pondered what to say, Abigail approached holding the *Breyadon*. "I was just about to try a spell that might let me talk to her," she said. "If it succeeds, we can find out exactly where she is."

"That's fine, but I still don't understand what's going on," Ed said, looking around and scowling. "I don't know who most of these people are. I don't know how I got here, why I'm here, or why Marta isn't here. Someone, please tell me what's happened."

Winnie Calder sidled up next to Ed, and Ed's features relaxed a bit as Winnie exercised her gift of imparting calm. Quickly Kyla said, "Yes, Abigail, go ahead and try to reach Marta. We need to know exactly where she is and what's happening with her."

Abigail glanced around her. "I can't do it here," she said peevishly. "I don't need an audience. I'll go into the kitchen, and—"

"We need to know right away whether the spell works," Kyla interrupted, "and if it does, I need to speak to Marta."

"I'll go with her," Veronica volunteered.

"No, absolutely not," Kyla said. "You've done enough."

"I didn't know she was going to do that to Ed's memories," Veronica declared, pointing at Renni. "She just did it without telling me."

"I don't doubt that," Kyla responded, glaring at Renni, "but you've caused other problems."

"I just tried to help," Veronica snapped. "Nobody else was doing anything."

"I'll go with Abigail, " Leah said, "and if she makes contact with Marta, I'll come back and report immediately."

"Fine, do that," Kyla said, smarting under Veronica's all-too-accurate accusation.

Carrying the large, leather-bound spell book, Abigail headed for the kitchen with Leah following her. That made two fewer people in the room, but Kyla still felt stifled, with everyone except Zauna gazing expectantly at her, waiting for her to say or do something when she had no idea what to say or do.

Zauna suddenly let out a horrific scream and toppled to the floor. Kyla rushed toward her and knelt beside her. Winnie joined her. "She's fainted," Winnie said. "I think I can bring her around. Just, please, everybody back away and clear the area around us."

Slowly and a bit grudgingly, they did as she

requested, leaving a large open space around her and Kyla and Zauna.

Winnie looked at Kyla. "You, too, please."

Kyla nodded and stepped back away from Winnie and Zauna. Ed made his way to her.

"Kyla, I have to know what's happening," he said.

"I know, Ed. Just please be patient a little while longer and let me see what Abigail learns and what Zauna saw that made her faint. Then maybe I'll know what to tell you."

A clap of thunder shook the house. A thump drew all eyes to the cleared space around Winnie and Zauna.

A body lay there, bathed in blood. "Mayzie!" Kyla screamed and ran to the wet nurse who had fallen out of nowhere. She slipped on the blood pouring from the young woman's chest and nearly toppled down beside her. Righting herself, she screamed again.

A long, deep gash between Mayzie's breasts exposed her breastbone and parted her chest enough to make visible her ribcage and lungs. Was she—could she still be alive?

"Veronica, get over here," she yelled. "And someone get Abigail. We need healers."

Veronica darted to her side.

Renni dashed to the kitchen and returned in moments with Abigail and Leah. "I couldn't reach Marta. I was still trying," Abigail said and then gasped as she saw why she'd been summoned. "It's Mayzie? Is she still alive?"

"Barely," Kyla said and added grimly, "I think."

Abigail dropped to her knees beside Mayzie, and Veronica joined her. They laid their hands on Mayzie's blood-soaked body.

Another thunderclap rocked the room, and Kyla

shuddered, fearing to see another body appear, but instead a voice boomed out, "Save her if you can, it matters not. You are all doomed." A bloodcurdling laugh followed, and then an awful silence.

They all gazed helplessly at one another. Someone started sobbing. Kyla looked around. Her gaze stopped on Veronica, whose hands covered her face while her shoulders shook.

"We lost her," Abigail spoke from beside Veronica. "Mayzie. We lost her when that horrible voice broke our concentration. She's dead."

"It's my fault," Veronica said between sobs. "It's all my fault."

Abigail shook her head. "We were sharing power, channeling it into Mayzie, stemming the blood loss. Veronica and I both stopped when the voice came. By the time we recovered, she'd slipped away."

"I should have held on," Veronica insisted. "I stopped because I recognized that voice. It's Jerome. I remembered all that anger he poured into me when ... when I killed ..." She burst into a fresh round of sobbing.

Leah knelt beside her and gathered her into her arms. "Hush, Veronica. It's all right. It isn't your fault. You mustn't think that."

"Jerome!" Ed exclaimed. "He's free? And behind all this? Why didn't you tell me? He's got to be stopped. We have to find Marta."

Veronica clung to Leah, her tears soaking the lovely dress Leah had worn to the Naming-Day ceremony. Her own dress was drenched with Mayzie's blood. Her inability to heal Mayzie, to save her life, was too much to bear. She'd failed miserably at everything she'd attempted. She'd let Aunt Kyla down badly, going off on her own, thinking she could make everything right. Instead she'd made it all wrong.

She hadn't been able to bring Dreama back, and bringing Ed alone, which she'd never intended to do, had stranded Marta somewhere, probably where Jerome could find her, and now Ed wasn't there to help her and couldn't even remember why he needed to find her, thanks to stupid Renni.

Aunt Kyla would have to explain everything to Ed, and that would take time, and they couldn't spare any time if they were going to save Dreama. And Ed didn't even know about Dreama, and if they didn't get her back, he'd have no memories of the little daughter he'd had for such a very short time. And Marta, if they got her back, would never forgive her for letting that happen.

She'd been so sure of herself—of her powers. She'd criticized Aunt Kyla for doing nothing, but doing the wrong thing was even worse than doing nothing.

She had to make things right. Somehow she would.

CHAPTER NINE
SEARCH

Frightened as she was and frantic with worry about Dreama and Mayzie and now Ed, too, Marta somehow managed to keep her wits about her. Ed had told her a great deal about this land, and even though it had changed so much, she recognized the streambed, a dry and stony depression winding where Ed had described a fast running stream, its banks lined with trees. The desiccated trunks of those trees still stood along it. By crossing the dry streambed and walking away from it she should come to the part of the land that Ed had declared not his. He'd described the ruined building where Jerome had been trapped when a wall had collapsed. Ed had explored that building and discovered a nexus there, a point of connection to the Dire Realms. He had even met Claid there, a brief encounter with the Dire Lord that had deeply affected Ed. If she could contact Claid, he'd help her rescue Dreama.

Stinging insects assailed her as she crossed the streambed. She beat at them and continued on, though they seemed determined to drive her back. The farther she went, the hotter the land felt. Waves of heat rolled upward from the baked sand. Even through her shoes the soles of her feet burned. Her thirst increased with every step. She could bear it only by keeping her mind focused on the image of Dreama.

Her thoughts, fixed on the infant and what Jerome might be doing to her and to Mayzie, kept her marching resolutely onward.

There! In the distance! A stone building that had to be her goal. With renewed drive she picked up her pace. The heat beat down with such intensity that as she drew nearer the building, she grew lightheaded. If only she had water! Her mind drew pictures of fountains of sparkling water and pasted them onto the desolate land. She had to ignore them. But she heard the tinkling of the water as it cascaded onto the rocks around a fountaining spring. She smelled the freshness, imagined she felt the dampness.

A mirage! To one side of and not far from the building. It looked and sounded and smelled so real! And she was so thirsty. A drop of water landed on her arm. She stared at it for the seconds before it evaporated, leaving a cool spot, a promise of refreshment. Of life.

She turned aside, toward the fountain. It was a trick. It had to be. But if it wasn't ...

With a groan Zauna woke from her faint. Kyla moved to place herself where she would block Zauna's view of Mayzie, guessing that a vision of Jerome torturing Mayzie must have caused the crystal gazer to faint. Winnie, still crouched beside Zauna, bent close and whispered something into Zauna's ear. Whatever it was, it calmed Zauna. She sat up, still facing away from the bloody corpse.

The silence in the room since Mayzie's death was broken only by the sound of someone sobbing. Kyla thought it was Veronica, but she didn't turn around to look, and the sobbing soon subsided. A hand on her shoulder made Kyla look up.

Leah bent down to say, "I've put a blanket over the ... over Mayzie. March and Lore are going to carry her body into another room. We'll have to notify her husband."

Kyla nodded. "I dread that. Isham will be heartbroken. I don't know what to tell him. And their little son ..." She paused to collect herself. It was hard to get the words out. "Have them put her in the room she used for nursing."

Leah moved away. Winnie helped Zauna rise and guided her to the chair from which she'd fallen. "What happened to Mayzie?" Kyla heard Zauna ask Winnie.

Zauna must have heard some of what she and Leah had said. Kyla got awkwardly to her feet and went to her side. "You don't know? When you fainted, what had you seen?"

Zauna shuddered, her face so pale Kyla feared she was about to faint again. But Winnie kept her hand on Zauna's shoulder, steadying her. "Hands. Bloody hands. Holding Dreama." Her whispered responses came out in gasps, and she shook her head all the while she spoke, as though she wanted to deny what her crystal ball had shown her. "I couldn't see the person, just the hands. And Dreama. I don't think the blood was hers. I didn't see Mayzie. Just those hands, dripping blood. And Dreama's face was all screwed up, and I didn't have to hear to know she was screaming, and ... and the hands were lowering her to the ground, and ..." Zauna sobbed, rocking back and forth.

"Go on, please," Kyla begged, though she dreaded to hear more.

"He was lowering her onto an ant hill. And the ants were huge and angry and bright red like fire." She spoke so rapidly that it was hard for Kyla to follow. As soon as she got the words out, Zauna collapsed in sobs.

"We have to get her," Kyla said.

"Did you see her actually placed on the ant hill?" someone asked. "Maybe it was a trick."

Kyla recognized the voice of Petros Birge. His acute hearing would easily pick up the words Zauna had spoken so low and hoarsely. How Kyla wished he were right, but it was no trick—not the sort Petros meant.

"No," she said. "Somehow he knows we're seeing what he's doing. He wants us to try to rescue her. She's nothing more than a means to an end for him. He wants us to go where he is."

"Well, we have to, don't we?" Veronica said, coming to stand beside her. "We can't let Dreama die."

"She won't last long on that anthill," Zauna said, shaking her head in despair. "Even if we knew where he was and how to get there."

"I know he's somewhere on the world I trapped him on," Ed said. "I can get there. But did you see Marta there?"

"No," Zauna answered. "I only saw those bloody hands holding the baby."

"Mayzie's blood," Abigail chimed in sadly. "He's a madman."

"A clever and very gifted one," Kyla said. "And very, very dangerous. If you go there, Ed, you could be putting yourself into his power."

She turned and looked at the others. "I have one idea. Rather than any of us trying to go where Jerome has Dreama, I think Ed should go to the world, take Lore with him, and then let Lore transport Dreama to them." She turned to Lore. "As soon as you have her,

Ed can return here with you and Dreama. It would be safer than trying to confront Jerome."

To Ed she said, "Lore can bring objects to him, and I believe he could bring Dreama, small and helpless as she is."

"I might be able to. I'm willing to try," Lore said. "But we don't know where Jerome is. We might appear right in front of him."

"I'm willing to take that chance," Ed told him. "It's a big place. The odds are in our favor. It's the best plan we have. If it works, I'll bring you and the baby back here, and then I'll return and hunt for Marta."

"Just do something, fast," Veronica begged. "We can't let her die at the hands of that monster. To do that to poor, dear Mayzie ..." She sobbed, unable to finish.

"Lore? Are you willing?" Kyla asked, skewering the young man with her glance.

He shrugged. "It's taking a big chance, and I've never tried to transport a baby—"

"It's the only chance Dreama has," Abigail snapped. "And you are the only one with that ability."

"Not quite," Ed said. "Marta has it. If we could only find her."

"She isn't here, and Lore is," Renni put in.

"All right, let's do it," Ed said, grasping Lore's arm. Before Lore could object, he and Ed disappeared.

"Oh, I hope it works," Veronica said, wiping away the tears. "It has to."

Ed gazed in horror at the devastation all around him. Until Lore pried his fingers loose, he didn't realize how hard he was gripping the young man's arm. "This isn't—this can't be my land."

Even as he spoke, he knew it was. He recognized

certain landmarks. The dry streambed, the withered trunk of what had been his apple tree, the hill, now barren and stony, that had been covered with wild flowers.

His rage grew. He wanted, needed, to find Jerome and make him pay for the destruction he'd wreaked. He turned to Lore and snapped, "Get busy. Find the baby and bring her here."

"Take it easy," came the shocked response. "I'm working on it."

He shouldn't take out his rage on this fellow, who was only trying to help, but he couldn't and wouldn't "take it easy." He offered no apology but stared off into the distance and muttered, "Just do it."

Maybe, if Jerome was still holding the infant, Lore would bring him along with the child. Ed wanted that. He longed to confront Jerome, imagining how he'd light into him, not using power, only his own physical strength. He needed the release that would bring, needed the pleasure of raining blows on his old enemy.

A weak wail followed by Lore's demand, "take me back, quick!" broke through Ed's thoughts and sent him whirling around.

Lore held in his arms a naked baby still crawling with ants the young man was frantically trying to brush off. The infant's flesh was red, swollen, covered with nasty-looking bites. Her face was so swollen Ed couldn't see her features. No longer wailing, she seemed to be struggling to breathe, her tiny chest heaving.

"Hurry, damn you! Can't you see she's dying?"

Ed grasped Lore's arm and pictured the room in which Kyla and her friends were gathered, waiting, depending on him. After returning there along with

Lore and the infant, he'd come right back here. But he couldn't think of that now, he reminded himself sternly. He had to concentrate on going there, where healers were waiting to save the child.

It seemed to Ed that he and Lore remained standing for hours, still as statues, going nowhere, the heat of the scorched land rising around them, the baby's gasping breaths fading into silence. If he didn't reach the healers in time, Marta would never forgive him.

He shut his eyes, closing out the sight of the ruined land and the dying infant, only visualizing Kyla, Veronica, Abigail, the others, waiting in that room that suddenly seemed so small, so far away. He couldn't remember the details. *Concentrate on Kyla's face*, he told himself. *Shut out everything else.*

"At last!" Kyla's voice.

Ed opened his eyes in time to see Abigail grab the infant from Lore's arms and Veronica place her hands on the child while Abigail rocked her. He stood, fascinated, as Veronica's skin reddened and swelled, welts appearing on her and on Abigail, while Leah reached in to brush off the vicious ants and stomp on them.

Abigail cried out in pain, and Leah had to support her arms to prevent her from dropping her precious burden. Veronica's face wore a grimace of pain and her hands shook, but she did not lift them from the infant, whose flesh was losing its fiery red tone and returning to a healthy pink even as Veronica's and Abigail's skin continued to redden and swell.

That meant the healing was going well. Veronica and Abigail were taking into themselves the poison the ants had injected and the pain they caused. That was how healing went; they would draw all the illness from little Dreama into their own bodies, and then disperse it. No need to watch longer—they'd saved the baby. He had to find Marta.

But having seen the land he could no longer think of as his, it occurred to him to supply himself with a canteen or water bottle. Skirting the healers, he reached Leah and whispered the request into her ear. She nodded, and without taking her eyes off Abigail, she told him where to find what he needed. Following her instructions, he went into the kitchen, filled two water bottles, and found a sack to carry them in.

He willed himself back to his violated land, shuddering again as he pictured the devastation. Finding Marta was his first priority, but after that he'd dedicate himself to healing the land.

Immediately on reaching his destination he looked for signs of her passage. He spotted her footprint in the dry creek bed, crossed it, and soon found other prints, easily visible in the dust. She must be heading toward the abandoned building. He quickened his pace. If he hurried, maybe he could catch up to her before she reached that site.

Renni stood near the wall, away from the healers, away from Ed, and, especially, away from Kyla. As usual, no one was paying any attention to her. Zauna was again seated in front of her crystal ball, but instead of looking into it she watched the process of healing. Lore also focused his attention on the healers, Renni was pleased to note. She, on the other hand, watched Ed. She couldn't hear what he whispered to Leah, but her gaze followed him as he headed for the kitchen.

A sudden intuition led her to move quickly to Petros's side, bend down, and whisper into the disabled man's ear, "Can you send your consciousness with Ed and stay with him? We can't risk losing him again."

He nodded. "Good idea," he said, and immediately a far-away look came into his eyes. He'd followed her suggestion. She wished she knew what had happened when Petros gave a start, but she didn't want to draw attention to herself by questioning him. His eyes remained unfocused, his face slack. Wherever Ed was, Petros's mind was with him. Satisfied that she had accomplished that much, Renni was content to wait until Petros was able to tell her and the rest what Ed was up to.

From his position on his wheeled platform, Petros couldn't see what the healers were doing. He could have sent his consciousness into Veronica or Abigail or someone near them in order to witness up close the healing of little Dreama, but it felt too much like spying. Still, it was frustrating not to be able to see the healing process unfold. Renni's suggestion appealed to him. Sending his consciousness to keep track of Ed might be interpreted as spying, too, but Renni was right about not wanting to lose him again.

So he sent his consciousness into Ed and watched as Ed found and filled two water bottles, placed them into a canvas tote, and slung its straps over his shoulder. Although he'd guessed what Ed was about to do, it still jolted him when suddenly instead of the large, airy kitchen filled with fading aromas of the food Kyla had served her guests for the Naming-Day celebration, a hot, dry, desert stretched before him. Only the twisted trunks of long-dead trees broke the monotony of the rolling sand dunes that continued to the far horizon. On that horizon a haze partially obscured what might be hills or could be only clouds. Petros wasn't privy to Ed's thoughts; his talent didn't work that way. He could only observe what Ed did and draw conclusions from his actions. He saw Ed stoop and examine a footprint that had to be Marta's, so he guessed Ed was following a trail he hoped would lead to her.

As Petros traveled along with Ed, an unobserved hitchhiker, he sensed the discomfort his host must feel due to the heat and the extreme aridity. Even though he couldn't feel the heat himself, he judged how hot and dehydrating it had to be to walk through this lifeless desert by the number of times Ed paused to take a swallow or two from his water bottle and how often he wiped the sweat from his face. But Ed never stopped for more than a couple of minutes except once when he stooped to remove one shoe, dump sand out of it, then repeat the process with the other. Another swallow from his water bottle, and then off he went again.

At last Petros spied something different in the distance. What he'd at first taken for a pile of rocks took on the form of an abandoned and crumbling building. Ed must have seen it before Petros did. They were now headed directly toward it. But as they drew closer, Ed slowed, studied the ground. Yes, Petros could see them—footprints turning away from the building and heading off in another direction. Ed shaded his eyes and gazed off in that new direction. Petros could see nothing, but Ed headed that way, anyway, following the prints that must be Marta's.

Because Ed's gaze focused on the ground, searching for prints, Petros echoed mentally Ed's cry of horror when he looked up and beheld a strange and terrifying sight. At first glance it looked like a fountain of sparkling water, with Marta standing in its center. But Marta, her hands upraised like a statue, did not move, nor did the supposed water. And when Ed reached out and touched it, Petros felt his shock and heard him mutter, "It's waxy, like the paraffin Marta uses when she cans vegetables."

Ed called Marta's name, but, held motionless in the false fountain, she probably couldn't hear—if indeed she lived. Ed dropped his pack with the canteens and pressed against the substance that looked like water but wasn't. It gave slightly beneath his fists but bounded back as soon as he released the pressure. He pressed harder. Petros could sense the tremendous effort Ed was putting forth to no avail. Defeated, he dropped his arms to his side.

"Maybe I can dig through it," he muttered, "if I can just find something to dig with."

"I'd be upset if you damaged my lovely sculpture," a voice behind them boomed.

Ed whirled around.

A tall figure loomed over them. Ed stared at the face peering down at them and laughing. What Petros saw through Ed's eyes was a skeletal form, flesh stretched taut over bone, a face little more than a skull with eyes, the deeply tanned flesh so near the color of old bone that at first Petros believed he was seeing a skeleton. But the eyes were startlingly alive, filled with a fiery glee that made Petros want to withdraw from Ed. He resisted that impulse. He would not give in to cowardice and fail Ed at this most crucial time.

Ed reacted first with a sharp intake of breath and then with the pronouncing of a single name: "Jerome!"

"Ah, yes, you recognize me, fool. You thought you were finished with me forever when you left me stuck in this land that you so stupidly called yours. But if any part of it ever was your land, it's all mine now. How do you like what I've done to it?"

Petros could not read minds, but he felt the rage boiling inside Ed's.

"What have you done to my wife?" Ed demanded.

"Oh, is that your wife? The former wonder worker? More fool she, to have married a simpleton like you. I see you've grown a beard. It doesn't make you appear any smarter. Still the simpleton, you've abandoned your wife here just as you did me.

The poor woman was so thirsty and tired, I took pity on her and led her to this fountain. But somehow, when she reached it and plunged her hands into the water, she was pulled in farther, and the water solidified around her. Never did get the drink she craved. No, she's not dead. She can't move, can't talk, but she's aware of everything. She can see you. She knows you've come for her. Wave to her, why don't you?"

Ed did not wave, but Petros felt him trying to do something, take some action. He tried to channel power to Ed, though he had little to spare, needing all his strength to keep his consciousness with Ed over such a great distance. Was distance the right term for whatever separated this odd, dead world from what Petros thought of as "the real world"?

Sparks shot from Ed's hands to fall harmlessly at the feet of the creature Ed had called Jerome. Ed shook his head, and his gaze fastened on Marta. Petros guessed by the strain he felt that Ed was trying to transport her from the fountain and bring her to his side. She remained firmly fixed in the odd substance. Had Jerome spoken the truth when he'd said she was alive and aware? Not even her eyes moved. Her fixed stare and frozen expression of terror could have been those of a corpse.

But Jerome, apparently aware of what Ed was attempting, said, "What a pity, Eddie. She can't join you. But to show you how thoughtful and considerate I am, I'll make it possible for you to join her."

He flicked a finger toward the fountain, and for just a moment it became water, sparkling in the harsh sunlight. And for a fatal second, struck by the sudden beauty, Petros failed to act, to withdraw and hurtle back to his own body. For in that fatal second, Ed, reaching toward Marta, plunged into the fountain, and, as he reached her side, the water returned to its solid state. Ed was trapped beside Marta. Then Petros tried to withdraw, only to discover that he, too, was trapped. He could not leave Ed's mind.

CHAPTER TEN
ERRANDS

Veronica lay on the floor, cushioned against Abigail. She had held Dreama in her arms until Kyla bent and took the infant, now completely healed, from her. The pain that had accompanied the healing had left, but now she felt drained, empty of power and empty even of the energy it would require to rise to her feet. Dreama had been so near death from all the ant bites that the healing sapped all Veronica's strength and probably all of Abigail's as well. If they both had not been here and able to work together, neither of them could have done it on her own.

So when she heard someone call out, "Something's wrong with Petros!" she groaned. If someone else needed healing, it was too bad. Neither she nor Abigail would be able to do anything about it. She closed her mind to the sudden stir and concentrated on gathering her strength. But she had none to gather.

Someone—she opened her eyes just enough to see that it was Renni—bent over her. "Marchion Blandry is sharing power with Abigail," Renni said. "Ask him to share with you. I think you need it more than she does."

Veronica remembered that Mr. Blandry was a power enhancer. But she lacked the strength to ask him. She could only manage to whisper to Renni, "You ask."

Renni must have done so, because a sudden infusion of power hit her body like a charge of electricity, and her mind cleared. She could sit up and look around. Kyla held Dreama and rocked her while standing near Petros. Zauna gazed into her crystal ball, but the others had gathered around Petros. Renni came back to her side. "Need a hand up?"

Veronica nodded and reached out; Renni clasped her arm and steadied her as she rose to her feet. "Ed's not back yet?" she asked.

"No, but right now everybody's worried about Petros." She lowered her voice to a whisper. "I know what's wrong, but I'm scared to tell them. I know they'll get mad at me."

Veronica frowned. "Why? What 'd you do now?"

Still whispering, Renni said, "I suggested he send his consciousness into Ed so he could keep track of him, and he did it. So he can't respond to anybody here because his mind is with Ed, wherever that is."

"That wasn't a bad idea," Veronica admitted rather grudgingly.

Renni shrugged. "I know they'd say it wasn't my place to tell him that. But I figured that way we could know what was happening with Ed and whether he found Marta."

Veronica hadn't forgotten that she was angry with Renni for taking Ed's memories without telling her or anybody else that she was going to do it. But she'd made her own serious mistakes. Maybe she should regard Renni as an ally. "Shouldn't Petros be able to tell us something?" she asked.

"I don't know. I don't really know how that consciousness transfer thing works."

"Well, it isn't really a transfer. That would mean he'd be in Ed's body and Ed's mind would be in his. I don't know of anybody who can do that. Petros's consciousness just goes along with Ed, but he can draw it back at any time. And I think he can tell us things, though it would kind of sound like he was talking in his sleep. Hasn't he said anything?"

"Not as far as I know."

"Let's see what we can find out." Veronica headed toward those gathered around Petros.

Renni put her hand on Veronica's arm, holding her back. "Don't tell them what I told you. Please."

"I won't," Veronica said. But she didn't promise.

She pushed past Lore and Winnie to get close to Petros. He was no longer sitting up on his wheeled platform, nor was he merely slumped over. He had toppled off and was lying on the floor beside it. Abigail had bent over him. As Veronica reached her side, she grasped Veronica's arm for support and stood, shaking her head. "It's nothing I can heal," she said. "It's like he isn't even there. He's sent his consciousness somewhere, I'd guess."

"But in that case, he shouldn't have collapsed like that," Kyla said, rocking Dreama. "He shouldn't be completely unreachable."

"What about if he sent it with Ed?" Veronica asked. "Maybe going to another plane would make him unreachable."

Kyla frowned and started to say something, but at that moment Dreama let out a loud wail, quickly followed by another. And another.

"She's hungry," Kyla said. "We've got to find milk for her."

"There's usually someone selling goats in the market in the old quarter by the waterfront," Leah said. "Shall I go and see if there's a nanny goat available? I'm not really needed here."

"That's not so," Abigail objected. "I need you."

Aunt Abigail hated for Aunt Leah to be away from her. Why was she selfish that way? Aunt Leah was right. Since she had no magic, she could be spared more readily than anyone else. But Veronica kept her thought to herself.

"All right, then. We do need someone who can go and get back quickly." Kyla bounced the infant in her arms as she spoke, trying to quiet the squalling child. "Veronica, you go. I'll give you money for the goat if you'll hold Dreama while I go get it."

Giving Veronica no chance to respond, she thrust the screaming baby into Veronica's arms and hurried from the room. While she was gone, Winnie came and took the child from Veronica, saying, "Let me try to calm her."

Veronica gave her a grateful smile, only too glad to let the wailing child be someone else's responsibility. In Winnie's arms the child quieted and sucked her thumb, letting out sad little whimpers but no longer screaming.

Aunt Kyla returned with a leather purse, which she handed to Veronica. "You'll have to hurry to get there before the market closes," she said.

"What if the goat seller isn't there?" Veronica asked.

"He's been there every time I've gone to the market," Kyla answered, frowning. "He just has to be there this afternoon."

"I'll go with her," Renni volunteered. "Goats aren't easy to handle. She'll need help."

"And what do you know about goats?" Kyla snapped.

"Plenty," Renni said. "I was brought up on a farm. I was sixteen when my folks sold the farm and moved to Port-of-Lords, but up until then I helped raise goats and chickens and a couple of horses."

Aunt Kyla's open-mouthed reaction almost made Veronica laugh. She could hardly refuse to let Renni go, after that revelation. Veronica sensed that Kyla mistrusted the girl and was still angry with her for having taken Ed's memories of coming here and of planning to raise Dreama as his and Marta's child. But Kyla hadn't seen the state Ed was in back in the arbor in the park, helpless with grief. What Renni did allowed him to function, to take action again. Where he was now and what he was doing she didn't know, but she hoped he'd found Marta and the two of them were dealing with Jerome.

As she and Renni headed for the door, Veronica had a thought. "We've all been in the market. We've seen the goats there. Why can't Lore bring a goat to us?"

Lore laughed. "Transport a goat? Are you crazy? I don't have that much power. Especially not after using as much as I did to get the baby to Ed. I haven't had a chance to let my power build up, but even if it was at full strength, I don't think I could transport a goat. Sorry, girls, you're on your own."

Aunt Kyla added, "None of us is at full strength now. We have very little power to work with, and we must conserve what we have. So go, and hurry. Don't waste time. Dreama needs that milk."

Although she had misgivings about having let Renni accompany Veronica, Kyla found it a bit easier to breathe with two fewer people in the room. She hadn't known about Renni's farm background, wasn't certain she believed the story. But if true, it would make it easier for Veronica to carry out her errand.

Marchion and Lore lifted Petros back onto his platform and wheeled it into a bedroom, where they hefted Petros onto the bed and arranged him comfortably. March returned to the living room, but Lore offered to stay in the room with Petros so he could alert the others if there was any change in the crippled man's condition, and Kyla agreed that would be the best use of his time for the present.

In the meantime, before seeing what could be done about finding Ed and Marta, Kyla had to enlist someone for another unpleasant duty. It might as well be done while they were too weak to use the power they'd require for anything else.

So she gazed around the room and said, "Mayzie's husband has to be told about her death. And the corpse will have to be cleaned up, because he'll want to see her, and we can't let him see her covered with blood. It's really my responsibility to give him the sad news, but I don't feel that I should be gone from here now. Is there—"

"I'll go," Leah said even before she could complete the request. "I'm not needed here. And Isham knows me and considers me a friend. I can talk to him more easily than anyone else."

Kyla nodded. "He should hear the news from a friend. I was Mayzie's employer. That's a different relationship. All right. Go ahead."

Abigail stood, and Kyla feared she'd either object to Leah's leaving or insist on going with her. Instead, the older woman said, "My clothes are already stained with Mayzie's blood. I'll clean her body and cover it. Then I'll go home and change clothes and get back here. Leah, don't let Isham come here too quickly. We need to spare his feelings as much as possible."

"I'll try to hold him back," Leah said. "And poor

little Bennie. How is Isham going to explain his mother's death to a two-and-a-half-year-old?"

No one had an answer. Leah kissed Abigail and left the house. As soon as she was gone, Abigail went to perform her self-appointed task. Saying, "She'll need help," Winnie handed the now quiet Dreama to Zauna and followed Abigail.

Exhausted and heartsick, Kyla sank into a chair, leaned back, and closed her eyes, meaning to rest only a moment. Zauna was again seated before her crystal ball, gazing into it as she gently rocked Dreama, but saying nothing. Marchion had taken a seat in a straight wooden chair near Zauna, and Kyla supposed he was doing what he could to channel power to her to enhance her ability to find Ed and Marta in her crystal. If she did find them, Zauna would call out. Now it was blessedly quiet and deceptively peaceful, and without meaning to, Kyla nodded off into sleep.

She awakened with a start at the sound of loud bleats and yells and jumped to her feet, fearing to see another dread sight like that of Mayzie's bloodied body. Marchion and Zauna stood staring out the window. Seeing them there, Kyla understood that the din was coming from outside the house, not inside. She hurried to the nearest window in time to see Renni and Veronica pulling a loudly complaining goat around the side of the house toward the back yard.

Dreama began to wail. "Soon, little one," Kyla said, taking the babe from Zauna, "soon we'll have milk for you." She hoped that was true and that the child could tolerate the goat's milk. Bouncing Dreama in her arms, she hurried through the kitchen and out the back door, where the girls were struggling with the unhappy goat.

"We'll tie her to the tree," Renni said, tugging the

rope and heading for a tall pine near the rear gate. Then, as Kyla approached with Dreama, Renni called out, "Don't get any closer. She'll need to calm down before we can milk her."

Kyla stopped and watched Renni wind the rope around the tree and tie it securely, while Veronica, looking disgruntled and disheveled, was too busy dodging the goat's butting head to be of much help.

"This goat's a demon. I've got the bruises to prove it," Veronica yelled somewhat breathlessly. "I'm naming her Butter, 'cause that's what she is."

"She's just nervous," Renni said. "And it's good I went along." This last she directed to Kyla. "This dumb girl would have brought home a billy goat instead of a nanny. You'd think she'd have known the difference, but—"

"I would have seen that it was male," Veronica interrupted, moving farther away from the goat. "You didn't give me a chance. I was too busy trying not to get bitten or kicked to check its under parts."

To Kyla's relief both girls laughed, not really angry but enjoying the adventure. She couldn't help thinking how easily their desperate situation faded from their minds. Triumph at their successful acquisition of the goat seemed to have banished danger from Jerome from their thoughts.

Then Renni proved her wrong by asking, "How's Petros? Has he revived? Have Ed and Marta come back?"

CHAPTER ELEVEN
PERSUASION

Seated beside the bed on which Petros lay, Lore had time to think and plan as well as to recoup his strength. His part in Dreama's rescue had left him tired and his power severely depleted. At least the rescue of the infant had succeeded, although he could not claim full credit for it. Ed had done as much as he had. And then Ed had returned to that strange and empty land. It galled Lore to contrast how quickly his strength had ebbed with how much of Ed's remained. He would have to learn how to build up his gift, to make it more powerful.

He thought about the various members of the Gifted Community, weighing the gifts of each. Many of those Kyla had sent home had more power than those who stayed. He questioned the wisdom of that. Oh, that poor weakling, Winter Whatever-His-Name, was better off gone. His only ability was to feel other people's emotions and get a headache from it. Lore didn't see that he even belonged in the Gifted Community. But Trille, now, she had great power. Yet Kyla had let her waltz off without the slightest hesitation. Trille was a famous singer; she had pull. That had to be the reason Kyla'd let her go so easily.

And Camsen. The Honored Camsen Wellner. He had plenty of power, but he was scared to use it. Scared of losing his place among the priests of Ondin.

Ran back to the temple with his tail between his legs. Why had the Power-Giver granted him so much power, when he didn't want to use it? Lore didn't understand why Kyla had even had him here officiating at the baby's Naming-Day Ceremony. Was she afraid to cross the priests of the established religion—she who supposedly could communicate with the Power-Giver? Why should she and no one else interpret the Power-Giver's will for the group? Didn't anybody in the Community question that?

Yes, Kyla organized the Community and found the gifted ones. But she didn't give the gifts. Bringing them, she called it. They came from the Power-Giver, she said. But Zauna Raye had been a fortuneteller long before Kyla arrived in Port-of-Lords, and he'd heard she'd done quite well at it. Professor Morence claimed that he had only discovered his gift of coercion on meeting Kyla, and he scarcely ever used it, but Lore had heard his students complain that he was arrogant and rude and no one liked him, neither students nor faculty, yet he boasted about being chairman of the Behavioral Sciences Department and in line for the position of dean. He'd already held that chairmanship when Kyla founded the Community. Lore was willing to bet that the good professor had used his gift of coercion to attain that position and would continue using it to be elevated even higher. It wasn't a gift he'd acquired through Kyla. Maybe he'd used it subconsciously, not knowing what it was until Kyla revealed it, but it had been there all along.

As for his own gifts, it would never have occurred to him to attempt to bring an object to him just by concentrating on that object. However, he did recall that as a child playing alone while his parents were at work, he had sometimes brought a small object that was out of reach close to him by willing it to move. At that young age he hadn't known that the ability was unusual and not shared by others. Later, as schoolwork took up more of his time, leaving little opportunity for play, he'd forgotten about the ability or dismissed it as imagination. It must have been real. He'd had the gift from early childhood; Kyla hadn't given it to him.

He'd point this out to Kyla, but now wasn't the time, not when she was upset about the disappearance of her friends and the wet nurse's killing. He did not want to anger her or turn her against him. Not when he could still learn so much from her.

He glanced at Petros. Still completely unconscious. Why waste time staying here with him? Enough time had gone by that the girls should be back from the market. He wanted to talk to Veronica about an idea he had for finding Marta and Ed.

Veronica flinched inwardly when Renni recounted the embarrassing incident of her nearly purchasing a male goat. She laughed along with Renni, and she was not sorry to see the story bring a smile to Kyla's lips. But Veronica resented being made a fool of before Aunt Kyla, who still regarded her as a child. And as irresponsible.

After she'd tied the goat, Renni busied herself making certain it could reach plenty of grass for grazing. "I'll milk her as soon as she calms down," she told Kyla, eyeing the fussy baby in Kyla's arms.

Not wanting to help with the goat, Veronica asked, "Have Ed and Marta returned?"

Aunt Kyla's smile vanished. She shook her head. "Not yet. I'm terribly worried about them."

"Well, what are you doing about it?" The question came out more sharply than Veronica intended. She didn't really want to anger Aunt Kyla. But Kyla's creased forehead told her she had.

"We're letting our power build back up," Kyla snapped. "Until it does, there's nothing we can do, no matter how much we want to."

Veronica knew she should drop the matter. Her own power had not fully returned, so she understood Aunt Kyla's dilemma. That streak of what Aunt Abigail called "contrariness" kicked in and made her say, "Marchion Blandry is an enhancer. Shouldn't you use him to—"

Kyla cut in, "He depleted his power feeding it to you and Abigail so you could heal Dreama. And to Abigail and you when you were trying to heal Mayzie." Her sharp tone made Dreama let out loud wails.

"Didn't do much good then, did it?" Veronica whirled away before Kyla could answer and slammed into the house. Mercifully, no one was in the kitchen. She stopped there to gather her thoughts.

She'd acted abominably, and she didn't even know why. Could Jerome be feeding anger to her as he had before when she ... No. She could not let that happen again. She loved Aunt Kyla. Aunt Kyla was like a mother to her. She should go right back outside and apologize.

She should. But she didn't. She'd let Kyla's anger cool a bit first. She walked slowly into the living room. Zauna was sitting at the table on which she'd placed her crystal ball, but she was slumped over, possibly asleep, certainly not gazing into the crystal. Marchion Blandry sat in a wing chair, and he most definitely was asleep. He let out a snore as Veronica neared. No one else was in the living room.

Thinking to go to her room, she tiptoed toward the hall door, but before she reached it, Lore came through it. He took in the sleepers in a quick glance and beckoned to Veronica. She approached and he stepped back into the hall. When she reached him, he whispered, "Come with me. I want to talk to you."

She nodded and he led her into Kyla's bedroom, where Petros lay. Someone had thrown a blanket over him. "We can talk here," Lore said. "He won't hear us."

Hesitant to speak, she nodded again, not out of concern for the silent figure on the bed but because she felt uncomfortable in Lore's presence. He was good-looking, with his dark, wavy hair, dark eyes with long lashes, his cleft chin, his warm smile. He was also, she reminded herself sternly, nine years older than she. To him she was just a kid. He wasn't attracted to her. Why should he be? She wasn't pretty. She was short for her age and overweight, with a plain face that impressed no one. Yet he'd called her in here. He wanted something from her. Something to do with power, no doubt. That was her one asset—her power. And it wasn't always an asset. Quite the opposite—it scared off any boy her age who might possibly take an interest in her. She tried to keep it a secret, but there were times at school that without thinking she'd used her talent in what to her was a small way. But it had frightened people, word had gotten around that she was "odd" and could do things no normal person could do. And her classmates, most of them anyway, avoided her. She'd never had a boyfriend. A few girls were friendly toward her, but only in a distant sort of way. They wouldn't share confidences with her as they did with one another. It had hurt when Renni laughed at her ignorance about the goat. She'd hoped she and Renni could be friends, despite the difference in their ages. After all, they were both gifted, so they had that in common. But maybe that wasn't enough.

She seated herself on the stool in front of the vanity, Lore having plopped down in the only other chair, an armchair positioned by the bed on which Petros lay so still he could be taken for dead were it not for the slow rise and fall of his chest. Lore hadn't spoken since they entered the room. He was regarding her with a speculative look that made her nervous. Tired of waiting for him to initiate the conversation, she said, "What did you want to talk to me about?"

He took his time about answering, first giving her a friendly smile that did nothing to alleviate her suspicions although it did set her traitorous heart thumping wildly. Leaning back in his chair, he continued to gaze into her eyes from beneath the long, dark lashes that any girl would die for.

Finally he spoke. "I think you're wondering just as I am why no one is doing anything."

And she knew what he meant. She had been wondering exactly that. But she said, "Doing? Everybody's doing something. Leah's gone to give Mayzie's husband the news about her death. Abigail and Winnie are trying to make Mayzie's body presentable so Isham can see her when he comes. Renni and Kyla are looking after the goat and getting milk for Dreama. And Petros has sent his consciousness into Ed—that I know for a fact. And either he can't or isn't ready to come back to his body, but I'm sure he'll have a lot to tell us when he does."

"If he can get back," Lore said in a calm, measured tone, all the while gazing at her, as patient as a cat stalking a bird.

He seemed to know what she was thinking. He wasn't a mind reader—was he? She thought she knew his gifts. She'd read the notes Aunt Kyla wrote to keep track of the abilities of each Community member. Lore could bring an object to him or send it to another person, so long as he knew that person's location. Also, he could transfer himself from one place to another, but that ability was limited to a short distance—or so Kyla had believed. Now Veronica wondered whether it had been Ed's power alone that had transferred him and Lore to Ed's ravaged land.

Lore subsided into silence while Veronica thought things through. "So what is your point, Lore?" she asked at last.

"My point is that those things you listed may be important, but not as important as getting Ed and Marta back. No one is doing anything about that."

"We don't know that they can't get back on their own," Veronica said without conviction. "We don't know what they're doing."

"Shouldn't we be trying to find out?"

"Zauna is looking into her crystal."

"Zauna." Lore gave a snort of disgust. "Who knows what she really sees in that globe—if anything. Even if she sees them, which she apparently hasn't, is that going to get them back?"

"Knowing where to look would give us a starting place."

"We know enough. We know it's somewhere in that place Ed says he created, or thinks he did."

Veronica didn't fail to notice that Lore tended to denigrate other people's powers. Yet she couldn't help agreeing with him. No one was doing anything to find Marta and Ed and rescue them if they needed rescuing. Which she suspected they did.

"Kyla will act as soon as her power rebuilds," she said, repeating the excuse she had been given when she'd made the same complaint Lore was voicing.

"You have power. A lot of it," Lore observed. "Is it depleted?"

"It was. After we healed Dreama. And I haven't rested. But going with Renni to get the goat gave it time to build up a bit."

"And I rested while you were doing that," Lore said. "I'd spent a lot of my power helping Ed rescue Dreama, but just sitting in here keeping watch over Petros was relaxing even though I didn't sleep. I don't think it takes as long to restore power as Kyla seems to think. I'll bet hers has built back up, too."

"If it had, she'd say so."

"Would she?" At her frown he added quickly, "Oh, I'm sure she would, but she's concerned about Dreama, about getting milk for her. And she's keeping Renni busy with that. And no one else will do anything until Kyla tells them what to do."

Veronica didn't miss his implication. No one else— but the two of them. "So what do you suggest we do?" she asked.

"Ah, that's the question I've been waiting for," he said, that warm smile illuminating his face. "I think you and I have the power between us to get to that world, whether or not it's truly Ed's world, and find Ed and Marta."

She frowned. "We might, but if Jerome has them ..." She shuddered. "You haven't seen what Jerome can do. I have."

The smile left his face. "I saw Mayzie. Saw her bleed to death from the way he sliced her open. That gives me a fairly good idea of what he's capable of. That's exactly why I think we shouldn't be wasting time. And I thought—hoped—you'd feel the same way."

"I do. I've been thinking along those same lines. But, honestly, I'm afraid of Jerome. I wouldn't dare face him alone."

"You won't be alone. I'll be with you." He was too confident, she thought, recalling the anger Jerome had fed into her. But she'd only been nine years old then. She was much stronger now.

So was Jerome.

"Look, I know it's frightening, but with our combined power, we ought to be able to best him. You have so much talent, and I've got quite a bit. Together we should be a match for him. And if we find Ed and Marta, look at the power they have. I don't know them well, but from what I've heard, Ed has amazing gifts. Even if he didn't actually create that land."

"He created part of it," Veronica said. "He didn't create the whole thing. Whatever it is, it's on a different plane of existence, and Dire Lords had something to do with it."

He stared at her. "You believe that?"

"I know that," Veronica stated firmly. "Kyla and Marta knew a Dire Lord. That's where Marta's power came from, and maybe Kyla's too. Some of it, anyway."

"Oh, I've heard that story," he said in a tone that to Veronica indicated disbelief. She found his skepticism annoying.

"Ed met a Dire Lord there," she declared.

"And he helped Ed, right? So if he's there and it's his land, he'll help us."

Veronica shook her head. "I don't think it works that way."

He shrugged and rose to his feet. "I'm sorry. I

guess I've wasted your time—and mine. I thought you'd help. I thought you felt the way I did, that we were losing time. But I guess I was wrong, and we've spent time talking and doing nothing, just like everybody else."

Stung by those words, she jumped to her feet. "No, you're right. I've wanted somebody to do something. And if no one else will, we should."

Again that marvelous smile. "Then you're ready to take action? You'll work with me?"

She nodded, suddenly breathless.

"All right, then. Let's get busy."

"What do we do?"

"I'm going to concentrate on the place I went to with Ed, and you feed me all the power you can. Take my hands." He walked to her, his hands outstretched. She extended her hands, he grasped them, and she felt a sudden warmth that was due to more than the power that flowed from his hands to hers.

She had to force herself to concentrate on sending power back to him. Something that normally came easily to her she now found difficult. *Concentrate on Ed and Marta, not on Lore,* she told herself. *This is power work. It isn't a boy-girl thing. He's only interested in my gifts, not in me.*

The stern lecture to herself helped. She focused her power and fed it to him. Something like electricity jolted through them both. And then they were no longer in the small bedroom but standing on burning sand being buffeted by a hot, sand-laden wind. Veronica freed her hands from Lore's so she could shield her face. In seconds her body was coated with sand and her hair was full of it. It stung and itched and abraded her hands.

They could die in this sandstorm. Coming here

was a mistake. She shouldn't have let Lore persuade her. They should go back right away. She opened her mouth to yell above the screaming wind, but sand flew into her mouth, and she quickly closed it. Her eyes shut tightly against the sand. She tried to will herself back home, back in the bedroom from which they'd come. Nothing happened. The wind continued, unrelenting. The pummeling sand drove her to her knees. Shielding her face with one arm, with the other she reached around her to locate Lore. He should be within reach, but her groping hand encountered nothing but sand.

Blinded, unable to shout over the wind, afraid to get back to her feet, she crawled in what she hoped was a circle but still encountered nothing. Where was Lore?

He must have seen how hopeless the situation was and returned home without her. But if so, he must be trying to bring her back. Why was she still here?

She gave up her futile search and huddled in a miserable crouch, her back to the wind, trying to protect her head and face. The sand built up around her body. If rescue didn't come soon, she'd die here, buried so no one would ever find her.

When Lore had come here before with Ed, it had been uncomfortably hot, with wind blowing some sand around, but nothing like this. He shut his eyes tightly against the onslaught. When he felt Veronica withdraw her hands from his, he slapped his freed hands over his face and hunched forward. They should return. They could do nothing in this sandstorm.

He hated to admit defeat. The thought of going back and confessing what a mistake his plan had been galled him. If he could just find some shelter from this storm, possibly he—they—could wait out the storm. He remembered he had a handkerchief in his pocket, fished around until he found it, and tied it over his nose and mouth. He turned to face the direction in which the wind was blowing so that his back was to the wind, and with his hands shading his eyes, risked opening them.

In the distance something glowed. A light? Out here? It seemed to be, but the blowing sand made it impossible to see clearly. He had to get closer. Without thinking, he stumbled through drifts of sand toward the glow. He couldn't have gone more than a few paces when he remembered Veronica. Calling out to her was useless in the howling wind. He turned around and squinted, trying to spot her. Sand flew into his eyes. Again he turned his back to the wind. He blinked his watering eyes until he could see again.

He should go back and find Veronica, but that would mean struggling against the wind, and sight was impossible. He could only find her by blundering into her, and how likely was that?

She could die out here. So could he. They would if the sandstorm kept up for long. But she had power, more than he had, he believed. She'd find a way to save herself. He hoped she would. If she didn't, he wasn't likely to survive either. But if the glow he saw was a light, it meant someone was out there. Maybe even that there was a building up ahead. Hadn't Ed spoken of a building here somewhere?

Why should both of them die, smothered in sand, their bodies buried, so no one would ever know what happened to them? It was difficult to walk with the wind, but walking against it was impossible. Why not head for the light and see what it was?

He slogged toward it, his feet sinking into drifts of sand that shifted beneath his feet. It was worse than wading through mud. He fell forward every few steps and had to pick himself up and move on. The glow still shone in the distance, brighter than before. It wasn't at ground level, but neither was it high enough above it to be a moon or even the sun shining through the dark storm clouds. Unless the sun was rising or setting—he had no idea what direction he was looking toward, and anyway, in this weird place the sun might even rise or set in the north or south.

After what seemed like hours, the light appeared closer, and he could see that it shone through a window of a building. Ed had spoken of a ruined building, long abandoned. But a light inside meant this building was inhabited. Maybe it was ruined but Ed and Marta had reached it and built a fire inside. They wouldn't need a fire for warmth, but for light. Kyla had told the group that both Marta and Ed had the gift of kindling a globe of cold fire that they could hold in their hands.

They had other powers as well. If he could reach them and explain what had happened, they could rescue Veronica. With renewed hope he plowed forward, and as he neared the building, the wind lessened. The sand ceased its pummeling. When he reached the building, the sand no longer flew and the wind calmed to a gentle breeze. The light flowed out from the window inviting him in.

The stone building's façade was scarred, with stones missing here and there. He walked to the window and looked inside, saw only an empty room, its stone floor strewn with rubble. The light shone from a doorway in the wall opposite the window. "Ed?" he called. "Marta?"

He heard no answer. The window was not so high that he couldn't climb through it, but the building must have a door. He walked around to the side. A long wall held high windows from which no light spilled, and he saw no door. He retraced his steps to the front of the building. As he passed the window there, he again looked inside. Glancing up, he saw that the roof over that room had fallen in. Anyone seeking refuge would go farther inside, under a roof. Marta and Ed must have done that and were probably not near enough to hear his calls. He'd walk around to the other side and look for a door. If he didn't find one, he'd come back and climb through the window.

He turned and walked toward the corner of the building. A voice behind him said, "You won't find what you're looking for inside this place."

He whirled around. The man he faced was taller than he by an inch or two and quite thin but muscular and looked to be no more than five or six years older than he was. His friendly smile and open and direct gaze made Lore question whether this could possibly be the formidable Jerome that Kyla and Marta had spoken of.

"How do you know what I'm looking for?"

The man's smile didn't waver. "Did I guess wrong? I assumed you were looking for your friends."

"I saw a light come from the building," Lore said. "I thought after that wild sandstorm I should find shelter. That looked like a safer place."

The man nodded. "It looks like that," he said. "Looks can be deceiving."

"Yes, they can." Lore did not return his smile. "Who are you and how did you get here?"

"I could ask you the same questions," the man replied.

"You could, but I asked first."

The man laughed. "I like your spirit," he said. "And I admire the way you battled your way through the sandstorm."

"I didn't have much choice about that," Lore said. "You haven't answered my questions. Now I have another. How could you have seen me battling through the sandstorm?"

He chuckled, a pleasant sound without any hint of derision. "I didn't see you. But the sand on your clothes and in your hair tells the story."

"Oh." Lore looked down, away from the amused expression on the man's face. "I guess it *is* obvious," he muttered.

"No reason to be embarrassed," the man said. "You've just gone through a really scary experience. And naturally the promise of shelter would attract you. But don't be fooled by that light." Lore looked up in time to see him gesture toward the window with its enticing glow.

"Why do you say I shouldn't go in there? And why are you sure what I'm looking for isn't inside? Someone must be in there, or where's the light coming from?"

"Some*thing* is in there, and it's nothing you'd want to meet. The light is a decoy. It's a trap."

"A trap?" Lore found himself wanting to believe this congenial fellow, but if this was Jerome, and all that Kyla and the others said about him was true ...

"Come with me. It's getting dark, and you don't want to be out here at night. Besides, another sandstorm could come up at any time. I have a place here—nothing fancy, but it's safe. You can get cleaned up. And I'll bet you're thirsty. Probably hungry, too."

"That sounds good," Lore said, trying not to reveal

the eagerness he felt at the thought of water and food and a place to rid of the sand that was making his head and body itch. A place to rest. So inviting, but ... "I'd like to accept, but I didn't come here alone. I got separated from my companion, and now that the sandstorm is over I need to go hunt for her."

"Her?"

The puzzlement and even shock that infused the question convinced Lore that his new friend had not known anyone else was here in this land. He nodded. "A young girl. I'm worried about her."

"A young girl! No wonder you're worried. Yet ... when I came upon you, you were looking for a way into this building. You don't think she might have gone in there, do you?" Alarm tinged his voice. Not feigned, Lore felt certain.

"No. Oh, no. I was looking for a place to shelter in. I planned to go back and find her and bring her here if the building proved safe."

"As I've told you, it is far from safe. But who is this young girl, and where did you leave her?"

"Her name is Veronica."

"Ah, the young Crowell girl. I remember her well." A quick quirk of the mouth as though he was trying to suppress a grin accompanied the words.

"So you are Jerome?" Lore dared to ask.

"Jerome Esterville, at your service." He gave a little bow. "I'm sure Veronica's grown quite a bit since I saw her last. She was, let's see, nine then, I think."

"You haven't seen her since?' Lore asked, stepping back, away from Jerome.

"No, how could I? I'm stranded here in this barren and forbidding place. But I do know it well, and I can certainly help you find Veronica."

"You—you stole that baby and nearly killed her.

And you did kill the wet nurse. After you tortured her."

A look of astonishment and horror appeared on Jerome's face. "I? I did those things? No. No, indeed. How could I, when I have no way of leaving this world? It wasn't I."

"Who was it, then?" Lore demanded, making no attempt to conceal his skepticism.

"There is an evil Dire Lord who visits here and who delights in tormenting people. He's tormented me often enough. It would be like him to do those terrible things and cast the blame on me. It would suit his perverted sense of humor."

Could Jerome be telling the truth? Lore wanted to believe him. And Jerome's voice sounded nothing like the voice they'd all heard thunder through Kyla's home. Nor did his appearance match the appearance of the being Zauna had described seeing in her crystal ball.

"Is that what's in the building? The thing you warned me against?"

Looking very solemn now, Jerome nodded. "That building is a nexus, a place where planes meet, giving a Dire Lord easy access to this world."

"To this world? What about access to my world? Where the baby was taken from?

"A Dire Lord can manifest anywhere, but it can't remain long in your world. I'm not sure why that is. It's not restricted here, though."

"So if it's in that building, can it come out of it and come after us? Are we safe anywhere on this world?"

Again that slight quirk of the lips as Jerome spoke. "Not completely, but the danger is greater the nearer we are to the building so we really need to move away."

"All right. Let's search for Veronica."

"I hope she's nearby," Jerome said. "It will soon be dark, and there's no twilight here. Night falls quickly. But surely you wouldn't have gone far from where you last saw her."

"I don't know. It was so hard, with the sand blowing all around. I could barely see. I may not have walked as far as it seemed." Lore gazed around. After the darkness that prevailed during the sandstorm, the daylight had seemed so bright he had failed to notice the gradual dimming of the day. But, yes, the light was fading, and rather quickly.

"Were you walking against the wind or with it?" Jerome asked.

"With it. It was impossible to walk against it. And it seemed to be pushing me along, which makes me think I could have come a considerable distance."

"I'm afraid we'd have no chance of finding her in the darkness."

The thought crossed his mind that Jerome might have deliberately kept him talking until it became too late to go searching for Veronica. But he'd seemed so genuinely concerned on learning that she had come here that surely that could not be true.

"I'm sorry," Jerome said. "I should have warned you sooner. I forgot that you wouldn't be accustomed to having so little time between daylight and dark."

"Couldn't we search by moonlight?"

"There is no moon here." He gave a little chuckle. "If this is Ed's world, as he believes, he was quite neglectful in failing to supply it with a moon." He grasped Lore's arm. "But I've always thought poor Ed was quite deluded about having 'dreamed up' this world, as I believe he once put it. Come on. Let me take you to my place."

"But what about Veronica? We can't just leave her."

"But you did leave her, and now it's too late to remedy that situation. Believe me, you would not find her in the dark, because when night falls here, it is very dark. Unless, you have the gift of summoning a light?"

"No, I don't. But what about you?"

"I have little power of any sort." Jerome's tone was rueful. "So you see, there isn't much we could do now. In fact, we'll have to hurry to reach my humble home before darkness falls."

He was right. The light was fading fast. Much as he regretted it, Lore could see that he had little choice but to accept Jerome's offer of shelter for the night. Still, he hesitated. He was, after all, responsible for Veronica's being here. He had persuaded her to come; he should not desert her.

"As I recall," Jerome said, "even as a young child, Veronica had a great deal of power. I suspect she can take care of herself. She may even have transported herself back home by now."

"She could have, I suppose," Lore said. "She *is* very gifted."

"There, you see! She'll be fine. We'll look for her as soon as it's light, but I'll wager we won't find her because she's found a way to get back home on her own, without waiting for you."

Veronica might do that. She was unpredictable. She had a lot of power, just as Jerome said. She could protect herself better than he could.

Jerome had not released his grasp on Lore's arm. He gave Lore a gentle tug, and Lore allowed himself to be drawn away through the growing darkness to whatever home Jerome had fashioned for himself. Any shelter, Lore told himself, would be welcome.

CHAPTER TWELVE
THREATS AND RESOLUTIONS

Kyla sighed with relief after finally getting Dreama to accept the bottle of goat's milk. She leaned back in her chair for a moment, but sat up in alarm when Renni rushed into the kitchen.

"I can't find Veronica anywhere," Renni said. "I can't find Lore, either. Where would they have gone?"

"I don't know. Wait a minute." Kyla hurried into the living room, Dreama held up against her shoulder. "Zauna," she said, and the older woman jerked forward and looked up at her with alarm. She must have been dozing.

"We need to locate Lore and Veronica," Kyla said. "Could you see whether you can find them in your crystal?"

Zauna rubbed her eyes. "They're missing?"

"Why else would I ask you to find them?" Kyla regretted her words as soon as they came out of her mouth. "I'm sorry. I didn't mean to snap at you. Renni says they're missing." She turned to Renni. "Did you look all through the house? And the yard? Maybe they're tending to the goat."

"I looked in every room, and I searched the yard and went out and looked up and down the street."

"Why were you looking for them?"

"Does it matter? I didn't find them, that's the important thing, isn't it?"

The girl seemed determined to anger her, but Kyla resisted the temptation to respond in kind and asked, "Did you check that little park Veronica likes to go to? It isn't far."

"No. I'll go look. But in case they aren't there, maybe you should come up with some kind of plan for finding them."

Kyla's resolve to hold her temper weakened. She snapped, "You just heard me ask Zauna to look for them."

Dreama started to cry. Kyla bounced her a bit and was rewarded by the baby's spitting up all over her shoulder.

"I'm going." Renni made a hasty exit.

Dreama's wails could mean the baby couldn't digest the goat's milk, but since they had nothing else to feed her, Kyla had to hope the infant was only reacting to her sharp tone.

Marchion had gone to stand behind Zauna's chair. "I'll feed her as much power as I can," he said.

Kyla nodded and did her best to comfort the crying child.

Winnie came into the room. "I heard the baby crying," she said, taking Dreama from Kyla's arms. "I thought I could help. There, there, little one," she cooed to Dreama. "Everything's going to be all right."

As she cleaned the regurgitated milk off her shoulder, Kyla wondered whether anything would be all right ever again. She had to get hold of herself. She couldn't let Jerome just pick them off, one by one, and she didn't know how to protect them, how to stop him.

Alair, I need your help. Now. She sent the mental call. No answer came. Even the Power-Giver had deserted her.

"Can you see them?" she asked Zauna, who sat forward, hunched over the crystal globe, her hands cupped on either side of it. She shook her head and continued to stare into the globe.

Kyla shouldn't break Zauna's concentration. If she saw anything, Zauna would tell them right away. But she felt so helpless, so desperate.

Winnie, with Dreama cuddled in one arm, placed her free hand on Kyla's shoulder. Kyla felt a warm, peaceful sensation flow through her for a moment. The moment ended when Zauna sighed and said, "All I see is cloudiness or ... I don't know, something like smoke or sand swirling around in the globe. No people, no objects, no place. Just a swirl of darkness."

Like my mind right now, Kyla thought.

"I'll go sit by Petros," Marchion said. "I don't feel right leaving him alone."

"Just don't let anything happen to either of you," Kyla warned, feeling that none of them were safe anywhere.

The front door burst open. Mayzie's husband, Isham, strode in and confronted Kyla with both fists clenched and raised. "Where is she? Where's my wife?"

Leah followed him in and closed the door he'd left wide open. Kyla's quick glance took in her friend's pale face and teary eyes.

Winnie turned to Isham. "We're all devastated by what happened. We have her laid out in the back room," she said soothingly. "I'll take you back."

"She can't be dead. She can't be." He broke down in sobs. "Our little boy ... What will he do without his mother?"

"Come with me," Winnie said again. She handed Dreama to Leah and led him from the room.

Kyla sank down into the nearest chair and rested her face in her hands.

Zauna rose from her chair and went to Leah. "Let me take Dreama," she said. "I'll put her in her crib and stay with her. I'm not doing any good here, and Kyla needs you."

Although Kyla didn't look up to see, Leah must have agreed, because moments later strong hands massaged Kyla's shoulders. She recognized Leah's touch.

"It's hard, I know," Leah said. "You have a terrible weight to bear."

"I'm not bearing it at all well, Leah," Kyla answered, her voice catching at the words. "I feel I'm making all the wrong moves. Poor Isham. I don't know what to say to comfort him. I've hardly had time to grieve for Mayzie myself. Not with Marta and Ed missing. And now it seems that Lore and Veronica are missing. I don't know what to do." The sobs came then. She could hold them back no longer.

Leah massaged her shoulders and neck, saying nothing, letting her cry.

After a few minutes Kyla's sobs ebbed. "I have to find Veronica. She's like a daughter to me. And Lore. He's young and he's new to his powers, but he shows so much promise. I can't lose them. Or Marta and Ed. Marta was my first real friend. We have to find them all. Jerome must have them. We have to stop him. But I don't know how."

"You're tired and you're hurting," Leah said. "You need to rest. I don't think you've even noticed how late it's getting. It will be dark in another hour. I also think you need the support of the Community. All of them. I understand why you sent several away, but you should bring them back first thing tomorrow morning. You may not need their gifts, but you do need their support."

"Too many of us get in each other's way, Leah," Kyla said with a sigh. "And I couldn't bear to lose anyone else. I'm afraid they'll be more vulnerable here. I can't put anyone else in danger."

"I think we're all in danger no matter where we are. But if we're together, we can lend each other strength. I don't have any magical gift, but I can offer encouragement and I can do this." Leah squeezed Kyla's shoulders harder, massaged vigorously.

"It does help," Kyla agreed. "But, Leah—"

Isham slammed into the room, his eyes red from weeping, his jaw set in a hard line. "I warned her," he shouted. "'Don't have anything to do with those people,' I said. 'They're an affront to the gods. They use powers no mortal was ever meant to have.' But she wouldn't listen. 'It's just a wee babe I'll be helping,' she said. She was so softhearted. 'I won't be around any of their magical goings-on. They've set aside a room for me to use for nursing the baby and caring for her. They know I don't want anything to do with magic, and they've promised to respect that.' So I gave in. I let her go, and now, now I've lost her." He paused, wiped tears from his eyes, and glared at Kyla. "Now I've got a motherless boy to raise by myself, thanks to you people and your accursed doings."

Kyla hunted desperately for words of comfort, but none came to mind. All she could say was, "Isham, I'm sorry. I'm so very sorry. We loved Mayzie."

"Loved her? You got her killed. Tortured and killed. That's not love!"

Kyla tried again. "Isham, none of us anticipated anything like this happening. I never imagined Mayzie could be in any danger."

"I don't want your flimsy excuses and your false sympathy. You're wicked, all of you. And now my poor Mayzie is dead because of your wickedness. She didn't deserve her awful death. You do. You all deserve much worse."

Leah, still behind her, leaned over and whispered, "It's useless to try to reason with him. He's out of his mind with grief."

Winnie and Renni had followed Isham into the room. Winnie shrugged helplessly. She must have tried to calm him and failed.

"I'm not done with you people," Isham went on, not shouting now, but his words burned with rage. "I've got to make arrangements for her burial. And figure out how to tell our little boy his mama won't ever come home. But then I'll go to the magistrates and bring charges and let everybody know how dangerous you people are. I won't be satisfied until the whole evil bunch of you are in prison for the rest of your lives."

He turned and headed for the door.

Renni hurried to Kyla and whispered in her ear, "I can erase his memories so he won't remember her and won't think to do anything."

"Absolutely not," Kyla snapped. "I take it you didn't find Veronica. Now just stay out of this."

Isham slammed the door behind him.

Renni's gaze followed him. She shook her head. "He's in so much pain. Why shouldn't I relieve it? What good is my gift if you never want me to use it?"

Kyla frowned. She had no time for this. "You have to learn when it's appropriate to use it and when it isn't."

Renni stood straight and crossed her arms in front of her chest. "When someone is that angry and he's threatening to harm us, I'd think it would have been very appropriate."

Before Kyla could issue the sharp rebuke that came to her mind, Leah squeezed her shoulder. "Let me explain," she said and turned to Renni.

"He's hurting too badly to think rationally right now, but he has to work through all that pain. You can't take it from him because he'll need all those memories you'd have to erase. Think about it. They include memories of the happy times he shared with Mayzie, memories of sharing the joy their son has brought them, memories of what a good mother she was, and what a good wife. Those are memories that will sustain him in his grief and help him heal. Furthermore, as his little boy grows older, he'll want to hear about the mother he won't otherwise remember. Isham will need memories to share with his son."

Renni relaxed her stiff stance. "Oh. I guess you're right," she said. "I hadn't thought about those things. But what if he carries out the threats he made?"

"It's a risk we'll have to take," Leah said. "I know Isham fairly well, and I think as he comes to terms with his loss, his anger will cool. He knows we cared about Mayzie. He just has to remember that. Right now his grief is blocking that recollection, but it will return. The memories you wanted to take might not ever have come back, and that would be a tragedy. You can't erase the fact of Mayzie's death. To ease his pain from that you'd have to erase all his memories of Mayzie. And if you have the power to erase memories that go that far back, you'd also erase his memories of his child. Where would that leave poor little Bennie?"

Renni was silent for several minutes, absorbing what Leah was saying. Finally she threw her arms around Leah and hugged her. "You're right. I don't know that I even have the power to take memories from that far back, but I can see now that it wouldn't have helped and might have hurt him even more. Thanks."

That crisis resolved, Kyla turned away from Renni and Leah and walked into the hallway. Winnie followed her.

"I tried to keep him from uncovering Mayzie's body and seeing what that fiend did to her, but he insisted," Winnie said, a catch in her voice. "The sight shocked him badly. It will take him a long time to recover from it, I fear."

Sighing, Kyla nodded. "I can hardly blame him for being so angry," she said. "It's just one more thing I can't cope with right now."

Winnie was trying to calm her, but her feeling of desperation was too great. The counsel Leah was giving Renni should have come from her. She was the founder and leader of the Gifted Community, and Leah was not even technically a member, since she was not gifted. If only she could remain calm like Leah instead of letting every little thing grate on her nerves. Alair used to tell her she was as capricious as the wind.

"Alair, where are you? Why haven't I heard your voice for so long?" She whispered the words instead of merely sending the plea mentally as she usually did. It was not merely a plea to the Power-Giver but to the man she had loved and lost when he had lost his humanity and had become the channeler of magic gifts, the near deity the gifted revered as the Power-Giver. When she and Marta had accepted the challenge of spreading gifts of magic throughout the land of Arucadi, her mental contact with Alair had been almost constant, but as time passed that contact had become less frequent. He and she had attributed it to many things: greater numbers of gifted needing the Power-Giver's attention, interference of evil Dire Lords who were jealous of their power and opposed to giving power gifts to receptive humans, Kyla's growing confidence in her gifts and therefore less need to rely on Alair's help. What Kyla did not want to face was the other possibility: that in becoming less human, Alair was less able to love her in the way he had. The love he had professed for her was the love of a mortal man for a mortal woman. With their changed circumstances, Kyla, a mortal woman, could not be the focus of his attention. As Power-Giver, Alair's loving attention must be spread to all those who received the gifts of power he channeled to them. Perhaps she no longer held more importance to him than any other devotee of the Power-Giver.

Not so, a voice in her mind protested. But was it Alair's voice or her own inner longing?

Wearily she turned into her bedroom and headed for her bed. Marchion rose from the chair by the bed as she approached. She stepped back. She'd forgotten this was where they'd put Petros. "No change I guess," she said, nodding toward the still form on the bed.

"No change at all," Marchion confirmed. "His breathing and pulse are normal, but he's not at home."

"I wonder how long he can survive without his conscious mind," Kyla said. "I don't think he's ever said."

"He probably doesn't know. I doubt he ever intended to stay out this long."

"No, I suppose not. But why hasn't he returned?"

Marchion rubbed his chin. "Maybe he can't."

"That's what I'm afraid of." Apparently she needed to add Petros to those lost in the past hours. Jerome's vendetta was going well. She had to find a way to stop it. "Try to get some sleep," she advised Marchion. "If he comes back, he'll wake you, I'm sure."

She left the room. She needed sleep too. They all did. Leah was right. Night had come without her noticing. Everyone was exhausted. They couldn't do anything until morning.

Leah was probably also right that in the morning she should call all the Community back together. She could not face this alone.

She stood in the hall, wondering where to go to rest. Veronica's room? But if Veronica returned, she'd be angry to find her bed occupied. Standing there, swaying from weariness, she became aware of someone sobbing softly and steadily. She headed toward the sound and reached the room where Abigail sat in a rocking chair beside the bed on which Mayzie's body was laid out. Abigail looked up when she entered. The older woman's eyes were red from weeping, and tears still ran down her cheeks.

"Oh, Kyla, Isham is so angry," she said. "He insisted on looking at her body, and when he saw it, saw the mutilation, he threatened terrible things. I don't know what he'll do, and I'm frightened, but I also feel so bad for him. We should have been able to heal her. He's right to be angry."

"He threatened me, too," Kyla said. "Leah doesn't think he'll carry out the threats. He just needs to calm down."

"I disagree," Abigail said. "I think he's dangerous. He'll be back soon to get her body, and he'll have friends with him. We'd better be prepared."

Kyla hadn't thought about that. It seemed that she

was to have no rest after all. Nor was anyone else. "You're right," she told Abigail. "I'll go and warn the others. You'd better come with me."

"I don't dare. Isham told me to stay right here until he gets back. He didn't want her left alone. I promised I wouldn't leave her. I don't think he'll hurt me or Leah, but you'd better get everyone else out of the way. And mind Veronica keeps out of it. You know her temper."

She didn't know Veronica was missing. And this wasn't the time to tell her. But something in her face must have alerted Abigail.

"What's wrong?" Abigail demanded. "Where's Veronica? What's she done?"

Kyla was too dispirited to try to cushion the blow. "I don't know. She's missing. Along with Lore. We don't know where they've gone or why. And Zauna hasn't been able to locate either of them in her crystal. I can't reach them with a mental sending, either."

Abigail paled, but whatever she might have said was halted by the sound of men's voices coming from the living room.

"Isham and his friends have already come for Mayzie's body," Abigail said, rising. "Quick, Kyla, go out back through the kitchen. Hurry!"

Kyla burst into a run before Abigail finished speaking. She dashed to the end of the hall and through the door into the kitchen. She paused there long enough to listen and verify that the voices registered anger and threatened harm. Zauna had come out of the room assigned to Marta and Ed, where Dreama's crib had been placed, and was begging them to be quiet and not wake the baby. Too late. Dreama's sudden wails rivaled the men's shouts.

Kyla hurried on through the kitchen and out the

back door into the yard. She took shelter behind the outhouse and the shrubbery that surrounded it.

She shouldn't be running, shouldn't be hiding. As the leader of the Gifted Community, she should be defending her flock, at least those members of it who were in her house because they'd remained to help her in this crisis. Suppose Abigail wasn't able to calm Isham.

Winnie would help with that, as would Leah, whose calming presence even without magic was almost the equal of Winnie's. But she couldn't risk being arrested and hauled off to jail at this critical time. Marta and Ed and Veronica and Lore and Petros were all depending on her to rescue them and bring them home.

Yes, depending on her. And here she was, crouching behind the outhouse like a craven coward, doing nothing.

What could she do? Even if her power was at full strength, she couldn't burst into the house and hurl fire at Isham and his friends. That was not a talent of hers, and it wasn't one she'd want to have. She'd seen the trouble Veronica had caused and the difficulty Veronica had in controlling that particular talent.

Four men slammed out of the back door, Isham in the lead. "We'll find that witch. She couldn't be far away," Isham shouted. "You hear that, witch? We're coming after you."

She hadn't heard shouts like that since the early days when she and Marta first set out to restore magic to Arucadi. They were always chilling, but with Marta at her side she hadn't felt the fear that made her flatten herself against the outhouse wall and will herself not to be seen.

Got to get hold of myself. My power is low, but

not entirely gone. I can't panic. I'm not helpless.

She hummed a low melody and sensed tendrils of power gathering around her. The men drew near. She heard them jerk open the outhouse door and walk inside. Good thing she hadn't taken refuge in there. She stepped away from the outhouse and moved carefully, using the moonlight to guide her away from shrubs and fallen branches that would snap if she put weight on them. The invisibility spell she'd cast around her would keep the men from seeing her but not from hearing her. She'd learned, though, how to walk very quietly.

She made it to the back door and waited to open it until she was certain none of the men were looking in her direction. They had fanned out through the yard, and Isham had opened the back gate and stepped through it to check the street. She eased the door open and slipped inside. After making sure none of Isham's friends had remained inside, she let the invisibility spell slip away. Quietly she went to the room where she'd left Abigail and found her friend stripping the bed where Mayzie's body had lain.

"Oh, thank the Power-Giver, you're safe," Abigail said. "However did you avoid those men?"

"Never mind that now." Kyla spoke more sharply than she'd intended. As the Community leader, she had to keep her emotions under control, but it was getting ever harder. The strain of losing first Marta and Ed and maybe Petros and now Veronica and Lore ... No wonder her thoughts and emotions were in a tangle. "They've taken Mayzie's body? They're finished in here?"

"They brought a long winding cloth to wrap her body in, and they put her in that cart they brought before going out back looking for you," Abigail told her. "They searched all through the house. I was afraid they'd cart Petros off when they saw him lying there helpless, but Marchion told them he was just fast asleep, and they let it go to could hunt for you. I understand Isham's grief but not his unreasoning anger nor that of his friends."

"Isham has them all stirred up." Kyla rubbed her arms, feeling suddenly chilled. "It's also very possible that Jerome is somehow fueling their anger. He has that ability."

She took a deep breath. "I need to call the whole community back to the house so I can talk to them," she told Abigail. "We have to work together. No more going off separately as Petros did and Veronica and Lore must have. We may all have different talents, but I hope we're all working toward the same goal."

Abigail rolled the sheets she'd taken off the bed into a large bundle. Holding it in her arms, she said, "I'll go round up everyone, and I'll drop these into the laundry basket on the way. Where do you want us all to gather?"

"In my room so Petros is included, even though he probably won't be aware of it."

Abigail nodded and left the room. After a few moments to gather her thoughts, Kyla went to the living room to look out the front window. The cart Isham and his friends had brought was gone. They must have taken Mayzie's body to be buried. She checked to be certain none of Isham's friends had remained behind. For now it seemed they'd abandoned their search for her, probably deciding they wouldn't find her with night so near. They might return in the morning—one more thing she had to worry about and somehow cope with.

CHAPTER THIRTEEN
LIES AND TRUTHS

While Marchion listened to Kyla, he scanned the others, noting their auras and also the shimmering threads connecting some in the room. Kyla emphasized that they all needed to work in harmony, consulting the others before taking action. She also declared her intention to summon all members of the Community to gather here once more, and although no member would be forced or required to come, she trusted that no one would refuse.

Her deep red aura reflected decisiveness, the color of a leader, but flashes of muddy gold indicated weariness. Leah's aura was a rich, nurturing pink. A shimmering green thread connected her to Abigail, revealing her as Abigail's anchor, the reliever of the older woman's fears. In Abigail's aura Marchion read those fears and the tension that he'd noted before between her giftedness and her distrust of magic, her wish to reject her own powers. A strange woman, but one whose abilities would be needed in their struggle.

The girl Renni's bright orange aura with flashes of red reflected her headstrong, excitable nature. The black thread that pulsed between Kyla and Renni was no surprise. He had observed the anger Renni often felt toward Kyla, and the lack of trust Kyla had in Renni was all too evident. That attitude on both their parts could endanger them all.

"We must get what rest we can tonight," Kyla was saying. "Tomorrow I intend to find a way to transfer some or all of us to the place I believe to be Jerome's stronghold. I think that's where we will find Marta and Ed and Veronica and Lore. How we'll get there, I don't yet know. I've never been there, but I've heard Ed's description of it—both what it used to be like and the devastation that marks it now. We cannot just stay here and let Jerome move against us at will. We have to seize the initiative, confront him, and fight his power with our combined strength. I'm convinced there is no other way to win."

As she talked her aura flared. A silver cord, visible to him alone, stretched from her to each of those crowded into the room, and the auras of everyone in the group revealed assent, though not without streaks of gray denoting fear. Marchion felt fear, too. They would face a powerful opponent on unknown territory, if they could even get there. Yet Kyla's confidence infused them.

Marchion was confident he spoke for all when he said forcefully, "We're with you, Lady Kyla."

"Good," she said, smiling at them. "We'll gather the other members of the Community and get started early. So right now, go find a place to sleep. There aren't enough beds for everyone, so some of you will have to make a bed of blankets on the floor."

She might have added something more, but at that moment Lore sauntered into the room. "Ah, I wondered where everyone had gone to," he said.

"Well! Where have you been?" Renni asked before anyone else could speak.

"Looking for Ed and Marta, since no one else was doing anything." He met her angry gaze with an insouciant grin.

"Did you find them?" Renni asked.

At the same time Kyla asked, "Where's Veronica? Wasn't she with you?"

He frowned then and looked around the room. "Isn't she back?"

"Back from where? Where did you go?" Kyla prodded.

"Why, to the place Ed calls 'his' world. That seemed the logical location to search." His gaze went to the window and the blackness beyond it. "Say, do you know that time runs differently there? It was midday when I left, just a couple of minutes ago."

"What about Veronica? Did she go with you or didn't she?" Kyla was growing angry. Her aura had changed from a bright, clear red to a muddied darker shade.

"She did. We combined power to get to the place. It's a barren desert. A sandstorm came up. Even if we could have kept our eyes open we wouldn't have been able to see anything. We got separated while trying to find some kind of shelter. When the storm finally died, I looked everywhere for her and concluded she must have come back here."

"Did you see any sign of Ed and Marta?" Renni asked.

"Not a trace. I don't think they're there."

"You couldn't have searched the whole land. From what Ed has described, it's quite large," Abigail commented.

Lore turned toward her. "It isn't that large. Ed's perception of it might not be wholly reliable."

Renni snorted. "And yours is?"

"Please, Renni, stay out of this," Kyla said, weariness and confusion clear in her tone and in her aura. "Did you see Jerome?" she asked Lore.

"No. I didn't see anyone at all. The place is completely deserted."

He was lying. Marchion studied his aura with care. Yes, definitely lying, and concealing something of great importance. The aura bathing his whole body was a muddy gray, bordering on black. What was he hiding?

"Ed once spoke of a ruined building there. Did you see it?"

"I saw what had been a building, Lady Kyla, but it's more a pile of stones than anything else. You can see where the walls were and get a general idea of the way the building was laid out, but there's no way to go in it. There is no 'in,' only rubble all over."

"That's not the way Ed described it," Kyla said, frowning.

"Maybe it looked different when he saw it," Lore said. "Time clearly progresses very differently there."

"And maybe you're not telling us the whole truth," Renni snapped, her aura a muddy orange and vibrating.

Again Kyla rebuked her: "Renni, I told you not to interrupt."

Marchion didn't understand why Kyla was being so hostile to Renni. The girl was right to be skeptical. Kyla should see that. She had doubts of her own, obviously. Maybe she just wanted to keep the peace and give Lore a chance to explain more fully.

Perhaps if he told Lady Kyla what he read in Lore's aura she would come down harder on Lore and be more tolerant of Renni. After all, Kyla couldn't see the aura that made clear to him Lore's untruthfulness. Why aura reading was not one of her talents, as gifted as she was, Marchion didn't understand. To him it seemed a gift requiring little effort and little power.

He cleared his throat, hoping that Kyla would grasp that he wanted to enter the discussion. Accusing Lore of lying would not be easy, but if she would listen, Marchion resolved to do it as diplomatically as possible.

Kyla was explaining to Lore her plan to gather the Community together in the early morning and mount a group attack on Jerome. Should she even be telling Lore this? Marchion tried to get her attention, but she didn't seem to notice him. He cleared his throat loudly, and said, "Ah, Lady Kyla, before you go further, there is something I'd like to say."

"Not now, Marchion," she said. "Wait until I've finished, please."

A wave of unease swept over him. Lore looked his way, a sharp, calculating look. He hadn't captured Kyla's attention, but he'd attracted Lore's. For an instant he found it hard to breathe. First a rush of heat swept over him and then a chill crept through his body.

Kyla finished explaining her plan and turned to Marchion. "Now, what was it you wanted to say?"

Confused, he scratched his head. He'd been going to tell her something. Something important. But what? It had gone from his mind. He must be more tired than he'd thought.

"Nothing," he mumbled. "It wasn't important."

Triumph at his success soared through Lore's blood. He fought to keep it from registering on his face. Jerome had told him the truth!

When Lore had told Jerome that his only abilities were to transfer from one place to another and to bring small items to him or send them to another person," Jerome had said, "Oh, no. You have many undiscovered talents. I can't see what all of them are, but one in particular is clear to me, and it's one you may have need of when you return. You have the gift of suppressing thoughts."

"Is that like making someone forget past events?" he'd asked, thinking of Renni's gift.

"No, although it may be similar. You don't remove memories. You remove a person's thought before he can verbalize it."

Puzzled, Lore had asked, "But how would I know that person had a certain thought? I can't read minds. I wish I could, but—"

"But you are good at reading facial expressions, aren't you?"

It didn't occur to Lore until much later that he should have asked how Jerome knew that. He'd only said, "Why, yes, I am. I've learned to be. It's helped me advance in my work."

"You are ambitious. That's good. I've always been ambitious, too. I was close to realizing my ambitions when I met Kyla and Marta and they ruined my life. And I wound up here."

Not missing the bitterness that infused that statement, Lore gathered enough courage to ask, "But it was Ed, wasn't it, who brought you here?"

"Yes, to what he calls 'his' world. The simpleton actually believed he could create a world just by imagining it."

"So this isn't really Ed's world at all?"

"Don't be foolish. Look around you." Jerome waved his hand in a wide arc that took in the ruins that had been a building, the empty space between it and the modest shelter Jerome had built using stones from the ruins for walls and dead branches for a roof, and then the mountains in the distance. "This is a very old world. You can see that. Oh, Ed may have temporarily altered one small portion of it, but in no way did he create it. After he abandoned me here, the part of the world he'd altered gradually reverted to its former state."

The story made sense to Lore, but a niggling feeling ate at him, an impression that there were other questions he should be asking. The questions, however, refused to come to mind.

He'd spent the night in Jerome's small home, and tired as he was, sleep had come easily. But in the morning he awoke hungry and wanting breakfast, and when he discovered that the only fare Jerome could provide was insects and cactus leaves, he decided it was time to return to his own world.

"By all means, go," Jerome had said when he expressed this desire. "I'm sure you'll be welcomed back. But weren't you going to search for Veronica this morning?"

Lore had forgotten. He was embarrassed to admit it.

Jerome reassured him. "I'll do a thorough search and let you know if I find her. But I'd guess she has already returned. She has the power, you know, and she isn't known for being patient. When she couldn't find you, I doubt she'd stay here alone."

He was probably right. He was certainly right about Veronica lacking patience. "How will you let me know?" he asked.

"If you'll allow it, I can send you a mental message. You'll hear my voice in your mind, but the channel will only be open so long as you want it. You can close it whenever you want. You can close it permanently if for some reason you so desire."

That seemed fair, but Lore had another doubt.

"I've never been able to project my thoughts into another person's mind or receive anyone else's thoughts."

"We'll test it," Jerome said. "Now concentrate." *When you return, I want you to tell them about losing Veronica in the sandstorm and wandering around, not knowing where you were or what to do. You can tell them you searched thoroughly for her. I know, you didn't, but I promise to do that and to let you know if I find her. She'll probably be back and worrying about you. Do not tell them about meeting me. They think I'm guilty of terrible things, and they won't believe you or trust you if you tell them all I've told you. Do you understand everything I've said? No, don't speak aloud; just transmit the answer mentally.*

Lore heard Jerome's voice clearly. He hadn't even known at first that Jerome hadn't spoken aloud. He'd started to tell him so but at Jerome's caution not to, he thought, *Yes, your voice is clear. I'll do just as you suggest.*

Good, came Jerome's response. *Now let's get you back to Kyla's house. You'll find that it is night there.*

A brief but biting cold was the only sensation Lore felt before finding himself in Kyla's living room. An oil lamp on a table provided enough light to let him see that the room was empty. A murmur of voices came from somewhere in the house. He'd followed that sound to Kyla's bedroom, where he'd found a large group crowded into the small room.

The shock he'd expressed at not finding Veronica among them had not been entirely feigned. He had let himself hope she'd returned, but somehow he'd known she hadn't, despite Jerome's expressed belief that she'd have gone back on her own.

Jerome's expressed belief, yes, but had he truly believed it?

Jerome, Veronica isn't here. Have you found her there?

He formed the thought clearly but had it reached Jerome? He should have asked whether the thought speech worked between worlds. There were many things he should have asked Jerome.

No time to think of that now, when he was being bombarded with questions. He had to appear confident. And he had to go on trusting Jerome.

And when that fool Marchion glared at him, it proved as easy to read his expression as Jerome had said it would be. The man knew he'd lied. Probably read it in his aura. But it proved pathetically easy to create confusion in Marchion's mind so that instead of accusing Lore, as he'd no doubt intended, he completely forgot what he was going to say.

What a great gift! Had he had it all along, or had Jerome passed it to him? It hardly mattered. He'd used it successfully, and visions of all he could do with it crowded out the small voice somewhere deep within that tried to remind him that it was wrong to suppress another's thoughts. He had a new tool to add to his kit. Why shouldn't he be proud? How many of those gathered in this room had talents as strong as his? Veronica did, but she was missing. Kyla was supposed to, but he'd seen little evidence of that. He saw no one here who could confidently claim to be his equal. A feeling of invincibility infused him as he saw all his life's goals come within his reach.

When Kyla's meeting broke up, everyone headed for a place to sleep for the few remaining hours of the night.

"I'm too old to sleep on the floor," Abigail declared imperiously. "Leah and I will use the guest room since Ed and Marta aren't here to use it. Leah, you get it ready for us while I get blankets for everyone." She turned and left the room, and Leah followed.

Zauna chuckled. "I'm at least as old as Abigail, probably a lot older, but I've slept on far worse than your floor. I'll get a blanket and just stretch out in the living room."

"No need," Kyla said. "You can use Veronica's room."

Winnie, holding Dreama, who was fast asleep, said, "I'll sleep on the floor by the baby's crib so I can keep watch over her and feed her if she wakes and fusses. There's still plenty of goat's milk in the cold box." She left to carry out that intention.

"Lady Kyla, you need to sleep, and we've got Petros in your bed," Marchion said. "I think we should move him back onto his platform so you can sleep in comfort. You need rest more than any of us."

"I'll help move Petros," Renni offered. "Even if he weren't unconscious, sleeping on his platform wouldn't be any different than sleeping on the floor. I don't think he'd mind, and you should have the bed."

Kyla gave them both an appreciative look. They lifted Petros onto his platform and wheeled it into the hall. Marchion settled down beside him, determined not to leave him alone. Kyla remained in her own room.

Renni held back while the others accepted the blankets Abigail was handing out. She intended to see where Lore went. He, too, held back. Was he being courteous, letting the older members choose first, or did he, like her, want to know where everyone else was located?

Finally he accepted a blanket and headed toward the living room. Renni took the last blanket and followed Lore. She didn't care what anyone thought. Lore was good-looking and personable, but her interest in him had nothing to do with sexual attraction. He was up to something, and she meant to ask him about it when she could do so without others hearing.

When they entered the living room, Lore turned from spreading his blanket down on the floor and grinned at her. "It's really chilly," he said. "Want to share blankets?" He sank down onto the blanket he'd spread out and patted the spot beside him.

She didn't answer, but she did kneel by him, careful, however, to hold the blanket in front of her, keeping it between them.

He grinned. "Come on, you aren't afraid of me, are you? I don't have any bad intentions."

"Don't you?" she said after looking around to make certain she and Lore had the living room to themselves.

"You sound disappointed."

"Not really. I want to know why you lied to Lady Kyla about not seeing Jerome. I know you did, and you somehow prevented Marchion from telling her you were lying. Sounds to me like your intentions were plenty bad."

His expression hardened. "What makes you think I was lying?" he demanded.

She was putting herself in a dangerous position, but she didn't care. "I saw how you squelched Marchion. He'd been reading auras, I'd guess, and saw something in yours that made him suspicious. More than suspicious, maybe, since he swears that auras don't lie. And then he couldn't tell Kyla about it.

What did you do to him? I didn't know you had that ability."

He grinned, not an inviting grin as before but a cat-that-caught-the-canary grin. "I'll show you what I did."

His boast gave her just enough warning to raise her mental shields. Even so, she felt the assault, like being hit on the head with a mallet. She rocked back on her heels, blinking.

"Now, weren't you about to agree we should share blankets?" he asked, that feral grin still gracing his face.

She needed considerable strength to ignore the pain and say forcefully, "No, definitely not. I asked you why you lied to Lady Kyla."

The shocked look that crossed his face gave her great satisfaction. She braced for another onslaught of pain. It came, but her shields held. "I'm still waiting for your answer," she said.

He scrambled to his feet, and she did the same. They glared at each other. He must still be trying to do to her whatever it was he'd done to Marchion, but the pain not only did not increase; it lessened. She smiled. "Your little trick isn't working, Lore. Now, why don't you answer my question? Could it be because you don't want me or anyone else to know that you met Jerome? And abandoned Veronica?"

"I didn't abandon Veronica. It happened just as I said. There was a terrible sandstorm, and we got separated, and after the storm died down I looked, but I couldn't find her."

Good. She had him on the defensive now. "And was it while you were looking for her that you met Jerome?"

"I didn't—"

"Oh, stuff it! I know you did. It's written all over your face."

He rubbed his face as though he took her words literally. "Look, you don't understand," he said. "Okay, I did meet Jerome. I lied about it because, well, Jerome isn't what they think. He's just a man, not a monster. I wasn't lying about getting separated from Veronica in a terrible sandstorm that made it almost impossible to breathe. It blinded us and in trying to protect our faces we got turned around and, I don't know, somehow we got separated. Even if we could have shouted, it would have been impossible to hear each other for the roaring of the wind that was driving the sand. I kept my back to the wind and walked with it rather than against it, hoping to find some kind of shelter, and—"

"And you left her. She could be dead."

"I really thought she'd send herself back here. She does have the power to do that."

"But she didn't. How much did you really hunt for her before you came back? Never mind, I doubt you looked very hard. Tell me about Jerome." She flopped into the straight chair by the table where Zauna usually sat to look into her crystal ball.

"He found me and gave me shelter for the night. He promised to help me find Veronica." As he spoke, standing by the table, he ran his hand over the crystal globe Zauna had left there. He continued slowly as though planning each sentence before speaking it. "But when morning came, I was starving, and all he had to eat, what he apparently lives on, was insects and cactus leaves. I wasn't *that* hungry. He would have shared the little he had with me, but when I said I couldn't eat it, he offered to send me back and to look for Veronica and send her back, too, as soon as he found her. But he thought, as I did, that she'd probably returned home on her own."

"So how hard do you think he actually looked for her? And how do you know he didn't find her?"

"He promised to let me know." As soon as the words left his mouth, his hand jerked free of the crystal. "I shouldn't have told you that."

"No, you probably shouldn't have. So you can communicate with him? Mindspeech, I suppose?"

He nodded, not meeting her gaze.

"But you claim he's just a man not a monster."

"That's how he struck me."

"You're an idiot."

"Am I?" He picked up the globe with one hand and slammed it down onto the table. "Am I?" he repeated. He threw his head back for a moment as if listening to something, then lowered his head and glared at her. "I'll show you just how much of an idiot I am."

With that, Renni felt a sudden deep chill and a moment of terrible nausea. Both the chill and the nausea ended when she fell onto hot sand. She blinked, blinded momentarily by bright light.

She got her eyes open and saw that it was no longer night but midday. A merciless sun beat down on her, its light and heat magnified in the sand's reflection of it.

A voice spoke from behind her. "Well, well. My friend Lore has sent me an attractive catch. Not the one I really want, but you'll do for the time being."

She stumbled to her feet and turned to look at the man standing behind her.

Man? Lore had said Jerome was "just a man," but that description didn't fit the towering being who leered down at her.

"Y-you're J-Jerome?" She could scarcely get the

words out past her fear. The face looking down on her was pure evil.

"Ah, yes. Sorry if my appearance isn't what you were expecting. Perhaps this will put you more at ease." In an instant a man normal in size and appearance replaced the terrifying apparition.

It had been an illusion, carefully crafted to petrify those to whom he appeared. She was angry with herself for having fallen for it.

"Don't think I'm any less powerful in my true form," Jerome said as though he'd read her thought.

"You didn't show yourself to Lore that other way."

"No. I have plans for Lore. He will be far more useful to me if he remains ignorant of my powers. You, on the other hand ..."

"I'm of no use to you," she finished his sentence.

"Oh, on the contrary. I have a very good use for you. But first you need to experience the full extent of my power."

CHAPTER FOURTEEN
GATHERING

Despite her exhaustion, Kyla couldn't sleep. She'd advised everyone to get as much sleep as they could to be ready for their attempt to confront Jerome, but she couldn't take her own advice.

Mayzie was dead. They had Dreama back, but Marta and Ed were gone. And now Veronica. Veronica, whom she loved like a daughter. How could she sleep, when Veronica might be in Jerome's hands? He'd shown what he was capable of by sending the dying Mayzie back to them as a warning—and a promise. What was he doing to Veronica? What had he done to Marta and Ed?

Concluding that sleep would never come, she arose, put on a robe, and walked through the house. Everyone else seemed to be sleeping. She checked the bedrooms and hall, and reached the living room. Lore lay on one blanket and had a second one wrapped around him. Abigail had given each person one blanket.

Where was Renni?

Had she lost another? Jerome had nothing against Renni. He was after those he blamed for his exile. If he already had Ed, Marta, and Veronica—and what other explanation could there be for their absence?—that left her, Abigail, and Leah. Although he could hardly blame Leah for anything. But Jerome didn't think rationally. That frightened her more than anything. He might well mean to destroy the entire Gifted Community. He had to be stopped.

She had to know whether Renni was another victim or had simply gone off somewhere on her own, as she might well have. She woke Lore, apologized as he sat up, yawning, and asked, "Do you know where Renni is? Didn't she come in here with you?"

He blinked as though trying to clear his mind of sleep. "Renni? No. I mean, yes, she did, but then she got angry about something and stormed out of the room. I don't know where she went."

"She left her blanket here," Kyla stated, pointing to the extra blanket.

"Oh, yes. She left in such a huff ..." He looked down and shrugged. "I guess I came across as, well, asking for something I shouldn't have. I thought ... She followed me in here, and I got the wrong message and acted on what I thought she wanted. Seems I was wrong." He raised his gaze to meet Kyla's. "I didn't mean any harm, and I'd never force her into anything she didn't want. I just misread the signals."

Was he protesting his innocence a bit too hard? Renni was a hothead and unpredictable. It could have happened just as he said. But if so, why hadn't she taken her blanket? And where was she? Kyla had gone through the whole house and hadn't seen her. Surely she wouldn't have walked home in the middle of the night.

She couldn't escape the feeling that Lore was not telling the whole truth. It was worrisome that Renni had gone off, no matter what the provocation. The girl should have come to her with a complaint against Lore if that was her problem. But maybe she hadn't wanted to wake her.

Whatever the situation, she could do little about it now. It was nearly morning. She told Lore to go back to sleep and headed for the kitchen to make tea. Soon it would be time to send for the other members of the Community. She hoped they would all be willing to come and help, but no one would be forced to do so. They'd be risking their lives by going up against Jerome, and she wouldn't compel anyone to do that. They'd either agree willingly to help or she'd send them home with her assurance of understanding.

She'd planned to ask Renni to take her message to the various members of the Community. Now she'd ask Lore. He rode a bicycle and could get around faster than any of the others. He could look for Renni as he went. She'd point out to him that he had an obligation to try to find her, and he also had mistakes to atone for.

Marchion awoke with a pounding headache. He'd been having dreams, disturbing ones. He recalled that much, though he could remember nothing more about them. He dragged himself wearily from the bed, dressed, and headed for the outhouse. If Abigail was up, he meant to ask her if she could heal his aching head.

No one was in the kitchen except Lady Kyla, but thankfully she'd brewed a pot of tea. She offered to pour him a cup, and he accepted gratefully, meaning to drink it as soon as he returned from the outhouse. Maybe it would help the headache.

He crossed the yard, heard a sleepy "Maaa," from the goat, and reached the outhouse door when a thought occurred to him. He had spoken to Kyla, but he hadn't seen her aura. Could the headache be responsible?

When he returned to the kitchen. Kyla was still seated at the table, and Winnie Calder had joined her, holding Dreama and giving the infant her morning bottle. He looked at both of them, consciously willing to see their auras.

Nothing. It had to be the headache.

He explained about his head pounding dreadfully and that he intended to ask Abigail to heal him as soon as she was up.

"Abigail always wakes early. I think she'll be out soon. But why not let Winnie try to heal you?" Kyla said. "She needs to work on her healing power."

"I don't care who does it," he said, groaning. "I just need to get rid of this pain."

Winnie handed Dreama to Kyla and went to stand behind him and place her hands on his head. "Oh! Oh, my!" she said. "It *is* a bad one."

"It's fading," he said. "You're doing it."

Her hands lifted from his head, and she collapsed into the chair she'd vacated and rubbed her forehead. "I could feel it," she said. "The pain's leaving now. How do you feel?"

He smiled. "You did it, Winnie. The headache's gone. I'm sorry you had to experience it to heal me."

"That's a normal part of healing," Kyla said. "Winnie, your healing skill is improving all the time."

Marchion gazed at Kyla and then at Winnie. "The headache's gone," he said, "but something else is wrong. I feel fine now, but I can't see your auras."

Kyla frowned. "Healing a headache shouldn't cause that."

"It didn't," he said. "I couldn't see them before Winnie healed me, but I thought the headache was the problem. It must be something else."

"Maybe I should ask Abigail to use her healing

powers," Winnie said. "Mine may just not be strong enough to have completed the healing."

"I hope Abigail can help," Marchion said. "I'll be of no use to you if I've lost my only power."

"But you haven't," Kyla protested. "I'm sure the ability to read auras will return. But it isn't your only power. Your gift as an enhancer will definitely be needed today."

Marchion felt a little better on hearing that, but only a little. The auras told him so much, and the threads of colored light connecting people even more. Those threads were gone, too.

Did he still have his ability as an enhancer? He wanted to test it, but at present he had no opportunity to do so, yet if he waited until it was desperately needed and only then discovered that it was gone, the results could be tragic.

He couldn't bring himself to ask someone to use power just so he could test his talent. Power should never be used without a reason. He would just have to hope that his gift of enhancement was intact and would function when needed.

Zauna rushed into the kitchen clutching her crystal ball and screaming, "Look! It's broken!" Sobbing, she held up the crystal and pointed to a crack that arced around the bottom of the globe, ending in a missing chip.

This could be the opportunity Marchion had wished for. "Now, now, Zauna," he said, "Your crystal may still be usable. The crack doesn't extend all the way through it, and the chip isn't that large. Why not check to see whether you can still use it? Let me enhance your power, and perhaps you can see in it just as before."

Her response was a withering look. "You know

nothing of how a crystal globe works," she said. "It can't receive visions when it's cracked and chipped."

"You can't be certain of that unless you try," he insisted.

"I don't need to try. I know."

"I understand how upset you are, Zauna," Kyla said, and Marchion hoped she was going to support his suggestion. Instead she continued, "You can't take your crystal with you when we go to confront Jerome. It would be of no use there. When we return we'll see about replacing it. For now, put it aside and calm yourself."

"But what use can I be without my globe?" Zauna asked, tears still trickling down her cheeks.

"You still have your power," Kyla told her. "You'll just have to use it in other ways."

"But I don't know any other way." Zauna set the crystal carefully on a shelf above the kitchen counter.

"Trust the Power-Giver," Kyla counseled. "He won't desert you because your globe is broken."

Marchion hoped Lady Kyla was right and that the Power-Giver would come to his aid as well.

With the goat milked and Dreama fed, Kyla was ready to put her plan into action. She sent Lore to fetch those members of the Community she couldn't reach through mindspeech. She thought it peculiar that some could receive her sendings and others could not. The nongifted could not receive, but all the gifted should be able to, yet of the Community members fully one-third could not receive. She'd asked Alair about it several times, but he didn't respond.

He'd told her when she'd discovered her own gift of mindspeaking that it was a way all the gifted could communicate with one another, a universal gift. Yet that had not seemed to be the case for many members of the Community.

No time to worry about it. The Community would soon gather; she had to be ready. Those with whom she could mindspeak were already on their way.

Lore whistled as he pedaled his bicycle over the roads, avoiding carriages and hansoms to reach his first destination. Kyla couldn't have given him a better assignment. And she'd agreed that he'd need to go by the shipping office and inform his boss that he wouldn't be in today. He was entitled to a day's leave. He rarely took a day off, and he hadn't used much of his vacation time. This wasn't a busy time of year, so he was certain there'd be no objection when he made his request. So far as he knew, no ships were due into port this four-day, and he was caught up on his work.

He'd get one stop out of the way before going on to Carnover Shipping Offices. Winter Salas lived in a flat near the art academy he attended, and that was right on Lore's way as he headed for the shipping offices. Winter would hate the thought of having to feel everybody's emotions, especially their doubts and fears, of which there were certain to be plenty. It would be fun to watch Winter squirm. He was such a weakling with his single insignificant gift that only made him miserable. He'd be no help at all with Kyla's grandiose plan. A hindrance most probably, and that would work out all the better for Jerome's plans.

He reached the apartment house where Winter lived, entered, found the door to his apartment, and knocked loudly. The disheveled young man who opened the door was not Winter. He glared at Lore and mumbled something that may have been, "Whadda you want?"

"I'm looking for Winter Salas. He does live here, doesn't he?"

"He's gone to class," the man said, starting to close the door.

Lore quickly inserted his foot to block that attempt. "I need to reach him as soon as possible," he said. "Can you tell me when he'll return?"

"No idea," the surly fellow said, tugging at the door while he shoved at Lore's foot with his own.

Resisting the man's effort, Lore said, "I need to leave him a message then."

"I'm not a messenger boy." He yanked the door from Lore's hand to pull it shut, jamming it against Lore's toes with a force he felt even through his leather shoe.

Lore exploded with a rage that sent a wave of power slamming into this boor, who clearly needed a lesson in manners. The nearly shut door absorbed most of the wave, buckling from its force. The fellow jumped back with a loud cry of pain. Lore withdrew his foot to let the now warped door close. Lore grinned to see that a gap remained between frame and door, preventing the door from shutting properly. It could no longer be locked.

Good. Served the guy right. But he still had to reach Winter.

He could mindspeak with Jerome. Maybe ...

Winter! He put enough force behind it to make the call the equivalent of a loud shout. He received no answer, but that didn't mean that his call hadn't reached Winter. As a precaution he repeated the call, adding, *You're needed at Lady Kyla's house. Go right away.*

That was the best he could do. He pushed his two-wheeler to its limit, reached the tall building housing Carnover Shipping, left the bicycle by the front door and rushed inside and upstairs to his office.

After apologizing to his supervisor for his tardiness, he made his request to take the day off. The supervisor looked reluctant, probably because of his late arrival. Lore tried a small mental push. It succeeded. The supervisor shrugged, agreed that Lore was entitled to take a day of compensatory time, and signed the request form he had Lore fill out.

Lore left, reclaimed his two-wheeler, and headed for Trille's home.

Winter arrived out of breath and clutching a large portfolio. As Kyla admitted him, he said, panting between words, "I got here as fast as I could, Lady Kyla. I left class early. The instructor called me back, but I ignored him. I'll probably get in trouble. I didn't know I could mindspeak, but your sending was so strong it gave me a headache. It's getting better, though."

He added the last apparently in reaction to her worried frown. The poor fellow must have run most of the distance from the Art Academy. She ushered him into the house, where several of the Community were gathered, some having already arrived in response to her mental sending. But none of those had complained about it being so loud, not even Professor Morence, who tended to complain about any perceived slight. And she had not directed her sending to Winter. She had not been aware that Winter could receive mindspeak, but that could be related to his being an empath. New as he was to the Community, she had not had an opportunity to test him for other gifts and had known only of his empathic ability.

He gazed around at the group looking rather like a startled rabbit. Winnie, holding Dreama, went to him and touched his shoulder, sharing her calming influence with him. Kyla suspected that his red face was due as much to nervousness and discomfort as to his rush to get here.

"Please, Winter, sit down and rest," she said. "And what is that you have with you?"

It was definitely a blush that reddened his face as he sank into the chair being offered and laid the large black folder across his lap. "A portfolio with my art work and sketchpad," he said. "I didn't have any place to put it. I had to bring it with me."

Under happier circumstances Kyla would have liked to see his art, but not now. She nodded and briefly explained to Winter why she had called the Community together.

"Veronica's missing?" he asked when she finished. "And Renni too? Did they go somewhere together?"

Kyla shook her head. "Veronica vanished some time before Renni turned up missing. I'm hoping Renni just went home. I asked Lore to stop by her house while he's summoning the other members."

"They couldn't hear your mindcall?" Winter asked, his brow furrowed.

Professor Morence spoke up before she could answer. "Obviously they don't have that gift, or Lady Kyla would have summoned them the way she summoned all of us."

Fortunately Winter was too worried about something—or someone—else to react to the professor's disdainful tone.

But Winter was one of those Lore was to contact. Lore would have gone to his apartment, but Winter had been at the Academy. Could Lore have sent the mental call? Did he have that ability? If he did, it must be a talent he'd acquired recently, unless for some reason he'd been concealing it. But that would make no sense.

New arrivals interrupted her thoughts. She went to the door and ushered in Gorvy and Darnell Mack. Now they only lacked Trille and Lore. She hoped they'd come soon. The gathering of the Community was taking much longer than she'd expected, and every nerve in her body tingled, demanding action. If there had been enough space in the living room, she'd be pacing, but the room was too full of people, all looking to her for calm, confident leadership. She couldn't let them see how tormented by fear and doubt she really was.

Winter must have sensed her fear. His face was no longer red. It had paled, and his hands shook as they grasped the edges of his portfolio.

Lore arrived at Trille's residence, an imposing house behind a high fence with a locked gate. His ringing a bell mounted on the gatepost brought a male servant Trille must employ as a bodyguard, judging by his muscular build and stern gaze.

"I need to see Lady Trille," Lore stated firmly. "I have an urgent message for her from Lady Kyla Cren."

"You may give me the message," the man stated with equal firmness. "I will deliver it to Lady Trille."

"It's an oral message. I prefer to deliver it in person." He infused the statement with some degree of coercion.

The man did not open the gate. "I'll convey that preference to Lady Trille. Please wait here." He turned and headed into the house.

Lore had had no idea that Trille kept a bodyguard

nor that she maintained such tight security, but he guessed it was understandable, now that she was becoming so well known as a singer. She did have a beautiful voice, but he wasn't particularly fond of the type of songs she sang. The traditional ballads and patriotic songs that were her specialty were too old-fashioned for his taste. Her fans adored her, though, and would-be suitors clamored for her attention. Given the irrational behavior of some of those fans, Lore figured she was wise to hire a guard and keep her gate locked.

The guard returned and spoke through the gate. "Lady Trille asks whether she is needed at Lady Kyla's home."

"Yes, she is," Lore answered. "I'm to accompany her there."

The guard frowned. "I see that you arrived by two-wheeler. How do you propose to accompany her?" Apparently he didn't expect an answer because he continued, "Please return to Lady Kyla and tell her Lady Trille will come by carriage and will be there soon." He turned away, leaving Lore fuming, his plans foiled. Trille had not even deigned to come outside and talk to him herself. She should have been curious as to what had been happening and why she'd been sent for. Lore had counted on that.

Apparently she felt herself too far above him to bother talking to him. But in the Community they were all supposedly equal. He'd show her he was as good as she was when it came to their special gifts. His were more useful than hers. What good would the ability to manipulate water do her when they confronted Jerome in a land so dry and barren? Jerome had told him how he trekked to the distant mountains to collect a bit of water from snowmelt. An onerous task, Jerome had said. He also extracted liquid from the leaves of cactus. Not an easy way to satisfy his thirst. In fact, Jerome had made it clear to Lore that staying alive in the harsh land to which he'd been consigned required all his time and strength. "So how," he'd asked, "do they think I'd possibly be equipped to do the kind of harm they're attributing to me?"

Lore had no answer except to agree that Jerome was being unfairly maligned. And Jerome had assured him that he welcomed the opportunity to clear his name and convince not just Kyla but the entire Community that he was as much an innocent victim of an evil Dire Lord as they were.

First, he needed Lore to help the Community members reach the desert land.

CHAPTER FIFTEEN
WATER

Veronica rose up out of the sand like a revenant rising from a grave. She shook herself again and again and then brushed off sand that still clung stubbornly to every bit of exposed flesh. Her skin itched and burned. Her eyes felt filled with grit. Sand had caught in her eyelashes; it lurked in her eyebrows; it rained from her hair when she ran her fingers through it. Her throat scratched and burned from thirst, the worst discomfort of all. She had to find water or find a way to get home.

Lore! Had he survived? She looked around, saw a sandy mound a short distance away, and moved toward it, her feet sinking into sand with each step, making progress difficult. She reached it and dug frantically into the mound, scattering sand about and plunging her hands and arms into the mound until she was as covered with sand as she had been when she first emerged.

Her efforts were futile. Her certainty that she'd find Lore, dead or alive, buried in this mound, kept her digging under the merciless heat of the sun until the entire mound was flattened to the level of the area surrounding it. Lore was not buried in it and likely never had been. The energy she'd expended had increased her thirst beyond what she would have thought possible. She had to find water. And shade.

But where was Lore? Had he returned home without her? She didn't want to believe that of him, but if he had, surely it was to bring help. She should wait here until that help arrived.

Her thirst would not let her wait. She had to move, had to find some moisture, anything that would ease the dryness, the sensation that sand filled her mouth. She could not even produce saliva to moisten her dry and swollen tongue. Nor did her thirst permit concern that she might encounter Jerome. Her fear of him, her hope of finding Ed and Marta, even her desire to locate Lore all retreated to the dim recesses of her mind, driven into hiding by her all-consuming need for water.

So she walked, hunting for a trail, seeking desperately for some sign of water. She crossed a dry streambed, so filled with sand that she recognized it only by the broken and decaying trunks of trees that had once lined its banks. As she continued, walking became easier because the ground became firmer beneath her feet, less carpeted with layers of sand. She could walk faster. She reached another dry streambed, more easily recognizable than the first because it had not filled with sand. She stopped in the middle of it and dug her fingers into the caked soil around her feet. She felt a slight bit of moisture there, not enough to allow her to extract any water, merely an indication that water had once flowed here.

An impulse led her to change the course she'd set and follow the streambed in the hope that upstream a bit of water might still flow. She hadn't walked far when she saw that the streambed led toward the distant mountains. Mountains wearing snowy mantles. Snowmelt must have formed this stream, but that water wasn't reaching it now. Not enough snow?

Or was something damming the stream? It was a long way to walk, and she doubted she had the strength to make it, but the hope of finding water at the end of the trek spurred her onward.

Soon she was stumbling, barely able to keep putting one foot in front of the other, weak from thirst and exhaustion, and the mountains looked no nearer. Her vision blurred. She fell to her knees, bruising them on the rocky streambed. With considerable effort she hauled herself to her feet and staggered forward, her gaze focused on a single point, a spot on the mountain just below the snow line. Her vision was restricted to a gray tunnel through which only that distant focal point remained visible, nothing else. Her mind, too, fixed on a single goal: *find water*. That tunnel vision and focused goal somehow kept her moving. She could no longer walk in the streambed, now filled with tumbled rocks.

Then the mountain loomed in front of her. She couldn't have come that far. She had no memory of traversing the distance that had spread between her last conscious thought and the present time. How, weak as she was, could she climb the mountain to the snow line well above her? She could barely walk.

She fell to her knees and crawled upward, still keeping her gaze fixed on her goal. She had come so far—she could not give up. She moved forward slowly, painfully. Digging her fingers into the soil, she pulled herself onward.

A wall of stones blocked her path. She dragged herself around it. Looking up, she saw the snow line hopelessly far above, the climb impossibly steep. Defeated, she relaxed her fingers, collapsed, and let her arm dangle over the edge of ... something ... a ledge of rock ...

Her fingers grew cold. And wet.

She gathered strength to rise up enough to peer over the rock ledge.

Water! Water—clear, cold—pooled behind a pile of rocks that formed a dam.

She cupped her hand, let the water fill it, and raised it to her mouth. The first mouthful she swished around and spat out to clean the sand from her mouth. At last she drank, water cool and clear and sweet. She savored every mouthful. When at last she'd slaked her thirst, she washed her face, hands, and arms, removing the sand that she'd been unable to brush completely off.

She felt revived. Her mind functioned again. The Power-Giver had surely led her to this place, had sustained her when her strength ran out. She breathed a silent *Thank you*, though that hardly expressed the depth of her gratitude. She should be dead. She would be if she had not received the Power-Giver's help.

Her power was still weak, but it would return. She was hungry, but she could do nothing about that. She needed rest. In her confused state she hadn't noted how low the sun was. Nightfall would soon be upon her. Gazing around, she spotted, a bit higher on the mountain, what looked like the mouth of a cave. If it was not the home of some wild beast, it might provide shelter for the night. And, she reflected, it was unlikely to house a wild beast. She'd seen no trace of any animal life remaining in this barren land.

It was a short climb to the cave, and by the day's last light she examined its interior. She could neither see nor smell any evidence of animal habitation. The cave was not deep, just a hollow, really, but exhausted as she was and as dark as it was growing, it offered the only refuge available. She bent and crept in, brushed an area free of loose stones and sand, lay down on the hard rock floor, and was soon fast asleep.

She awakened to see bright sunlight flooding the small cave, sat up and stretched, wincing as muscles aching from her long trek and her sleep on hard ground protested every movement. Despite the aches, she crawled from the cave, stood, and peered around. With her mind fully functioning again, her fear of Jerome reawakened. But she saw no sign of life anywhere.

That absence lessened her fear that Jerome might come for water and spot her hiding place. The pool she'd found had to be his water source, the dam of stones his construction to provide a reservoir for the precious liquid. It would be a long and difficult trek for him, but as she examined the site she saw that it was an ideal place to create a pool of water. The dam had been placed in the narrowest part of the channel that ran between two high, stony banks. He would have needed less work to dam the flow in this particular spot and would have been rewarded with a more sizable pool than he could get anywhere downstream. No doubt he had found or crafted some type of vessels in which to transport and store the water, so he would not have to come here often. Still, she would have to guard against the possibility of his coming to replenish his supply and finding her here.

The climb down from the cave proved more difficult than the ascent had been. Clambering from ledge to narrow ledge, she made her precarious way to the pool, where she again drank her fill and washed. Pangs of hunger assailed her. Her power, she sensed, had built up from the night's rest. Maybe she could use it to return home. She had come here via Lore's power, and whether she had the ability to transport herself she did not know. She would have to test it.

But not now. She felt a sudden compulsion to undertake a difficult task. Driven to deprive Jerome of his water source, she descended to just below the dam, lowered herself into the damp but waterless streambed, and set to work pulling and prying the stones of the dam, bit by bit dismantling it until water trickled over the lowered barrier and flowed over her feet. Her shoes, already badly scuffed and scoured by sand, their soles worn thin from climbing over rocks, would be ruined, but she refused to let that matter.

Some of the lower stones were so firmly wedged together that she had to use power to budge them and pry them loose. Icy water now swirled over her ankles, numbing her feet. Still she labored, rolling aside the lower stones, too large and heavy for her to lift.

The water now reached halfway between her ankles and knees, but she judged correctly that it would go no higher because it flowed downstream more rapidly with each rock she removed. When she cast aside the last layer of rocks, the pool emptied and the water rushed past, giving her only moments to clean her hands in the flow and capture a couple of mouthfuls before the water tumbled down the mountain to soak into the thirsty ground below.

She climbed out of the stream and rested a bit before attempting to go home. While she labored at the destruction of the dam, she'd decided that she would not search for Lore. He might have returned home without her, possibly believing her dead, or he might be dead. Jerome might have captured him. She worried about him, but by now Aunt Kyla, Aunt Abigail, and Aunt Leah would be worried about her. If she could transport herself, she would need all her power to do it. Better use that power to get home and let Aunt Kyla and others of the Community locate and retrieve Lore if he had not returned.

She removed and discarded her ruined shoes and rubbed her feet and legs to restore circulation until the numbness wore off. Warmth returned quickly as the hot sun beat down. She stood. It was time to try to return home. She breathed a plea to the Power-Giver and, picturing Aunt Kyla clearly in her mind, she willed herself to be at Kyla's side.

CHAPTER SIXTEEN
CONFUSION

Trille was the final member of the Community to arrive. Kyla rapidly filled her in on her plans, and Trille declared her willingness to help, adding "Though I don't know what use my gift will be in the barren land you describe."

"None of us knows exactly what gifts will be needed or what will be required of us," Kyla said. "I believe each of us has something important to contribute."

Only Leah and Winnie would stay behind to care for Dreama and keep watch over Petros. The rest all agreed to try to be transported to the land of Jerome's imprisonment, though Abigail objected at first, wanting either to stay with Leah or to have Leah accompany her. Although Kyla reminded her that Leah, not being gifted, would be in too much danger and that Abigail, being a powerful healer, would be a vital part of the group, it took Leah to persuaded Abigail by saying that as one of the Community's oldest and most gifted members she was obligated to set a good example by going with the others.

So at last they were ready and the time arrived to go. Everyone gathered in the living room and formed a circle. They joined hands. Winter, looking frightened, kept his portfolio with him, clutched firmly between his arm and his side, leaving his hand free to grasp the hand of Darnell Mack, next to him. Holding the portfolio that way looked awkward, and she should tell him to put it down, but Kyla guessed that having it with him helped to calm him, so she said nothing.

Camsen Wellner cleared his throat. "Should we not pray to Ondin for guidance before we undertake this unlikely journey?" he asked, no doubt prepared to offer such a prayer.

Kyla didn't want to anger the priest. They would almost certainly need his talents for sculpting and throwing fire and for creating illusions. Yet to her the worship of Ondin was based on delusion. "It is better to ask the Power-Giver's help," she said as gently as she could. "You may pray to Ondin on your own. But let us ask for the Power-Giver's guidance and for the power needed to defeat Jerome."

She took a deep breath and sent a silent plea, *Please don't let us fail. Keep me from making a terrible mistake, please, Alair.* Aloud she said, "Power-Giver, we beg you to infuse us with power, both individually and jointly, sufficient to the task ahead of us. We ask your guidance and your help in this rescue effort."

I will do all I can, Alair's voice spoke in her mind, startling her. It had been so long since he'd spoken to her. *There is more at stake here than you know,* he continued. *I must warn you that Jerome owes much of his power to an evil Dire Lord, who has given him gifts you will find difficult to combat.*

Kyla shuddered. *Why didn't you tell me this before? And why haven't you spoken in so long?*

I didn't want to worry you, came his familiar voice *And Claid has been rationing my power.*

She sighed. Alair hadn't changed much, even as

Power-Giver, from the arrogant and infuriating mage he had been. But was Claid, the Dire Lord whom Alair had held in thrall for many years and on whom his present existence depended, really rationing his power? She recalled how often Alair, when a human mage, had blamed Claid for failures that were Alair's own.

Claid will help us, won't he?

Claid is even more unpredictable as a powerful Dire Lord than he was when he assumed a human guise. You can't count on him.

Kyla didn't believe that. Alair had always refused to trust Claid. If she needed his help, he would give it, she felt sure. They had to go ahead with their plan. Too many lives depended on it.

And how many lives would be lost if the plan failed? Or even if it succeeded? No, she couldn't think of that. Come what may, it was time to take the group to confront Jerome. She tightened her grip on the hand of Trille, on one side of her, and Lore on the other. "We're ready," she told Lore.

Renni glared at Jerome, tempted to tell him that letting her see him as human made him no less a monster in her eyes. She held back, knowing how dangerous he was. If she could erase his memories as far back as she could, which was probably not more than a month or two, it wouldn't undo the damage he'd done in that time, but it might prevent his doing more. He met her glare with the kind of amused look one might bestow on a naughty child. She did not avert her gaze but launched her power at him and waited for the look of confusion that typically followed memory loss.

He burst out laughing. "You think your puny

power is a match for mine? You can't harm me, little fool. Let me show you what my power can do."

They were standing on sand, hot and dry, and Renni felt that sand shift beneath her feet and seep over them. She began to sink, being drawn deeper into the sand, which rose to her knees, then to her hips. It didn't stop until it reached her waist. Now she had to look up to Jerome, who had remained standing firmly on the surface of the sand.

"Let's see," he mused. "Shall I let you sink further?"

As if in answer she fell deeper, so that the sand covered her breasts. Its weight against her chest made it hard to breathe. Her feet had grown numb. She had lifted her arms when the sand reached her waist, so her hands and arms remained above the sand. The urge to dig at the sand and push it away from her body was almost overpowering, but she refused to yield to it. She would not give Jerome that satisfaction.

"It would be amusing to bury you deeper and watch you die," Jerome said. "I may do that, but not right now. Let me take you to some friends of yours first." He waved his hand and the sand fell away from her body, spreading out so smoothly that it no trace remained of how it had piled up around her.

Jerome reached out and grabbed her arm. She tried to pull away, but his hold had the strength of a steel clamp. She could not break free. He grinned at her discomfort. "Come," he said.

And with that single word he and Renni were swept up in a rushing wind and seconds later set down on stony ground, a welcome change from soft sand. At first her mind refused to accept the scene that met her eyes. In front of her a fountain of sparkling water seemed to surge mysteriously from the flat soil. In the center of that fountain, the water gushed over two figures. She blinked at the astounding sight, slow to take in the horrible truth. Ed and Marta stood like statues in the midst of that fountain.

"Wouldn't you like to join your friends" Jerome asked, his hand still clamped around her upper arm.

Jerome's question jolted her from her bemusement. She looked more closely at the fountain. The water wasn't moving. Carefully she stretched her free arm toward the fountain and brushed her fingertips across the surface of the supposed water. That surface was waxy and dry, definitely not water. Stalling for time, she gave it another tentative touch. Like wax it was smooth, cool, and slightly resilient.

"You haven't answered my question," Jerome observed.

"Are you giving me a choice?"

He wasn't, of course. She had to come up with a plan. Fast.

Petros strained to hear through Ed's ears the conversation going on between Renni and Jerome outside the solidified fountain in which Ed and Marta were imprisoned, trapping him along with Ed, who was unconscious, perhaps due to something Jerome had done. Fortunately, Jerome did not know about the hitchhiker in Ed's mind.

Although it was difficult even for him, with his special ability, to hear through the strange stuff that imprisoned Ed and Marta, Petros could distinguish enough of the conversation to gather that Jerome intended to add Renni to the collection within the false fountain. To do that, Jerome would have to release briefly whatever spell kept the fountain solid. That moment could give Petros his only chance to free himself. Ed's unconscious state might allow him to move Ed's body.

He'd lost his legs so long ago. Would he remember how to walk? But he'd only have to lurch forward, toward Jerome. If he could catch Jerome unawares, possibly Renni could do something. Or Marta might awaken. He'd heard she had lots of power.

A lot of ifs. But he had to try. He searched for and found the link in Ed's mind to the muscles in his legs. That was all he had time for. Even though he'd been expecting it, when the stuff that looked like water but was not pooled around Ed's feet the suddenness of his release jolted Petros.

Jerome dragged Renni into that gooey pool and slammed her up against Marta. Petros caused Ed's body to lurch forward. The stuff he'd been standing in sucked at his feet, but Petros managed to keep Ed upright and moving in an awkward stumble. Somehow that haphazard motion brought Ed's body around in a circle, so that he came to a stop just in front of the action.

Jerome released his hold on Renni to grab Ed. Renni grabbed Marta and yanked her out of the sticky stuff. Now the pool was empty, though Jerome had grabbed Ed and was pushing him back into it. Petros lacked enough control to resist.

Marta grabbed hold of Ed's arm and pulled. She didn't free him from Jerome's hold, but she must have awakened him. He took control of his body, and once again Petros became only an observer.

"Go ahead, Lore," Kyla said. "Focus on the land, and we'll all feed you as much power as we can."

He nodded and closed his eyes. The room around them dimmed slightly and then brightened again.

"Hey, what's happening?" a familiar voice called out.

Veronica!

Lore's eyes popped open. Veronica walked around the outside of the circle to stand just behind Kyla. She glared at Lore. He cursed silently.

"So you did come back here," she said. "Why didn't you look for me? I came that close to dying." She held up her hand, her thumb and index finger little more than a hair's breadth apart.

"I thought you'd come back on your own," he said. "And when I learned you hadn't, I was afraid you'd died in that sandstorm. But we're just getting ready to go back there. We'd have looked for you immediately."

Instead of responding, she looked at Kyla. "You're going there? All of you?"

"All of us except Winnie and Leah. They'll stay here to care for Dreama and watch over Petros. The rest of us will try to get there," Kyla said. "We have a better chance with you to help us.

Did you see Jerome? Or Marta and Ed? Or Renni—she's gone missing now too."

"I didn't see anyone," Veronica said. "I didn't look for anyone. When I got out of that sand, all I could think of was finding water. I did find some, or I would have died."

Lore wanted to ask her where she found water, but the question might lead Veronica to probe more deeply into what happened to him in that land. If only someone else would ask. No one did, not even Trille, whose talent depended on the presence of water.

"Well, I mean to try to find Marta and Ed and to

rescue them if Jerome has them," Kyla addressed Veronica. "It's time that we all confront Jerome. Now that you're here, we'll be that much stronger when we face him."

Veronica shook her head. "I don't have much power right now. I haven't had anything to eat for way too long. I wasn't sure I could make it back here."

"You did, so you should be all right to go with us. We're ready. A few seconds later and you would have missed us. The Power-Giver must have delayed us just long enough for you to join us. Come on, get in the circle and take my hand." Kyla held out her hand.

Veronica shook her head and made no move to take Kyla's hand.

Lore was relieved that Veronica hadn't, after all, died in the sandstorm, yet he did not want her going back with the group. Jerome would almost certainly prefer not to have to deal with the temperamental girl.

And, fortunately, she was being temperamental now. "I have to eat something," she said. "You don't understand what I've been doing. I'm starved. You go on. I'll join you later."

"That's unwise and selfish of you," Kyla said sharply, continuing to hold out her hand.

Lore chuckled to himself. Kyla had said exactly the wrong thing.

Veronica's cheeks reddened with anger. "I'm not being unwise. I need to rebuild my strength. If you think that's selfish, I'm sorry, but I know what I need. You can either wait awhile or go without me." She flounced off toward the kitchen.

"Come back here," Abigail called. Veronica kept going, and Abigail broke from the circle and started after her.

"No, Abigail. It's no use," Kyla said. "In that mood

she'd be no help to us anyway. If she can't see how important this is, let her go." Reclaiming Trille's hand and squeezing Lore's, she said, "Let's get there."

As soon as Abigail returned to her place Lore clasped Kyla's hand tightly, and his other hand gripped Marchion's. He closed his eyes and sent a mental message to Jerome: *We're coming—finally.*

Undeterred by the lack of response, he pictured Jerome in his mind and focused on that mental image as he received an infusion of power from all those in the circle, drawing especially on Marchion, who fortunately retained his power of enhancement, though equally fortunately, he must not have regained his power to see auras.

Lore felt the sudden chill and then a rush of wind. "Hold tight," he said, though he doubted anyone would hear. His feet rested on solid ground. Someone near him let out a heavy breath.

A loud scream made him open his eyes on an unexpected scene.

Renni let out a shrill scream when Jerome slung her into the puddle of thick goop that had been the fountain. And that stuff started moving upward, quickly covering her ankles and oozing up her legs. She tried to pull free of it but could not. Jerome grabbed hold of Ed and shoved him into the goop beside her. He reached for Marta. But Marta had moved beyond his reach and through her power was lifting rocks and sand and hurling them at Jerome. He shielded himself and remained unhurt but distracted, not only by the barrage Marta was sending at him but by—Renni's eyes widened—the circle of Gifted that appeared so close that when Kyla released the hand of Trille she could reach out and touch Jerome's arm.

Instead, still holding Lore's hand, she backed away from Jerome.

Renni lost sight of the group as Ed swung his body in front of her, grabbed her around the waist, and, grunting, lifted her free of the goop. It surrendered its hold on her legs with a loud gurgle and pop. With a strength she wouldn't have thought he had, Ed tossed her clear of the sticky fountain. She landed on her rump, yelped, and struggled to her feet. "Marta," she yelled, "We've got to get Ed out of there."

Marta was already running toward her husband. Renni yelled again, "Be careful! Don't get into that stuff."

By now the goop had risen to Ed's groin and looked more like water, though Renni was well aware that it would neither feel nor act like water. Ed had saved her from it but he could not save himself.

She ran to Lore. "Get Ed out of there," she said, shaking his shoulder. "Transport him. Hurry."

"Calm down," Lore said, jerking away from her clutch. "He isn't going to be hurt."

"Lore, you're a fool. Jerome will kill us all if we don't do everything we can to stop him."

"No. Listen, everyone," Lore shoved Renni away and raised his voice to address the rest of the group. "Jerome just wants to talk to you. You need to hear what he has to say."

"Idiot!" Renni screamed.

"Stop it, Renni," Kyla ordered. "We didn't come here to fight among ourselves." She turned to Lore. "Lore, what are you saying?"

"He's saying he's a traitor," Renni yelled as she rushed to help Marta pull Ed from the stuff climbing up his body.

It was no use. They could grasp his hands, but no

matter how hard they pulled, they couldn't free him, and they couldn't get close enough to grab his body and lift without stepping into the goop and getting caught themselves.

"Leave me," Ed said. "You'll get trapped too."

"We could use some help here," Renni shouted, ignoring Ed's plea, as did Marta.

Gorvy Darnell and Marchion Blandry ran to their aid. They were taller than Marta and Renni and could lean in far enough to grab Ed beneath his armpits, but no matter how hard they tugged, they could not extract Ed from the stuff that had climbed above his waist and come perilously close to his would-be rescuers' hands and arms.

With a loud whoosh the stuff of the fountain spurted up and over Ed, covering him completely. Renni and Marta barely had time to jump back as the fake water rained down on them. Marchion also stumbled out and away from the sticky stuff, but Gorvy was not so lucky. Renni looked back and saw him, one hand still clasping Ed's arm, swallowed up by the surge. In seconds he and Ed were like two statues in the middle of a fountain. A fountain whose water wasn't really water at all.

Burning with rage, Marta swung around toward the group. It would have been gratifying to see so many of the Gifted here to help her and Ed except that no one was doing anything constructive. Renni, who had tried to help and had in fact accomplished more than anyone else, now was shouting a whole arsenal of epithets at a young man who shouted back and seemed, incredibly, to be calling on the group to calm down and listen to what Jerome had to say. Kyla, her hands on her hips, faced the two shouters and was trying in vain to quiet them. A middle-aged woman with tears running down her cheeks was standing by the figures caught in the now solidified fountain. She must be the wife of the man caught with Ed. The man who had nearly been caught also stared at the fountain, looking dazed as he pulled gobs of the fountain stuff off his clothes and out of his hair.

His effort reminded her that she, too, was peppered with globules of the waxy substance. It clung stubbornly to her fingers when she tried to pull it off, and she had to tug it free. Meanwhile, Jerome stood to one side observing all the confusion. His amused look told her that he'd orchestrated that confusion.

She held in her hand the stuff she'd pried from her fingers. It wasn't a lot, but ...

Using her power she hurled the sticky substance at Jerome's face. Her accurate aim plastered the stuff over his eyes. It stuck to his face like a mask. He let out a howl of rage.

Marta rushed to the man still peeling the substance from his body. "Give it to me, quick," and at his uncomprehending look added, "the goop you're taking off yourself. Give it to me."

Not waiting for him to respond, she clawed a wad of it out of his hand and sent it flying at Jerome. It molded itself over one of his ears. In seconds Marta scraped another bit off the man's shoulder and sent it after the first to cover Jerome's other ear, then targeted his nose and mouth. By that time her unwitting helper caught on to what she was doing and joined her in a hunt for more bits she could turn into weapons.

Jerome clawed at his face, but Marta used her power to keep the stuff, now hardening, plastered tightly to him, blinding, deafening, and silencing him. And could he even breathe through it? She and Ed had when they were encased in the fountain. So it couldn't kill Jerome, but maybe it would render him helpless enough to allow the group to find a way to imprison him.

Having nothing more to throw, she glanced around, expecting to see others rushing to attack Jerome while he was vulnerable. Instead, Kyla kept trying to separate Lore from Renni, who was now attacking him physically as well as verbally. The priest who'd brought the blessing at Dreama's Naming-Day service stood to one side praying, and though Marta couldn't distinguish the words, she guessed he prayed to Ondin rather than to the Power-Giver. The wife of the man caught along with Ed still stood by the fountain, weeping. Abigail stood by her, consoling her. A dowdy woman in a ridiculous gown wrung her hands helplessly as she watched the fight between Renni and Lore. Most incongruously, a pretty young woman was singing, a recognizable melody. And the shy young man whose name she couldn't now remember sat on the ground a considerable distance away, hunched over what looked like a large drawing pad. Marta wanted to scream at them all to stop the nonsense. But what good would it do? They had become marionettes with Jerome pulling their strings.

Another man, whose name she didn't recall but remembered that he was a professor, stood with brows furrowed and hands clenched, apparently trying to use his power. It had no noticeable effect. Or did it?

Jerome stopped clawing at the clear substance covering his face. His arms and hands lowered and clamped against his side. Marta remembered: the professor's gift was coercion. He must be forcing Jerome to remain still and refrain from removing the mask.

Marta's helper must have noted the same thing. "I'm feeding the professor all the power I can," he said. "While Firstan holds him, we need to secure him."

"How?" Marta asked. "With what?"

She looked around, saw only dry sand. But the sand gave her an idea. "Kyla," she shouted. "Sing the wind. Have it throw sand on Jerome."

Kyla didn't seem to hear. She remained preoccupied with the shouting match between Renni and the young man. The other singer paused, staring at Kyla as if she hadn't known the Community leader sang the wind. Was it possible that Kyla had never revealed that gift?

Marta could not escape the conviction that Kyla had failed the Community in many ways. She couldn't think about that now. Jerome might be blinded and deafened by the clingy substance she'd thrown onto his face, but that didn't mean his power was diminished. He must be controlling the actions of Renni, the young man, and even Kyla in some way. *He won't control me,* Marta resolved, firming up her defenses.

She turned to the young woman who had been singing. "You," she called to her, "can you sing the wind?"

The woman hurried toward her. "No," she said. "I can control water by singing. There's no water here, but I'd hoped the fountain, even though it's not real water, might respond." She shook her head sadly. "It doesn't."

Marta nodded. No hope from that quarter then. At

least the woman had tried to do something. She turned to the man who had been helping her. "What are your abilities?" she asked.

"I see auras—or did. Something took that ability from me. I can enhance other people's gifts. I've been feeding you what power I can while you tossed that stuff at Jerome."

"Good work, thanks," Marta said. "Keep it up."

She turned to Abigail. "Abigail, what are you doing?"

"I'm trying to use a spell to contact Veronica," she said. "We need her here, but the spell isn't working."

"Forget that. Help me break Kyla and Renni out of whatever spell Jerome's put on them."

"I don't know how—"

"Try. Use your ability to heal." Marta grabbed Kyla's arm and swung her toward Abigail.

Kyla seemed to be in a daze. She kept repeating, "Lore, Renni, stop. We can't fight among ourselves."

So now Marta knew their names. Lore and Renni paid no attention to Kyla. Like her, they were repeating the same phrases over and over. Lore kept shouting, "Just listen to him. Let him explain things." Renni kept yelling, "You're a traitor and a liar." Locked in that cycle of recrimination and pleading, they seemed unaware of anything or anyone else.

Marta tried to step between them and hit something like an invisible wall. She had to let them go and look for help somewhere else. If only she could remember the names of all these people. Kyla had introduced her to all of them at the Naming-Day ceremony, when she'd been in such a state of nerves that she hadn't even tried to commit their names to memory.

The dowdy woman in the gaudy gown sidled up to

her while casting wary glances at Jerome. "You probably don't remember, but I'm Zauna." She spoke in a whisper as though fearful of being overheard. "I'm a crystal gazer, but someone cracked my crystal ball so there wasn't any use in bringing it. I can't do anything without it, but Kyla insisted I should come. If I can help in any way, I will. And so will the rest of us. We just need direction."

Marta had expected her to say she wanted to be returned home. Gratified by the offer of help that had come instead, Marta said, "I've forgotten the names and abilities of these people. Can you tell me?"

Zauna nodded toward each of her companions in turn. "That's Marchion. He's an enhancer. He also sees auras, but that won't be much help now. She turned her head toward another man. "That's Professor Firstan Morence. He can force people to act against their will." She indicated the young man hunched over the drawing pad. "That's Winter Salas. He's an empath. He won't be much help."

Marta remembered how Veronica had embarrassed him with her effusive introduction. Why had Kyla brought him here? He'd feel all the tension, the anger, the fear. "He must be suffering terribly."

"Yes," Zauna agreed, and echoing Marta's thought added, "He shouldn't have come." She turned to the young woman who'd tried to control the false fountain by singing. "That's Trille. She could use water as a force, but there isn't any here."

Marta frowned. Such a diverse group, but very little talent that could be used against Jerome. She cast a worried glance at him. He'd free himself before long. They'd never be ready for it. If only Kyla could tell her what her plan had been. Zauna must know. "What did Kyla intend to do?"

Zauna stared down at her sandaled feet. "I don't think she had a plan," she mumbled. More clearly she said, "She just wanted us to pool our power and throw it against him." Her voice trailed off. "Somehow."

"So she came here, brought everyone here, with no plan?" Marta had suspected as much.

"She was desperate to rescue you and your husband," Zauna said, once again studying her feet.

"And Dreama. Don't forget about the baby," Marta snapped. "She's the important one."

Zauna lifted her head, her eyes round. "But—oh, that's right. You didn't know! Baby Dreama is safe. Lore and Ed rescued her. Winnie and Leah are caring for her. And they have a nanny goat to provide milk."

"She's safe?" Marta could scarcely believe what she'd heard. Zauna deserved a hug for that news. But wait! "Ed and *Lore* rescued her? The fellow Renni's screaming at, calling a traitor? The one who keeps telling us to listen to Jerome?"

Zauna took a step backward as she nodded. "Lore Kaplek. I think," she said, her voice again lowered to a whisper, "he's the one who broke my crystal ball."

Marta didn't care about the woman's crystal ball. "We have to free him from the spell Jerome's got him trapped in. And Renni and Kyla, too, before Jerome breaks loose and out of that glop I threw on him."

The ground shook. Jerome zoomed up to twice the height of a normal man. With one hand he peeled the hardened waxy stuff from his face, freeing his eyes and ears. Laughing wildly, he loomed over them, clapping his hands. Zauna screamed.

"You've been so wonderfully entertaining," his voice boomed. "Such a mismatched, sorry group with such big ambitions. I let you think you'd incapacitated me. But did you really think you were strong enough and coordinated enough to overpower me? You have no idea of my strength and a greatly inflated idea of your feeble abilities."

Everyone froze. They all gazed up at Jerome, varying degrees of horror written on their faces. Even Winter looked up from his drawing tablet, a charcoal smudge on his face and a stick of charcoal clutched in one hand, to stare open-mouthed at the monstrous figure.

Marta sensed that Jerome was lying about only having let them think they'd blinded and deafened him. He'd been furious and more than a little afraid for a time. It hadn't lasted long, and he'd pretended to be incapacitated longer than he actually had been, but they had proven that Jerome was not invincible. They could defeat him, but they had to find stronger measures to use against him.

The spell that had held Kyla and Lore and Renni in an endless round of shouting and pleading, recriminations and admonitions vanished, leaving them shamefaced and afraid. Lore shook his head in disbelief. Marta stood near enough to hear his low mutter: "You lied to me. You misled me. And you probably won't let me keep the gifts you gave me."

Gifts? What abilities had Jerome given this young fool, and how had he used them?

Jerome had heard him, too. "Oh, no, my friend Lore," he boomed, "the gifts are yours to keep. They are your reward for being so helpful to me. You can only lose them by trying to use them against me. Not that you could do any harm to me if you tried."

At that speech, everyone turned to glare at Lore.

"So Renni was right," Kyla said. "You are a traitor."

"No, I—"

Marta cut in. "Drop it, both of you, before you get caught in another shouting loop. You're playing right into Jerome's hands." She looked at Lore. "I don't know how Jerome got to you, but you did something wonderful before that. Thank you for helping Ed rescue our baby."

"*Your* baby?" To Marta Jerome's surprise sounded feigned. "I thought it was the child of the woman who clung to it so tenaciously, trying to wrest it from my grasp. I had to teach her a lesson. Too bad I made it so severe. I'd have reserved that treatment for you if I'd known."

"Lesson? Is that what you call what you did to poor Mayzie? You murdered her!" Kyla shouted.

"Monster!" Marta leapt toward him, her fists clenched. Jerome put out a hand, palm forward. She fell back as though he'd given her a hard push, although he hadn't touched her.

Jerome laughed. "Such delightful drama," he crowed. "I never knew you people could provide so much entertainment. Look at the poor fools, Lore. Stick with me. Stay on the winning team."

"Winning? We'll see about that," Kyla said, her hands on her hips, her chin tilted defiantly upward.

"Release my husband!" Marta demanded with equal defiance.

"No indeed. Simple Eddy is staying right where he is, where he can't blunder into any more trouble." Jerome peered down at the wife of the man trapped along with Eddy. "Sorry about your husband, madam. He'll have to stay where he is, as a consequence of choosing such troublesome and foolish friends."

"You haven't seen how troublesome we can be," Marta said. "We'll see who's foolish."

Jerome's loud laughter again poured over the group. "Indeed we will. Although it should be obvious already. Look at you, a pathetic bunch who can't even work together or formulate a plan. A match for me? Hardly. I've had years to hone my skills and sharpen my intellect. I've already outwitted and outmaneuvered you. I let you get the baby back. Taking it accomplished what I wanted. It brought you all here, where I needed you. Now the real fun can begin."

CHAPTER SEVENTEEN
TEARS AND TRIALS

Veronica let anger override her guilt at refusing to accompany the group. Aunt Kyla should have understood. She knew what it felt like to have her power depleted and should have understood what it was like to have just come from a harrowing experience. True, she didn't know about the hard work of tearing down the dam and releasing the water reservoir. Would all that work prove of any use? Jerome could easily use his power to rebuild the dam and collect the water he needed.

At the time it had seemed vitally important to destroy the dam. She'd felt compelled to do it. Had it been no more than a foolish impulse? Here, alone, she felt unsure of herself.

From somewhere in the house she heard the baby wail, reminding her that she wasn't alone. Leah and Winnie were here. She should go find them and look in on Baby Dreama. And rest a bit to recover her powers. But first she needed to eat.

She took two eggs from the cold box, put a pan on the stove, added a bit of butter, and scrambled the eggs. The breadbox held a loaf of Leah's wonderful baked bread. She cut off a big slice and sat down at the kitchen table to eat the eggs and bread.

"Veronica! You're back! What happened to you?" Leah hurried to the table and took a seat opposite her.

"I smelled something cooking and couldn't imagine who was here. We've all been so worried about you. The others have gone to confront Jerome. Did you see him? Where have you been?"

Leah's warm welcome, which contrasted so with Aunt Kyla's, comforted Veronica. She responded eagerly. "Lore and I went to Ed's world, or what used to be Ed's world. We got caught in a sandstorm. It was horrible, impossible to see or hear anything. We got separated. Lore says he looked for me, couldn't find me, and figured I came back without him. I think he's lying. He talked me into going. It wasn't my idea. So he had a lot of nerve, just leaving me there." Sudden tears poured down her cheeks and she started shaking. "I thought I'd die of thirst." She choked out the words between sobs. "I had to walk and walk to find water."

Leah rose and came around the table to put her arms around Veronica. "But you did find some?"

Veronica nodded.

"And you're back, safe."

"Yes, I got back just as the group was ready to transport to Ed's world, and Aunt Kyla wanted me to go with them, but I couldn't. Aunt Leah, I just couldn't. I was hungry, and my power was all gone, and ... and I'm so tired."

"Of course you are," Leah said, letting Veronica sob into her shoulder while she patted her back. "Kyla couldn't think straight. She's too worried about Marta and Ed. Do you know what's happened to them?"

"No." Veronica told her about walking to the mountains, finding the dammed stream, and tearing down the dam. "I wanted to keep Jerome from getting water. But he'll just build it back up." That realization brought a fresh paroxysm of wrenching sobs.

"Maybe not," Leah said. "At least, not right away. It may have an effect you can't anticipate."

"You're just trying to make me feel better," Veronica said as the tears streamed down her face.

A hand rested on her shoulder. She heard Winnie's voice say, "No, Leah's right. We can't know what will result. You just need to finish eating and then sleep for a while."

Winnie must have come in long enough ago to hear most of what she told Leah. The comfort offered by these two dear women calmed Veronica. Gradually her tears subsided, and she followed Winnie's advice, finishing her bread and eggs, and even enjoying a second piece of bread slathered with Aunt Abigail's delicious peach jam.

She hugged Leah and Winnie. "I do need to rest a little," she said. "I have to get my power built up so I can join the others. Right now I don't have enough to transport myself anywhere but to bed."

"That's where you belong," Leah said.

"Don't let me sleep too long though," Veronica begged. "Wake me in a couple of hours, no more. That should be enough to build my power back up."

Leah promised, and Veronica went to her room, lay down, and fell asleep immediately. She thought she'd been asleep only a few moments when Leah shook her awake. "Wha— Wha's wrong?" she mumbled.

"You asked me to wake you in two hours," Leah said. "It's been two and a half. I would have liked to wait longer, but I'm worried about Kyla and the others."

Veronica sat up, rubbing her eyes. "No word?"

"No, and I can't think about what could be going on where they are."

"I guess I'd better see if I can get back there."

Leah gave her a hug. "I almost hope you can't. I don't want to lose you too."

"You haven't lost anyone yet," Veronica said, hugging her in return. "They're all there—in Ed's world. Except ..." She hesitated before adding, "except it isn't Ed's world anymore. I guess it's Jerome's world now."

Leah burst into tears. "That's why I'm so worried," she said, sobbing. "I wish you didn't have to go back. But if you don't ..." She was crying too hard to finish.

Veronica didn't know what to say. She'd never seen Leah like this. She was always calm, always a steadying influence not just on Aunt Abigail but on everybody, even Aunt Kyla. It frightened her, gave her an icy feeling deep inside. If Aunt Leah was this scared, was there any hope at all?

Suddenly Veronica just wanted to go back to bed. She still felt tired. And cold. And scared. She did not want to return to "Jerome's land."

The wail of a baby jolted her. Dreama! She'd almost forgotten about her.

Dreama needed a mother and a father. Veronica couldn't back out. She had to help defeat Jerome, help rescue Marta and Ed. Frightened or not, she had to go where she was needed and do whatever she could to help.

Because the waxy substance encasing Ed and Gorvy was transparent, and because Ed was conscious, through his eyes Petros saw everything that happened within Ed's range of vision. Ed couldn't turn his head, but he could roll his eyes to shift his gaze. Unfortunately, while he could see, he could hear only a little of what was occurring. That was enough to show him how easily Jerome defeated the valiant efforts of Marta, Darnell, and Marchion. Judging by Jerome's expression of triumphant glee and the fearful gazes of most of the group, they had little hope of victory or even of saving themselves. If only Ed and Gorvy, and he with Ed, could be free to help instead of being trapped in this weird, waxy stuff. Petros had never felt so isolated and helpless.

If he could mindspeak to Ed, he'd feel less alone. But how would Ed react to having an uninvited rider in his head? He might resent it, especially after having had Renni erase so many days of memories without his consent. He should have asked Ed's permission, but there hadn't been time. And there was no assurance that Ed would give it. So here he was, trapped along with Ed and without Ed's awareness of his presence.

He recalled that Lady Kyla had said Ed had heard the Power-Giver's voice in his mind. That wasn't really an analogous situation but maybe, Petros thought, Ed could hear him if he tried hard to mindspeak. His consciousness was already in Ed's mind, which should make it easier.

Deciding to take the risk, Petros concentrated, putting all the force he could muster into calling, *Ed, Ed, can you hear me? It's Petros. If you hear me, respond by thinking back to me.*

He got no response, but kept trying. And finally, after many tries, he heard, *Petros? I'm sorry. I don't understand. Who are you?*

That's right, Ed wouldn't remember him. Renni had wiped his recent memories, and he'd had no time to become re-acquainted with the Community members. Kyla had been right in scolding Renni for doing that to Ed.

I'm the fellow that uses a wheeled platform to get around because my legs are gone. Although I can't walk, I can travel by sending my consciousness into someone and following them to a distant location. I sent my consciousness into you so I could follow what happened when you returned to this place to find Marta.

There followed a pause so long that Petros feared Ed had heard none of that explanation. But finally came Ed's clearly suspicious sending: *So you're in my mind? My thoughts?*

Petros immediately sent back, *I'm not in your thoughts at all. I'm not a mind reader. I'm just a hitchhiker. I can see what you see, hear what you hear, but I can't know what you're thinking. And up until now I've never tried to mindspeak with anyone I'm hitching a ride with. But I'm trapped in this fountain-thing along with you, and not being able to speak to anyone or hear anything was getting to me. I didn't know whether I could get through or not, but I had to try.*

Again a long silence, then a question, *How does this help? With what's going on out there, I mean.*

Petros had no good answer to that question. *I guess it doesn't. Not right now, anyway. It just keeps us from feeling so isolated.* It wasn't a satisfactory answer, and Petros knew it. *It gives us a bit of a reason to hope,* he added a bit lamely.

Does it? was Ed's only response.

But another response came from a different source. *Hey, fellas, I'm in here too, and I think it does.*

Gorvy! Petros had momentarily forgotten that he was trapped along with Ed. It had never occurred to him that his mental speech could reach Gorvy. It must have been possible only because of the three of them being trapped together in such close proximity.

Yes, the *three* of them—they were not two but three. And Jerome didn't know that. That might give them some advantage. How or what was not apparent at the moment, but Petros had faith that it would become so, and wasted no time communicating that belief to his fellow prisoners.

She could do nothing to Jerome at present, so Marta concentrated on building a shield of protection around herself. She wished she could mindspeak so she could warn Kyla to do the same. Kyla ought to think of it on her own, but would she? She seemed to have become totally ineffective. Coming here with no plan had been foolish, and having been caught up in the loop of shouting and recriminations was inexcusable in Marta's estimation, even if Jerome had trapped her and Lore and Renni in it. He'd been able to do it only because Kyla had not resisted. When Kyla joined Renni in hurling accusations at Lore, Jerome easily formed the loop that kept that argument going.

"Well, Marta and Kyla, Wonder Workers, what wonders are you dreaming up?" Jerome's voice boomed. He was enjoying this, curse him.

"And speaking of dreaming, how's little Dreama doing? Cute little thing. I think I'd like to take another look at her. Lore, go and fetch her for me."

Marta whirled around to confront Lore. "Don't you dare!"

At the same time, Kyla cried out, "No, Lore. Resist him."

The young man gaped at Jerome, then glanced at Kyla. "I wo—"

"Now, Lore, you want to keep those very helpful

gifts I gave you, don't you?" Jerome smiled that false smile Marta knew all too well. "Just bring the child here to me. That's not asking much, is it?"

"He's asking you to betray all the rest of us," Marta snapped.

"I don't want to do it. He's forcing me. I can't help myself."

"You mean he's using coercion?" Marta demanded. "I don't think so. I'd sense it."

"And so would I." A well-dressed, middle-aged man stepped toward Lore. Marta couldn't remember his name, but she recalled that he was a professor of something or other. "As coercion is one of my gifts," he continued, "I recognize it in others."

Jerome sneered. "Do you now? Do you really think that just because you have a certain talent, you can recognize that talent in someone else? What a foolish idea. I'll show you just how foolish."

The professor drew himself up proudly and glared indignantly at Jerome, whose raucous laughter told Marta how much he was enjoying this.

"I'm not using coercion on my friend Lore, but you could have used it to prevent his carrying out my command. Now, though, I think you'll find it no longer possible."

"Lore, bring Veronica back with you, not Dreama," Kyla said.

Did Kyla really think Jerome would allow that?

The professor slumped like a deflated balloon. Jerome must have blocked the man's gift of coercion.

"Go on, now, Lore. Bring the baby here to me. Hurry."

Lore disappeared from their midst.

Marta's fury needed an outlet. She wanted to slap sense into Kyla, prod her into action. Knowing how much Jerome would enjoy seeing that display of temper, she resisted the urge. Better to seize the initiative and act on her own to get the Community together, get them organized. How could she do that with Jerome watching her every move?

She tried to recall what gifts each person had. Veronica had told her what they were as she'd introduced each one to Marta and Ed, but Marta had not seen the gifts in operation, and the stress of all that had happened and was happening drove the memory from her mind. She needed help.

Help came from an unexpected source. *Miss Marta, Jerome took my power of coercion, but I also have the ability to project my thoughts into someone's mind. I'm testing to see whether he took that power as well. If this thought reaches you, just nod.*

The professor! She gave a slight nod.

Can you transmit your thoughts to me? came the question.

If only she could. But that was not one of her gifts. She had to find another way to communicate with the professor.

"No," she said, looking up at Jerome. She paused before adding, "No! You will not get Dreama again."

Lore had not returned—with or without Dreama—or Veronica. Could that be a good sign? Jerome seemed unconcerned. "We'll see about that," he said.

I assume your first "No" was in answer to my question, the professor's words entered her thoughts.

"Yes," she said and again paused briefly before adding, "we will."

The professor had the information she needed. He could send it to her if she could let him know. She had to proceed very cautiously.

"Look, Jerome," she said, "you're making a game out of this, having great fun playing with us like a cat with a mouse. And like that cat, you have every advantage, so it isn't really a very fair game. I suppose you don't care about that, but couldn't it be just a bit more fair? I don't even know what skills most of these people have, so I have no idea whom to call on for help. How can I offer you any challenge?"

"Your friend Kyla knows their gifts. She brought them all here to stand against me. She must have come with a plan."

"I suppose she did, but she's not doing anything. I guess you have her under some sort of spell."

"No, he doesn't," Kyla snapped. "I am doing something, though it may not look like it to you."

Kyla's response bewildered Marta. She had believed Jerome had somehow bespelled Kyla. If not, what *was* Kyla doing?

The answer came to her in a sudden flash of insight. Kyla must be communicating with the Power-Giver. Probably begging him for advice and help. But Marta had no confidence in Alair. She preferred to rely on the professor. She cast him a covert glance.

And as she'd hoped, he understood what she wanted. *I can tell you each person's talents. But you'd better seem to be preoccupied with something else so as not to arouse Jerome's suspicions.*

Recognizing the wisdom of that advice, Marta walked over to the false fountain in which Ed and another member of the group stood unmoving. They could see her, even if their immobility allowed no hint of their awareness. "Ed," she said loudly, "Even if you can't hear me, maybe you can read my lips. I love you and I will get you out of here."

"Ah, how sweet," Jerome cooed. "So tender. But

making a false promise like that isn't really very loving."

"It's no false promise," she snapped, and again looked at her husband. But she concentrated, not on Ed, but on the information she was receiving from the professor. Her back to Jerome as she faced Ed, she mouthed the names and talents that the professor was placing within her mind. Maybe Ed could read her lips and derive some hope from her listing the names and talents of the gifted, but she was doing it as a mnemonic device.

Winter, the young man hunched over the sketchpad, was an empath. Not much help. Trille, the pretty young woman standing off to herself, was a singer, and used song to control water much as Kyla used song to do such things as read the Breyadon and open locks. And windspeak, but if the professor knew that, he didn't mention it. Without water anywhere nearby, Trille's talent was of little use. Zauna could see distant places and sometimes future events in her crystal globe. Not much help there, either.

The Honorable Camsen Wellner, priest of Ondin, had more to offer. He could create illusions and could throw and sculpt fire. *Unfortunately, he hesitates to use his talents,* the professor noted. *He feels that the gifts of magic are an affront to Ondin. But I believe he will use them to save lives when it comes to that.*

It has come to that. Marta wished she could send back that thought.

Darnell Mack, the wife of Gorvy, the man in the fountain with Ed, is a shape-shifter. She transforms into a wolf.

Marchion, the gentleman standing just to the left of Darnell, can see auras and read the person's mood and mental and physical condition from them. That may not be of much use, but he is also an enhancer. That can most definitely be of help.

Renni was, she learned, a new member of the Community. So far as Professor Morence knew, her only gift was to suppress a person's memories. However, the professor suspected she had other gifts as yet undiscovered. That, he confided, was Kyla's suspicion as well.

Lore had the gifts of transferring an object from one place or person to another so long as the destination was familiar to him. But clearly Jerome had somehow bestowed additional gifts on the young man, including that of transferring himself to another place. What other gifts he might have been given, the professor didn't know. He did opine that Lore seemed ambivalent about aligning himself with Jerome and could perhaps be persuaded to aid the Community instead.

As if on cue, at the moment the professor sent that thought, Lore reappeared, holding a squalling infant. "Sorry to be so long," he said. "The kid was being fed when I arrived, and I had to wait until she finished her bottle, and then she needed a change, so I waited for that too."

At last, Kyla acted. She sent a loud, high song soaring into the dry air. A wind sprang up, carrying a load of sand in its trail. The wind spun between Marta and Jerome, bringing with it a whirl of sand that hid Jerome from Marta's sight and allowed her to edge close to Lore. The roaring, sand-filled wind drowned Dreama's loud cries. Marta snatched the wailing baby from Lore's arms, at the same time extending her protective shield to include Dreama. She gathered the baby into her arms and hugged her to her breast. The child's wailing ceased.

The wind slowed, lessened, dropping its load of sand bit by bit until the hot desert air was clear again. Seeing the infant in Marta's arms, Jerome sent out a blast of power that hit but did not penetrate her shield.

Jerome laughed, but this time the laughter had a false edge to it. He was more annoyed than he cared to let on. But, Marta reflected, being annoyed isn't the same as being afraid. Kyla's act had not frightened him. Maybe Marta's next move could.

Kyla, her wind song concluded, shouted at Lore, "You fool! Can't you see you don't need to do Jerome's bidding?"

Lore did look a bit chagrined, but he perked up when Jerome said, "Need to do my bidding? No. He's an intelligent young man. He's smart enough to ally himself with a winner rather than losers like you, Kyla Wonder Worker. Let's see how easy *you* find it not to do what I tell you to. Bow to me."

Jerome waved his hand, and Kyla fell to her knees, facing Jerome, and bent to touch her head to the sand.

Poor Kyla! Jerome had to demonstrate his power over Kyla to counteract her sandstorm summoning. Marta could do nothing to help her. She was expending most of her power on the protective shielding that now safeguarded Dreama too. Marta thought about what she'd learned from the professor. Which member of the Community might be of help?

If only she could mindspeak! Marta had an idea, but it required Professor Morence's help. She had to act while Jerome's attention was on Kyla. She moved near the professor and whispered, "Send to Renni. Tell her to see whether she can bind his powers."

That isn't one of her known talents, came the

professor's thought. *Nor, so far as I know, is mindspeech.*

"Let's find out," Marta urged. Both using mindspeech and binding power were related to finding and deleting memories. And the professor had said Renni might have powers she was as yet unaware of. And not trained in. But the girl was clever; Marta had seen that.

Marta watched Renni, saw her eyes widen for a moment, and surmised that the girl had received the professor's thought. Renni glanced at her, and Marta gave a quick, encouraging smile.

Nothing happened. Renni shrugged. Apparently she could neither bind power nor, despite having received the professor's mental sending, could she respond through mindspeech any more than Marta could.

Marta risked another whisper. "Send to all the others. Ask if anyone else can bind or quench."

The thought boomed in her brain. *Gorvy Mack is a quencher. That doesn't do us any good, does it?*

Gorvy—the man trapped with Ed. No, it didn't do any good—unless they could free him and Ed.

The stuff of which the "fountain" was made was a waxy substance. Would fire melt it? The professor had said Camsen the priest could throw fire. Veronica had that talent, but she wasn't here and Camsen was.

She rocked Dreama in her arms and bent down as though murmuring comforting words to the child. Actually she whispered to Professor Morence. "Tell the priest to throw fire at the fountain to try to melt the wax. And if it works, tell Abigail to be prepared to heal them if Ed and Gorvy are burned."

Kyla had not moved; she must be trying to break Jerome's power over her, but she could not. But by expending power to keep Kyla in the humiliating position in which he'd placed her, he'd had to allow Marta more freedom. His power was not limitless.

Jerome's attention again focused on Marta. "No muttering and whispering," he ordered, glaring at Marta. "But you never could keep your mouth shut, could you? I'll have to impose silence on you."

A force pounded against her shield of protection. The professor's thought popped into her mind: *He's sealed my lips shut. I can't speak aloud. Fortunately he must not know I can send my thoughts.*

She wished she could send back to tell the professor that her shield had protected her. But she had to pretend it hadn't. She clamped her lips shut and glared at Jerome, who laughed at her. Yet the laughter had a hollow ring. He might know that she was shielded and therefore had to be faking the inability to speak. But he must *not* know about the professor's gift of sending his thoughts.

I've relayed your instructions to the Honorable Camsen Wellner, and he's thinking it over. At least that's what I presume he's doing. He hasn't thrown fire as yet. Abigail also received your instructions, but as yet she has nothing to do.

So Camsen, the idiot, was holding back, afraid to use the power that could save them. If only Veronica were here! She could throw fire, and she wouldn't hesitate.

As though in answer to her wish, Veronica appeared, with Winnie clinging to her arm and looking terrified. They materialized almost on top of Marta. Coincidence? Or was someone helping out?

"Oh, thank the Power-Giver, you have Dreama!" Veronica said to Marta, thus foolishly issuing a challenge to Jerome.

Did Professor Morence know that Veronica could throw fire? That particular gift of hers carried with it sad memories that led her not to speak of it. She considered it unlikely that Veronica would have told the Community of that gift, but Kyla might have.

But as moments passed and no fire was thrown, Marta could only conclude that Kyla had not. She looked, no, glared at Camsen. Winnie gradually released her hold on Veronica and said, "Veronica brought me with her in case Dreama needs me. Do you want me to hold her?"

"No, we may need your healing talent," Marta said without looking away from Camsen, hoping he'd understand and act on the thought the professor had sent him. Hadn't he received and understood it?

"What's the matter with Aunt Kyla?" Veronica demanded, going to Kyla, bending over her, and trying unsuccessfully to lift her to her feet.

"Just teaching her humility," Jerome said. "Maybe you need a similar lesson."

No! Camsen had to act. Now! Marta called out, "For the glory of Ondin."

The priest turned toward the false fountain with its trapped occupants, regarded them, his expression sad, almost apologetic. Slowly he lifted his arm and pointed toward the fountain.

Flame shot from his fingers and struck the fountain. Flame swirled around it. Jerome let out a roar of rage and pointed at Camsen. The priest fell backward and lay still. Had Jerome killed him? If so, Marta had to accept part of the blame.

Veronica reacted by throwing fire at Jerome. It faded out without touching him.

"Be careful, Veronica," Kyla called out. "He's shielded. You can't harm him like that."

Marta turned and saw that Kyla had lifted her head and risen to her knees. Veronica must have distracted Jerome enough to partially free Kyla. Good.

"So what was The Honorable Camsen Wellner trying to do?" Veronica demanded.

"Melt the fountain," Marta said, abandoning any attempt at secrecy.

"Oh. Great idea." Veronica sent a stream of flame arcing toward the fountain.

"That's it for you, you little meddler," Jerome said. He took one step toward Veronica, swung forward as if to take another step, and jerked back as though caught on something. He looked behind him, but nothing or no one was there.

Again his foot moved forward, and he seemed to try but fail to take a second step. His face reddened with rage.

Marta gave the professor a questioning look and heard his answering thought: *I don't know what's happening. It's nothing I suggested to anyone.*

Could Veronica have caused it? But the girl was concentrating on sending fire at the fountain, careful, Marta noted, to narrow the stream of flame and aim it at those portions of the fountain not directly touching Ed or Gorvy.

Slowly the wax began to melt. Jerome let out a bellow of rage. "I'll get you, you little brat. You won't survive this."

CHAPTER EIGHTEEN
SMALL VICTORIES

Ed found it maddening to see what was happening but be totally helpless to lend aid. He rejoiced to see little Dreama safe in Marta's arms, but what Jerome did to Kyla frightened him. Marta could be next. With Veronica's arrival he saw Jerome's attention shift from Marta to the girl. His hope soared, followed by pangs of guilt for feeling relief that Marta would be spared while Jerome punished Veronica.

That concern was forgotten in an instant as one of the men in the group outside pointed at Ed and Gorvy, and flames shot from his finger and danced around the waxy fountain that imprisoned them. Was this an attempt to kill them?

The flames stopped as suddenly as they had come. Ed saw the man who had sent them lying on the ground, perhaps dead.

Only moments later Ed watched Veronica step toward the fountain and launch a stream of fire at the fountain, more carefully aimed than the man's had been. *Hey, fellas, I think they're trying to melt this thing and get us out.* He passed the thought to Petros and Gorvy.

Hope they know what they're doing and don't fry us, Gorvy sent back.

Looks like Veronica's being careful, Petros put in. *But is it working?*

I think so. It's getting uncomfortably warm. As he spoke, Ed tried to move his arms, and the waxy substance holding him immobile gave a bit.

He pushed harder. *It's loosening up,* he told his companions. *It's working!*

I'm burning up! Gorvy said. *Those healers better be good.*

Ed pushed harder against the imprisoning stuff and felt it give way. A block of it fell, and one arm was free. The flames shifted to another area. Marta thrust Dreama into Winnie's arms, ran forward, and grabbed Ed's hand. He pushed and she pulled, and in moments, as the fire stream shifted away from his side, he tumbled free.

"Get Gorvy out," he gasped. Sweat poured down him. Marta drew him well away from the melting wax fountain.

Darnell ran to Gorvy and thrust her hand through the soft wax. Ed watched her worriedly while Abigail fussed over him, finding and healing minor burns. Ed could see that Gorvy would need her far more than he did. Darnell pushed and pulled at the softened wax until she could grasp Gorvy's arm. She tugged. The flames stopped; they'd done all they could without endangering Darnell.

Marchion hurried to help her, and the two of them were able to extract Gorvy from the melting wax. "Go heal his burns," Ed told Abigail.

Ed expected Veronica to go to Gorvy's aid too, but she went to the man who'd first thrown fire and knelt beside him. "He's still alive. Winnie, come help me heal him," she called.

Relieved at that report, Marta took Dreama back from Winnie, who then hurried to join Veronica.

"What—or who—is stopping Jerome?" Ed asked.

"I don't know. And neither does Professor Morence." Quickly, speaking in a low voice, Marta told Ed how the Professor had listed for her the talents of each member of the group. "Gorvy's a quencher," she said. "Could he have been able to do that from inside the fountain?"

Ed shook his head. "I'm sure he couldn't. It had to be someone out here."

"No one out here has that talent. Well, Kyla probably does. I'd ask her, but if she's doing it, I don't want to distract her."

"I just hope whoever it is, they can hold him," Ed said, looking around. Marta was probably right. It must be Kyla. She was staring fixedly at Jerome.

Abigail had Gorvy stretched out on the sand and knelt beside him, her hand on his chest. The redness that had infused his flesh when he fell free of the waxy substance was rapidly fading. Abigail took on the red hue, but only briefly. Soon she rose, and Darnell helped Gorvy to his feet and embraced him.

Relieved to see Gorvy healed of his burns and heat sickness, Ed smiled at Marta and the baby in her arms. He touched a finger to the infant's cheek. "So this little girl is ours now?"

"She is, and we must keep her safe."

Yes, they must. It no longer mattered that his memories of first meeting her had been taken from him. The sight of her in Marta's arms awakened his paternal feelings. This was their daughter, and he would keep her safe no matter what the cost.

Veronica knelt beside the Honorable Camsen Wellner. She'd felt clearly the pulse in his throat when she'd pressed her fingers against his neck. It was strong and steady, yet now with her hands on his chest she should sense healing taking place, but she sensed nothing.

Winnie came and knelt on his other side, opposite her. "Do you get the feeling that there's any healing going on?" Veronica asked her.

Winnie, too, placed her hands on him. "No," she said after a long pause. "I don't feel anything."

"Let's keep trying."

Winnie nodded assent, but soon said, "It isn't working. Could Jerome have taken our power?

Veronica was still considering that possibility when Abigail joined them. "I don't have much strength left after healing Ed and Gorvy," she said. "I'll use what I have."

"It may not do any good," Veronica told her. "Neither of us can sense any healing happening."

"Well, let me try anyway." Abigail crouched beside Veronica and reached out to put her hands on the priest's arm. "Oh!" She jerked her hand away as if it had been burned.

"What happened?" Veronica asked.

"I don't know," Abigail answered, examining her fingers. "I've never felt anything like that before. It was like putting my hand into a fire."

"Maybe that's where the trouble is centered," Veronica suggested. "That's the arm he used when he threw fire. Maybe that's where the healing has to be concentrated."

"Maybe," Abigail said, but her dubious tone told Veronica she didn't believe it. "It didn't feel like healing. Why don't you try it?"

Abigail rose, allowing Veronica to scoot over a bit and reach for the Honorable Wellner's hand.

"Be careful," Abigail cautioned as Veronica wrapped her fingers around the priest's wrist.

Flames shot up Veronica's arm before she could pull it away. She rolled over on the ground and scooped sand onto the flames until they were extinguished. She cradled her badly burned arm with her other hand and arm. "It hurts so bad," she said, sobbing. "Why did it do that?"

Abigail was beside her, gently touching the burned flesh.

"I'm cursed. Ondin has cursed me."

Veronica turned her head and was amazed to see the Honorable Camsen Wellner sit up, tears streaming down his face. "I shouldn't have accepted or used the cursed gift," he said. "Ondin has punished me for it."

"Looks more like he punished me," Veronica snapped. "I don't see any burns on you."

"Now, now," Winnie soothed, "be calm, both of you. Veronica, I can see that Abigail is healing you, so you'll feel better in just a moment or two. And Camsen, I understand your feelings as a priest of Ondin, but I strongly suspect that it was Jerome and not Ondin who cursed you."

"Of course it was Jerome!" Veronica said, still feeling snappish despite Winnie's spreading her mantle of calm. Winnie was right; Aunt Abigail's healing already eased the pain of the burns, and the flesh of her arm was returning to its normal hue. It would be Abigail who'd feel the pain now, though only for a short time.

"Maybe Ondin is dealing with Jerome right now," Zauna put in, nodding toward Jerome, who still remained immobilized though he was clearly struggling to free himself.

Kyla walked toward Veronica, shaking her head. "It isn't Ondin. I feel power flowing from someone in the group, but I don't know who it is. I can't trace it to its source."

"Well, whoever it is should say so," Veronica stated, gazing around the group.

"Maybe they don't know," Marta put in, joining Kyla and Veronica. "Could it be a newly awakened talent?"

"That's possible," Kyla said. "I've suspected that the newer members of the Community may have talents they haven't yet discovered."

Veronica cast a nervous glance at Jerome. "Instead of talking we'd better find who's doing it, and feed the person more power before Jerome breaks free."

"Marta, try tracing the source," Kyla said. "You're better at that than I am. I'll hold Dreama."

"Hurry!" Veronica said, barely able to keep herself from shoving her adoptive aunt into action.

Marta surrendered Dreama to Kyla and moved away. Veronica looked around, craving action, searching for something—anything—she could do.

Marta went first to Professor Morence. "Professor, can you speak now?"

He shook his head, and his voice spoke in her mind. *Alas, it seems our foe is physically bound but retains his powers.*

"Who are the newest members of the Community?" she asked, as though musing to herself.

The professor's answer formed in her mind: *Winnie Calder, Renni Natches, and Winter Salas.* Marta knew Winnie and Renni. "Winter's the empath, right?" she asked in a low voice.

Yes. He's sitting a considerable distance away from the rest of the group, doodling on a sketchpad, came the disdainful response.

An empath would be suffering and trying to shut out the rampant emotions flowing from the group. That wouldn't leave him with energy for anything else even if he had the ability.

Winnie had been busy healing, so she wasn't likely to be the binder. That left Renni, assuming it was one of the newer members of the group. That wasn't necessarily a valid assumption. A long-time member could discover a new talent, especially under great pressure. She couldn't rule out anyone.

Marta cast a nervous glance at Jerome. His muscles taut, he strained at the invisible binding that held him immobile. It wouldn't hold much longer. His face was scarlet with fury. He met her gaze with a stare so filled with hate that she couldn't repress a shudder. Quickly she looked away, located Renni, and headed toward her. She felt his eyes drilling into her back, his hatred buffeting her. She refused to turn around to meet his gaze but kept her eyes fixed on Renni. The girl was standing away from those clustered near the priest and the healers and idly moving one foot, making circles in the sand. A random motion, or was it some sort of spell casting?

She hurried to Renni's side. The girl gave her a startled look. She apparently had been so deep in thought or deep in casting and maintaining a spell that she hadn't noticed Marta's approach. If the latter, Marta didn't want to interrupt her and break the spell. Again she wished she could mindspeak.

Renni looked down at the circles her foot had traced. "Distraction," she murmured so softly Marta wasn't sure she'd heard correctly.

Distraction? Did she mean that Marta was distracting her? In that case it would be best to leave her alone and let her work.

Marta backed away. As she did, Veronica came up to them. "Hey, Renni. I need you," she said, making no effort to lower her voice. "We need to get Dreama back to the house and get her some milk. And you're nominated to milk the goat."

Marta's cry of "Veronica! No!" made Veronica aware that Marta thought Renni was responsible for binding Jerome. Veronica was certain she wasn't.

"It's okay," Renni said quickly, confirming Veronica's belief. "But is it safe to go back?"

"Safer than here," Veronica said. "But we have to persuade Lore to send us." Although she could probably transfer them herself, she'd expended a lot of power using her fire-throwing gift to free Ed and Gorvy, and she'd expended even more trying to heal Camsen Wellner. Besides, she wanted to talk to Lore away from Jerome and from Aunt Kyla.

"I don't trust Lore. Do you?" Renni asked.

"Keep your voices down," Marta cautioned. Dropping her own voice to a whisper, she asked, "He may be bound physically, but he can still cause trouble. Do you know who's binding him?"

"Not for certain," Renni whispered. "But by process of elimination, I've figured who it must be."

"Who?" Marta asked eagerly. Veronica leaned closer to Renni, as eager for the answer as Marta was.

Renni shook her head. "Jerome's listening, and I'm guessing he can hear every word we say, even when we whisper."

"But we need to know who—"

"Marta, I figured it out. So can you," Renni insisted.

"Then so can Jerome," Veronica said, growing impatient. "But come on. If you're not going to tell us, then let's get Dreama and talk Lore into sending us back."

"Wait a minute," Marta held out her arms as though she could hold them back in that way. "I don't want you taking Dreama and going off by yourselves. And I don't trust Lore."

"We don't trust him either," Veronica said. "We'll be careful. Dreama has to eat, and there's no way to feed her in this place."

Marta shook her head. "I know Dreama's in danger here, but she'll be in just as much danger back in Kyla's house. Here I can give her some protection."

"But for how long?" Veronica said.

"I'll go with them."

Veronica hadn't sensed Ed's presence until he spoke. He must have been standing right behind her for some time.

"Oh, Ed! That's all right then!" Marta said, her objections erased.

Veronica hid her annoyance that her plan to get Lore away from Jerome and talk some sense into him was ruined.

But then Ed said, "Lore can go, too. That way, I can come back, and when the girls are ready to return here, Lore can bring them back. Will it be okay, you think, to leave Dreama there with Leah?"

Veronica guessed that Ed really meant, *Is it safe to leave Lore there with no one to keep him in check?*

"I can stay there to help her," Renni offered as Marta hesitated. "I'm not doing any good here."

Renni must have understood Ed's concern also. She was clever and might be of great help in defending against an attack by Jerome. But she would also be helping to keep Lore away from Jerome's evil influence.

"All right, but be sure that Lore returns with Ed," she said. "Let's get Dreama from Kyla, and we'll check our plans out with her."

"No, stay here. I'll get Dreama," Veronica said and ran to Kyla without giving Marta a chance to object. She'd been keeping an eye on Jerome, and she saw him strain visibly against the mysterious bonds that held him in place. He could break free at any moment.

She grabbed Dreama from Kyla's arms. "Good luck with Jerome," she said. "We're taking Dreama back home."

She ran back to where Marta, Ed, and Renni waited. "Lore," she called, after handing Dreama to Renni. "Come here."

He came. He'd been watching their discussion and also, Veronica guessed, watching for any sign that Jerome was only toying with them, pretending to be bound, and would soon burst into laughter and punish them all."

"You can see Jerome isn't the all-powerful wonder you thought he was. We're giving you a chance to prove that your loyalties still lie with the Community. Give me your hand." She reached out her hand."

Lore, looking embarrassed and puzzled, took the offered hand.

"Now transport us back to Aunt Kyla's house," she ordered, using her power to supplement his and adding an element of coercion, a power she'd known she had but had kept that knowledge to herself.

A brief sensation of bitter cold and the two of them stood together in the sitting room of Kyla's house.

Ed lingered long enough to hug Marta and kiss her cheek. "I know you're worried, and I know how much you hate being away from Dreama. Be brave. We have to trust the girls. Leah will keep them in check. And she'll take good care of Dreama until we can get back to her. Not only that, but here's a surprise. A man named Petros has been sharing my consciousness and was trapped along with me in the fountain. He'll be going back with me and going back into his body. So he'll be there with Veronica and her friend. He'll be a help to Leah, I'm sure."

That unexpected news cheered her a bit. Marta had completely forgotten about Petros. He was clever. He'd be another person to help Leah with Dreama and help keep Lore under control.

Ed kissed her again, on the lips this time. "I love you, Marta. I'll be back as quickly as I can."

"I know you will. I'm relieved that you're going with them. They can be so reckless. And I know you'll keep a close eye on Lore." Marta reluctantly withdrew from his embrace. "Go now, before I start to bawl."

She blinked back tears as he walked away. *Ed will see that no harm comes to Dreama. I have to concentrate on the situation here.* With that thought, she resolutely set her mind back on the present need to find out who was binding Jerome before that person's strength ebbed. Why was Renni so certain that Marta could figure it out on her own? There must be something that made it obvious.

Whoever it was had accomplished something no other member of the Community had succeeded in doing. Since it was the only attempt against Jerome that had had any effect, Marta felt that the best hope the Community had of defeating Jerome was to feed power to the person responsible, thus holding Jerome helpless while they found another way to deal with him more permanently.

She reviewed what she knew of each member of

the Community Kyla might have the power, but she'd said she wasn't doing the binding, and anyway, rightly or wrongly, she was too preoccupied with other things. Abigail was a spell caster, but she'd been busy healing, as had Winnie. It wasn't Veronica or Renni.

Lore? No, or Renni wouldn't be helping Veronica take him away from this world. Professor Morence could certainly be eliminated. He'd been mindspeaking, attempting in his own way to discover the binder. Gorvy Mack had been in the fountain with Ed, and at the time of Jerome's binding he was getting the burns healed that he'd suffered from Veronica's fire. His wife Darnell was hovering over him, so concerned that Marta didn't think she'd have had the presence of mind to perform a binding spell, if she had that talent, which she didn't, according to the professor.

That left—Marta thought carefully—Zauna, the crystal ball gazer; Marchion Blandry, the enhancer; Winter, the empath, and Trille, a singer who used song in her feats of power, which, according to the professor, always involved water. Could he be wrong about her abilities? She and Winter consistently stayed off to the side, apart from the rest of the group. It could well be one of them, and Trille was more likely than Winter, who the professor said had no power other than being empathic, which, since he hadn't yet learned to shield, was more of a liability than a gift.

It must be Trille. Marta walked over to where the young woman stood, looking forlorn and uncomfortable.

As soon as Marta reached her side, she said, "Please tell me what I'm doing here? There is nothing for me to work with in this desert—not a drop of water. I'm utterly useless. And the monster seems to be restrained, so someone's power is effective. I want to go home."

"So—you aren't using your power to ... do anything?" Marta frowned. She'd been so certain Trille was the one she was looking for.

"No, how can I? Without water to work with, there is nothing I can possibly do."

"I'll see what I can do to help you get home then," Marta said, understanding the young woman's frustration all too well.

If it wasn't Trille, could it possibly be Winter? Or had she overlooked something? It occurred to her that Renni, too, had probably concluded that Trille was the binder, but she hadn't bothered to check.

Marta supposed she should go and talk to Winter. But then another thought came to her. She recalled that Ed had met Claid in the ruined building on this world. Could the Dire Lord be somewhere nearby? He certainly had the power to bind Jerome. And really, it didn't seem that anyone among the gifted gathered here had that much power. It had been Kyla's idea to bring all of them so they could pool their power, but they hadn't done that and weren't doing that now. Maybe collectively they could overcome Jerome, but separately none of them, including Kyla, had enough power.

She glanced at Winter. He sat cross-legged on the sand, hunched over his sketchpad just as he had since they'd all arrived here. He seemed to have closed out everything and everyone. Sitting well away from everyone else, his shoulders slumped, his head lowered, gazing only at his drawing, he had isolated himself so thoroughly that Marta doubted he'd seen or been aware of anything that had happened.

Still, she started toward him. She'd taken only a few steps when she heard a cry that sent her whirling around.

Veronica ran toward Kyla. Ed followed much more slowly. It was Veronica who had cried out, calling, "Aunt Kyla! Aunt Kyla!"

Renni and Lore had not returned.

CHAPTER NINETEEN
WIND AND SAND

Alarmed, Kyla glanced around as Veronica raced toward her. The girl's shout had drawn everyone's attention, including Jerome's. His head turned to follow Veronica as she skidded to a stop before Kyla.

His head turned! He hadn't been able to move at all. The power that held him in check had lessened. The panic in Veronica's voice and her dash to Kyla must have distracted the person who'd bound Jerome enough to allow him some movement.

"Look!" Veronica thrust a paper at Kyla. "Leah's gone. Isham has her."

She hadn't bothered to lower her voice. Kyla took the paper and read it hastily.

I came for you, Kyla Witch, but no one was here but your friend Leah, so I've taken her. I'll exchange her for you, or I'll do to her what I wanted to do to you—the same thing that was done to Mayzie. I want your answer by Dora rise. Isham

Dora rise—the moon would rise toward mid night. Here it was midday, but time ran differently here than back home. She had no way of knowing when it would be the midnight there. Even if she knew the time, how could she return?

"What did you say about Leah?" a very agitated Abigail demanded, reaching them and grabbing Veronica's arm.

"Ouch! Aunt Abigail, you're hurting me." Veronica tried to pull free of Abigail's tight grasp.

Kyla handed Abigail the note. Abigail read it and burst into tears. "I have to go back. I'll talk to Isham, offer to trade myself for her. He's got to release her."

"What time is it there?" Kyla asked. "How much time do we have?"

"It's midafternoon, but that doesn't really help, does it?" Veronica answered. "I mean, we don't know whether time here moves faster or slower or sometimes one and sometimes the other."

Loud laughter burst over the area. Jerome strode toward Kyla and those grouped around her.

He'd broken free.

Veronica looked up in shock. Jerome was free, and it was her fault! She'd distracted everyone with her yelling, causing Aunt Abigail to panic and Aunt Kyla to divert her attention from Jerome. And whoever had bound him had lost that hold. So how could they go and rescue poor Aunt Leah when Jerome was loose and threatening everybody again?

Aunt Kyla was screaming at her. Jerome was bellowing now—something about punishing all of them. Aunt Abigail was wailing that they had to go rescue Leah. Veronica couldn't think.

"Maybe if everybody just calmed down a bit—" she said, trying to make herself heard. Nobody was listening.

Aunt Kyla put her hands on Veronica's shoulders and shook her. "Listen to me! Where is Dreama? Who's taking care of her?"

Veronica tried to focus. Dreama. Yes. "We left her with Renni and Petros. Petros is okay now. He said she'd be safe with him."

"Safe?" Kyla groaned. "Renni's not reliable, and Petros can't take care of a baby."

"Where's Lore?" a man's voice asked. In all the confusion Veronica couldn't tell who'd spoken.

Ed came up beside her then. "He's going to try to rescue Leah. Said he wants to redeem himself."

"And you believed him? You trusted him?" Marta's voice verged on hysteria. "Kyla, I've got to go back."

"So do I," Abigail said. "Right now. Ed, send us back."

"Ed, why didn't you stay and take care of Dreama?" Kyla demanded. "She's your daughter."

"I had to bring Veronica back. I would rather have brought Renni, but she wanted go with Lore to rescue Leah." He paused when Kyla groaned at that announcement, but when Kyla didn't speak, he added, "Veronica thought she should be the one to break the bad news to you—and to Abigail."

He added Abigail as though she were just an afterthought, but Abigail was growing hysterical, insisting that they needed to return right away. Veronica's sense of guilt increased. She should have sent Renni and stayed to go with Lore. She had more power than he did and could more easily have overcome Isham. What could Lore do?

Truthfully, she didn't know what new powers Jerome might have given Lore.

Jerome. *Why isn't anyone worrying about Jerome? He's threatening to kill us all. And why do they act like transferring between worlds is as easy as walking from one room into the next?*

Trille—*where did she come from?*—was saying, "I want to go back. I can be of more help there than here, where there's no water anywhere, so I have nothing to work with."

No. She's wrong. She needs to stay here. Before Veronica could say anything, something slammed her to the ground. She lay helpless on her back, feeling as though a great weight was pressing down on her, though nothing was there.

Jerome had chosen to start his acts of vengeance with her.

Aunt Kyla gasped. "Veronica! What's wrong? What happened?"

What does she think happened? Why does she keep ignoring Jerome? Veronica tried to ask the questions aloud, but she couldn't make a sound.

I'm helpless! she thought, trying desperately to move or even to speak. If she could have, she would have burst into tears, but even that was denied her.

Veronica's collapse urged Marta into action. She had to do something before Jerome picked them all off, one by one.

Winnie fell to her knees beside Veronica and placed her hands on her, apparently attempting a healing. But Veronica wasn't injured. Jerome's power held her in some sort of paralysis. Winnie could do nothing for her. Marta sensed power flowing from someone near her toward Jerome. She looked around. Gorvy. A quencher, he was trying to quench Jerome's powers.

It was like trying to stop a flood with only a few sandbags. She moved to Gorvy's side, placed her hand on his arm to lend him power. Too late. He sagged, and she carefully lowered him to the ground beside Veronica. Gorvy's body felt as stiff as a wooden carving. And, like Veronica, his open eyes stared unblinkingly at nothing.

Marta rose, leaving Gorvy and Veronica to

Winnie's useless ministrations. Remembering that she'd been going to check on Winter when Veronica's loud arrival deterred her, she almost turned and looked at Winter before stopping herself, lest she draw Jerome's attention to him. Anyway, how could Winter have bound him?.

Kyla whispered, "Marta, what shall we do?"

Jerome heard the whisper. "Do?" he crowed. "Why, my dears, there is nothing you can do. Nothing at all."

As if to prove his point, Winnie flopped over on top of Veronica. A short distance from them Professor Morence toppled to the ground beside Gorvy.

No point in whispering. Marta rebuilt her shield, moved beside Ed to include him in it, and said, "Ed, Dreama's in danger, and Petros can't protect or care for her. Take Abigail and ... and Zauna. And go. Now."

Ed's frown told her he didn't want to leave her here with Jerome.

"Hurry! For Dreama!" Marta prodded, recalling that Ed needed to feel a sense of urgency in order to transport back from his world.

Abigail had grasped Ed's arm and hung on as soon as she heard Marta's plea. Zauna came up behind them and put her hands on Ed's shoulders.

"Oh, no!" Jerome said. "I mean to have fun with Simple Eddy. He's not going anywhere."

Marta poured all the power she had into her shield of protection. It had to hold! A force pummeled against it, causing her to stagger.

Jerome let out a roar of rage and the force increased, doubling, tripling, until she was gasping for breath and sweat poured down her face and arms. Then with a suddenness that jolted Marta the pressure was gone.

Ed, Abigail, and Zauna were gone, too. As she toppled to the ground her last thought was, *Thank the Power-Giver, the shield held just long enough.*

When she saw Marta fall and lie still like Veronica and the others, Kyla felt a sense of despair. She steeled herself, expecting to fall like the others and, like them, lie helpless on the hot desert sand.

A hot wind blew sand eddies around her feet, reminding her that she was not helpless. She could sing the wind again. Filled with sudden rage, she raised her voice in an angry summoning song.

The wind swirled around her, hot and wild. As she poured her fury into it, it matched her anger with its own. Catching up sand, it flung it about, until she stood at the center of a swirling tornado of sand. Someone screamed—Trille, she thought. Someone else was coughing. The sand must be blinding them all and making it hard for them to breathe. The others weren't important right now. The sandstorm had to affect Jerome as much as it did the others. She could see nothing but the sand roaring all around her. She concentrated on hurling the wind and its burden of sand toward the spot where she hoped Jerome was still standing.

The wind howled and screamed around her, drowning out all other sounds, but still she sang. Until a voice spoke over the wind and the pelting sand. "Enough," it said.

The wind stopped. The sand fell. For a moment she found herself in utter darkness. Then a strange light—neither sunlight nor moonlight nor artificial light—blinded her for a few moments. As her eyes adjusted, she saw that she had been brought to a place she had visited once before, in the company of Alair.

At that time the being who now stood before her had been in chains, but he had not been chained for some time. He now looked every bit the fearsome Dire Lord that he was.

A Dire Lord! One of those dread beings that inhabited the Dire Realms and are often spoken of in frightened whispers. But this Dire Lord was well known to her, although she had known him best in another form. His bearded face smiled down on her from a height well above her own. "Greetings, Mistress Kyla," he said. "We must talk."

She sank to her knees before him. "Lord Claid," she said.

He bent, took her hand in his, and raised her to her feet. "Come, Mistress, no need for that. It's just Claid. I'm still your friend. Though what I must say to you will not please you, I fear."

CHAPTER TWENTY
SO MANY DEATHS

Fortunately, Renni knew where Isham lived. Not only did Lore have no idea, but it was all he could do to keep walking beside her while he struggled to shut out the voice in his head. The voice that urged him to do terrible things—and gave him the power to do them.

I have the power to give gifts and I have the power to take them away, the voice warned.

He wanted more power; he didn't want to lose the power he had. But that desire warred with the thought of being a hero by rescuing Leah and thus winning back the favor and trust of the Community. And what did Jerome care about Leah? She wasn't gifted. She was no threat to him or anyone.

If he could be sure that Jerome would be the victor in his struggle with the Community, Lore would cast his lot with him unhesitatingly. But something—someone—had bound Jerome, and when Lore had come back here, the last sight he'd had of Jerome had shown him unable to move or speak. He could still mindspeak, obviously. Could he use other powers? Lore rather thought he could, but the fact that someone in the Community had been able to bind him proved that he was not invincible.

Lore preferred to keep his options open. But the voice in his mind persisted. If only he could block it out!

"Something bothering you, Lore?" Renni asked, casting a shrewd look his way.

"Just thinking about what we'll do when we're face-to-face with this Isham."

"Were you? I wouldn't think it would worry you that much. I mean, he's not gifted. It should be easy to get Leah away from him."

"Not if he has friends with him and they have guns pointed at us," Lore said, although until he spoke the words he hadn't given that possibility a thought. It did deserve consideration though. "Do you have a plan?"

"Yes, I do," she said, giving him a sidelong glance as she marched along beside him. "I have a plan, but you have the power, so the plan depends on you. That means I have to be able to trust you, but I don't."

"Hey, I'm here with you, aren't I, putting myself in danger? So you'd better tell me this plan of yours."

"Fine. It all depends on our being able to talk to Isham without his cronies being there. You need to stand by and let me do the talking. I'm going to tell him I understand how upset he is and how he wants revenge. I'll say that we can take him to the person who killed his wife. I'll persuade him to let us do that. Then you whip us to Jerome's world. Just him and us, not any of his friends. And we let him deal with Jerome—or let Jerome deal with him. However it turns out, it will distract Jerome and maybe let us marshal our powers while they confront each other."

It wasn't a bad plan, Lore reflected. It could work except for one major flaw. Renni had no idea that Jerome could listen in on their conversation, hearing everything that Lore heard. If Renni's plan worked, Jerome would be prepared for their coming. He would not permit the Community to marshal their powers.

Lore took care not to react when Jerome's voice

spoke in his mind. *I can fit those plans into mine,* the now hated voice said. *By all means, tell Isham you are taking him to confront his wife's killer. That will be delightfully amusing.*

Lore felt trapped. He could confess to Renni his bondage—he now thought of it as that—and beg her to call off her mission and return to Kyla's house. But if he did, Jerome would strip him of his powers. Probably not only the ones Jerome had given him but also those he'd had before encountering Jerome. He'd be left with no power at all. He could not endure that. So he merely nodded his assent to Renni's plan, not trusting himself to speak.

Renni didn't trust him, and that gave him pause. Her plan probably involved more than she'd told him. She'd have held something back. He would have, were he in her place. So far as he knew, her only power was that of removing memories, but she could, like him, have powers the Community didn't know about. It would be like her to conceal a special power. Lady Kyla had been distracted enough since Marta and Ed's arrival that she wouldn't have suspected anything.

"Here we are."

Renni's announcement brought him to a sudden halt. He'd been too deep in thought to pay attention to his surroundings. They stood in front of a small house of weathered brown wood, its slate roof slanting sharply upward to a peak that defined the house's center. It would be, then, one of those houses of probably no more than four rooms arranged one after another in a straight line from front door to rear door.

In front of the house a child's wagon reminded him that Isham and Mayzie had a young son. A son who would be orphaned if Jerome killed Isham, as Lore expected. What would happen to the child? Lore thrust the nagging thought aside. Renni had stepped up to the door and knocked.

"If Isham opens the door, be ready to grab him and go," she whispered.

He got no chance to respond. The door swung open, and Isham stood in the doorway holding a rifle.

He grinned. "Figgered I'd be seeing some of you filthy witches before long." He cocked the hammer and aimed the gun directly at Renni. "I mean to pick you off one at a time. See, I found the perfect bait for hooking witches."

Renni stood perfectly still and spoke with a steady voice. "You can kill every member of the Community of the Gifted, and you still won't have touched the man who killed your wife. He isn't a member of the Community, and without our help he isn't anywhere you'd be able to find him."

"Hah! Good story, but it won't save your life." Lore saw Isham's finger tighten on the trigger.

Renni must have seen it too, but she didn't flinch. "His name is Jerome," she went on. "He's our enemy just as he is yours. He's a ruthless killer. He wants to kill the members of the Community, just as you do, and he used Mayzie as bait to bring us to him, just as you are using Leah. If you kill us, you'll be playing right into his hands. You'll be carrying out his plans. I understand that you want to avenge Mayzie's death, but the way to do that is to kill Jerome, not us."

Lore took a deep breath. Isham had listened to Renni's speech. But his scowl made Lore doubt that he would believe her—that and the fact that Isham's finger had never relaxed its pressure on the trigger.

"At least hear our offer," Renni said. "We'll take you to Jerome if you take us to Leah."

Isham shook his head. "I'm not falling for your

tricks. If this Jerome is your enemy, you'd use your witchcraft to defeat him. You wouldn't need me to kill him for you."

"We may have what you call 'witchcraft,' but we don't have guns. We've used our power against him, but he has power of his own with which to counter it. He can stop our powers, but he couldn't stop your rifle just as we can't."

The fool girl was practically daring Isham to shoot her. She was right—she had no power against his rifle. But Jerome did. And if he'd let Lore use that power, even for just a few moments, he could grab Isham and take him to Jerome. He sent Jerome a frantic thought to that effect.

I'll lend you the power to stop a bullet, but there is a price.

A price. That sounded ominous. But it would save his life. And probably Renni's too, though that was incidental. *I'll pay the price,* Lore sent. *Just do it.*

He felt an immediate surge of power flow through him. But for how long? No time to waste! He jumped in front of Renni and reached for Isham. The gun went off. Renni screamed. Lore lunged for Isham, grabbed his arm, and held his hand out for Renni to take.

She'd either thrown herself or fallen to the ground when Isham fired. When he saw the blood pouring from her arm, he guessed she'd fallen. The bullet had struck her in the arm. Not a fatal wound, surely. But he couldn't wait for her to rise. Isham was struggling to get free from Lore's grasp while holding firmly onto his rifle.

Lore sent the mental request for power to Jerome, and the next moment they stood before him. Lore gasped at the sight that his eyes took in as he gazed around. He didn't see Lady Kyla—or many of the others who should be here. He saw only Trille, Winter, and Camsen Wellner. Trille, whose magic required water, was helpless in water's absence. Winter remained seated a considerable way off and still hunched over his drawing pad, his hand grasping the stick of charcoal but not moving across the paper. Apparently he'd left off his foolish sketching. Wellner knelt on the hot sand, his head in his hands, probably praying to Ondin. Sand covered his clothing, Trille's, and Jerome's too. Sand had piled in some places and in others formed mounds that resembled graves.

"We had another sandstorm while you were away," Jerome said, his gaze following Lore's. "I'm afraid it's too late to help those who were lying on the ground when it happened. They've surely suffocated by now."

Lore released his hold on Isham's arm and stepped back, putting a greater distance between him and Jerome. Could the rest of the Community be under those mounds, dead? He hadn't believed Jerome would really kill so many. Marta. Marchion. Gorvy and Darnell Mack. Professor Morence. Winnie. And Lady Kyla? Surely the leader of the Community couldn't be dead.

"Where is this? What have you done?" Isham asked, his voice trembling. "What kind of evil magic brought us here?"

"I told you I'd bring you to the one who tortured and killed your wife," Lore said, suddenly hoping Isham would kill the monster who'd slaughtered so many. "There he is." He pointed at Jerome.

Jerome laughed uproariously. "Do you believe this lie?" he asked. "You must know that the enemy of your enemy is your friend. Look around you. See how I've reduced the number of the so-called powerful."

"What I see is another worker of witchy magic." Isham punctuated the statement by spitting forcefully on the ground, where with a small puff of steam his spittle vanished into the dry sand. He raised his rifle, cocked it.

The barrel of the rifle melted. With a shout Isham dropped it and shook his hands as though he'd been burned. His eyes filled with fear. He backed away from Jerome so fast that he collided with Lore. "You're demons, all of you," he shouted, turning in a circle, his eyes wide with terror. "Well, know this. If anything happens to me, my friends have sworn to kill Miss Leah. So nothing you do to me will save her."

Lore grabbed Isham and tried to restrain him, but it was like trying to restrain a rabid dog. Kicking, striking with fists and feet, Isham burst free of Lore's grasp and ran, blindly it seemed to Lore, blundering into stumps of long dead trees and tripping over stones, only to rise and keep going until he was only a moving dot in the far distance.

"The fool!" Trille exclaimed. "He'll run himself to death in this desert."

Rubbing his face and arms where Isham had struck him, Lore gazed around the group, taking stock. "Where's Lady Kyla?" he asked. "And Miss Marta?"

"Miss Marta collapsed like the others," Trille said, her eyes filling with tears. "She's under the sand along with the rest. We don't know about Lady Kyla. She caused the sandstorm. Sang it up. It stopped all of a sudden, and she was gone. But the storm had already done its worst."

That was odd, but Lore wasn't given time to think about it. Trille grabbed hold of his arm and said, "Take me home. I can't bear this another moment."

"You'll have to bear it, little lady," Jerome said with a cruel grin. "He doesn't have the power."

Even as he said it, Lore knew it was true. His power wasn't just exhausted. It was gone. Jerome had taken it from him, leaving him utterly helpless. He had been a fool, and he would pay for that folly with his life. He had little doubt that he would soon occupy a mound in the sand along with the rest of the Community.

But was it his fault? No! Lady Kyla was the real cause. The blame was hers, not his. She had led the Community to their deaths. Not intentionally, no. He didn't think that. But carelessly, without having a plan. And now he, along with the rest of the Community, would die because of her carelessness.

"Oh, don't worry. I've merely suspended the power to teleport yourself and others. I can't have you bouncing back and forth between worlds, now can I? But I can restore it if you continue to cooperate with me.

Renni hoped she'd done the right thing in avoiding going back to what was now Jerome's world with Lore. She'd intended to go with him, but only after they'd rescued Leah. They hadn't even found her. Lore should have waited.

Lore wasn't to be trusted. For that reason, it may have been a mistake to let him return to Jerome with Isham. But she'd really had no way to stop him, short of wiping out his recent memories. That could have had fatal consequences for him and for her and probably for Leah too. And he had saved her from getting killed. The wound on her arm was only superficial. Isham's bullet had just grazed her. Already the bleeding was stopping.

She got to her feet. Isham's abrupt departure had left the front door of his house standing open. Cautiously Renni stepped inside and peered around. She saw no one, heard nothing.

"Leah?" she called softly.

No response. She hadn't really expected one. She ventured further into the house. Where was Isham's son? She saw a few toys scattered about, but no sign of the little boy. Sleeping perhaps?

She went from the front room into a bedroom, then another, both empty. The child was probably with a neighbor. But where was Leah? Finally she came to the kitchen and dining area—one long room with a door leading outside at the far end.

She walked to that door and put her hand on the latch, but paused and went to the window instead. Carefully she pulled aside the curtain and peered out—and quickly ducked back in. A rifle shot shattered the window. Glass slivers peppered the arm closest to the window. She threw herself onto the floor.

She'd seen her assailant in that quick glance through the window, and unfortunately he'd seen her. She didn't recognize him, but he had to be one of Isham's cronies. He'd been guarding the outhouse and watching the house at the same time. So Leah had to be imprisoned in the outhouse.

He probably wasn't alone. There could be others outside whom she hadn't seen. She wasn't safe in the house. But she had to find a way to reach Leah.

She scuttled to the other side of the door, got to her feet, and ran into the next room. As she closed the door to that room behind her, she heard the back door open. She raced through the next room and into the front room, footsteps now thundering through the rooms behind her. She burst out the front door—and collided with Abigail.

"Where's Leah?" Abigail demanded, disentangling herself from Renni.

"A man's coming," Renni panted, pulling Abigail off the walkway. "He has a rifle. Leah's in the outhouse. It's guarded."

As if to reinforce her words, the front door swung open, and the gun-bearing man stepped outside and swung his gun toward them. Abigail shoved Renni behind her and shouted words Renni didn't understand. The man stiffened and stood still as a statue. Abigail must have cast a spell from that book so prized by Kyla.

Abigail started toward the front door, but Renni called out, "Not that way. There may be more armed men. Go around the side of the house. Be careful."

Abigail turned and ran the way Renni had advised. Renni ran to the man Abigail had bespelled and pried the rifle from his hand. A repeating rifle. Good! Her father had one, and she knew how to use it. With it, she followed Abigail, proceeding more cautiously than the older woman. As she rounded the back corner of the house, she saw Abigail race toward the outhouse.

A man stepped out of the shadow of the outhouse, a shotgun in his hands. "Stop!" he yelled at Abigail. "You want your friend? I'll get her for you."

He reached for the handle on the outhouse door. Abigail stopped. He swung the door open. Leah, bound hand and foot, her mouth gagged, her eyes wide with fear, perched on the edge of the outhouse seat, away from the hole from which a noxious odor poured.

Abigail shouted, "I'm coming, Leah dear, hang on." She'd taken her eyes off the man with the gun.

He raised the gun and aimed it as she hurried to the outhouse door. Renni shouted a warning. Too late.

The bullet flew past Abigail and struck Leah. She toppled forward, falling into Abigail's arms.

Renni raised her purloined rifle and fired at the man who'd shot Leah. Her aim was good. He fell and would not rise again. Renni looked around, checking the shady spots, the corners of the house, the area around the outhouse. Seeing no other assailants, she went to where Abigail now sat on the ground, cradling Leah's head in her lap. Blood poured from the wound in Leah's chest. Abigail was trying frantically to heal her. Renni could see it was already too late.

Ed had been talking to Petros while Zauna rocked Dreama. Suddenly Zauna looked up and said, "Abigail—where is she?"

Ed looked around, but instinctively he knew exactly where Abigail was. He rose from the chair he'd been sitting in, relaxing just a bit. *A bit too much*, he thought now.

"Stay here and protect Dreama." He gave the order as he headed for the door.

He had no idea where Isham's house was, but that was where Abigail had gone and probably where Renni and Lore were. He fixed the image of Abigail in his mind and willed himself to be at her side.

And he was there. In a back yard cluttered with a child's toys and carelessly abandoned gardening tools. Standing beside Abigail, who did not seem to take note of his presence as she rocked, keening, crying, "Come back to me, Leah. Come back. I can't bear life without you."

The deep wound in Leah's chest told Ed that Abigail's pleas were futile. He placed a hand on her shoulder. She shook it off without so much as glancing up to see who was there. Ed had not felt so helpless since he met Kyla and Marta five years ago. He wished he could go to his special place. But it wasn't his any more. It was Jerome's now. It was ruined. Ruined as their lives would be if they couldn't defeat Jerome. And they weren't having any success at doing that.

He looked around. A man's body lay on the ground not far from the outhouse. Ed was certain the man was dead, shot he believed. "Who shot him?"

He wasn't aware of having asked the question aloud, but he had, and a voice answered, "I did. Too late."

He saw her then. Renni leaned against the side of the outhouse wiping her mouth. She must have just vomited.

"I never killed anyone before," she said, walking toward him. "I had to do it, but it was too late. He shot Miss Leah before I could even aim the gun. I thought he'd fire at me or Miss Abigail, but he shot her. I couldn't stop him." The catch in her voice and her trembling hands exposed the grief she tried to hide.

"I can heal her," Abigail said. "I have to."

She must know Leah had already died, but she couldn't accept it. "Miss Abigail," Ed said softly, "Please, I think it's too late for healing."

She shook her head so violently her hair flew about her face like a gray mourner's veil. "No," she said, "No. I need Veronica. And Winnie. And Marchion to enhance our powers. We can bring her back. We have to."

"Veronica and Winnie and Marchion aren't here," he said. "But even if they were, they can't bring someone back from the dead."

"She isn't dead. She can't be. Please, if you can't bring them here to me, take me and Leah to them."

"But we don't know what's been happening in ... in Jerome's land." He'd almost said *in my land.* "We don't know what danger we'd arrive in the middle of."

"I'm willing to take that chance." Abigail raised her head to gaze directly at him for the first time. Her eyes were red-rimmed but empty of tears. "Are you too afraid to go?"

"I'm afraid for you and for Renni," he said. "And I don't think it would save Leah."

"We won't know unless we try," Abigail insisted.

"I want to go back," Renni said. "Jerome has to be stopped."

"And you know how to stop him?" Ed felt defensive.

"I know someone who may," Renni said. "And I can't do any more here. Let's go."

"I don't know that I can take so many."

"You can try," Abigail snapped, glaring at him.

"Shouldn't we go back to Kyla's house first and tell Zauna and Petros what we're doing?" He was grasping at straws. He wanted to return, wanted to be with Marta. He did not want to take Abigail and Leah. Why transport a dead body to a dead land?

"Zauna can look into her crystal ball and see where we've gone," Abigail said.

"Her crystal ball is cracked," Renni put in. "She says it doesn't work."

"That's her problem," Abigail said, refusing to accept any answer but the one she wanted. "Take us, Ed. Right now."

"All right. I'll have to carry Leah. You can't." He bent and gently lifted Leah from Abigail's arms. Her body was already cooling, and the blood that had flowed from her chest was coagulating around the wound. "Grab my shoulders and hang on," he told Renni and Abigail.

Renni helped Abigail stand. Abigail leaned against his right side, her arm around his back, her hand resting on his left shoulder. Renni, standing on his left, took hold of his arm with one hand and helped support Leah's body with her other.

Ed closed his eyes, took a deep breath, and pictured the land with the terrible desolation Jerome had brought to it. He opened his eyes when he felt the hot sand beneath his feet, burning even through the soles of his shoes.

Petros had never felt so helpless. The feeling had nothing to do with his physical condition. He could get around just fine on his wheeled platform. But he could not leave Zauna alone, unguarded, with Dreama in her care.

Zauna had dragged Dreama's crib into the living room, saying, "We need to stay together." She sat beside the crib, watching the baby sleep. Petros found the silence maddening.

Too much time had gone by since Lore and Renni left. When Abigail and Ed had come back, Petros had considered sending his consciousness into Ed once again, but Abigail had run off to find Leah and then Ed had announced his intention of following after her, so Petros knew he had to stay with Zauna and the baby. He wouldn't be much protection, but he would be better than none. He could at least keep her from panicking and from feeling lonely and abandoned. But as time stretched and Ed and Abigail failed to return with or without Leah, not knowing what had happened to them became unbearable.

"Can't you try again to use your crystal ball?" he asked Zauna. "Dreama is sleeping. You have time."

"I've told you it's cracked. That makes it useless," she answered crossly.

He tried to answer calmly, knowing her snappishness was unlike her and indicated that the same tension that tormented him tortured her as well. It wouldn't do for them to argue. That could only make them both feel worse. "I know you've told me that, but you could still try."

Perhaps his calm voice had an effect. "All right, I'll try. Will that satisfy you?"

He smiled. "I can't ask any more than that."

She went to the table on which her crystal rested in its stand. After gazing at it ruefully, one finger tracing the crack that marred one side, she turned the crystal so that the cracked side no longer faced her, cupped her hands around it, and gazed into it.

He waited, watched her shake her head despairingly, and said, "Don't give up. You may not see anything because you don't *expect* to see anything. Try to forget that the ball is cracked. Look into it as you normally would, expecting to see something."

She sighed but kept staring into the globe. Petros suddenly became aware that he was drumming his fingers against his platform. He curved the fingers into a fist and sat perfectly still.

"Something's taking shape," Zauna cried, and bent closer to peer more intently into the crystal.

Petros waited eagerly now, suddenly more hopeful.

"No, no, no!" Zauna sat up straight and pushed the crystal away from her. "I can't look anymore."

"What did you see?"

She turned toward him, tears filling her eyes and spilling down her cheeks. "Dead," she said. "They're all dead."

CHAPTER TWENTY-ONE
EXCHANGE

Abigail lowered Leah's body to the ground and looked around, her eyes wild and filled with fear.

Ed stood still, only his eyes moving as his gaze roved across the desolation. "Marta. Where is she?" he murmured.

That was not the question Renni most wanted answered. She saw no one but Trille, Camsen Wellner, and Winter. Trille rushed to Ed and grabbed his arm.

"You have to take me home. Now. Before he kills the rest of us."

"Where's Marta?" Ed asked more firmly.

"Under there with the rest." With a sweep of her hand Trille indicated the mounded sand. "That mound, I think." She pointed to a mound not far from where Camsen Wellner knelt. Wellner seemed unaware of their arrival.

Ed pried Trille's hand from his arm and ran to the mound, sank to his knees, and began digging frantically.

Trille would have run after him, but Renni caught her arm and swung her around. "Get hold of yourself," she told the singer. "You're needed here."

Trille gave a loud laugh that bordered on hysteria. "I'm useless," she said. "There's no water any where."

Renni slapped her face, leaving a red splotch on her cheek. "Calm down. Where is Jerome?"

"I don't know, but he's going to come back. He took Lore and said Kyla had deprived him of too much of his fun. He was going to arrange something special for the toys he had left. He meant us!" Her voice rose to a scream.

Renni slapped her again. "There's no time for hysterics," she said. "We have to act fast."

Renni ran to Winter, took hold of his shoulders, and shook him until he looked up at her. "Draw dark clouds," she ordered. "Draw rain, lots of it, falling from them. Hurry!"

He gave her a puzzled look. She reached down grasped the hand that still held a stick of charcoal, and positioned it on his sketchpad. "Draw dark clouds and rain. Now!"

His hand moved on the paper. She watched long enough to see a cloud take shape, see him shade it in darker and darker. "Good," she said. "Keep going."

She ran back to Trille. "Sing rain," she ordered.

"Why? What good will that do?"

"It may save our lives," Renni said. "Now sing."

"I can't make it rain," Trille objected. "There would have to be rain clouds."

"Pretend there are. Sing as if the sky was covered with clouds."

Trille looked at Renni as if she thought Renni had lost her mind.

"Look up!" Renni said and pointed at the sky. A dark cloud hovered above them, and as they both watched, a second joined it. And a third.

Trille sang. Tentative at first, her voice grew stronger, instilled now with confidence.

Renni felt a raindrop on her arm. More, on her face, her shoulders. In moments rain pelted down from the clouds. It fell hissing onto the hot sand, sending up clouds of steam. It formed pools on the hard sand, ran in rivulets through the valleys between the mounds.

Ed gave a strangled cry, drawing Renni's attention away from Trille. He held Marta in his arms. "She's dead," he cried. "She can't be dead."

Unable to witness his grief, Renni turned away and saw Abigail trying to shield Leah's body from the rain.

Trille's voice faltered. "Don't stop!" Renni shouted at her.

Renni hurried back to Winter. He looked up at her in wonder. "Did I bring the rain? With my drawing?"

"Yes. You've discovered a power you didn't know you had."

"But we're all getting soaked, and my sketch pad will soon be too wet to draw on."

A furious roar told Renni that Jerome had returned. She looked around, saw Jerome standing near Ed, saw him shove Lore, whom he must have brought back with him. Lore lurched forward, then broke into a run, zooming toward them. Through it all, Trille continued to sing.

"Quick, turn your pad over. The back should be dry enough to draw on. I'll shelter you. Draw Jerome bound like you did before."

She leaned forward, hands on Winter's shoulders, shielding his sketchpad with her body. Winter had only begun to sketch when Lore barreled into them, knocking her into Winter and toppling Winter backward, with Renni falling on top of him. She felt Lore throw himself on top of her, so that she and Winter sank into the wet sand.

"Sorry," Lore hissed in her ear. "Jerome sent me to kill you both."

Ed stroked Marta's hair, holding her head against his chest. The rain had washed the sand from her body. It would revive her, he thought. It had to. She couldn't be dead. Not Marta!

The rain was slowing now. It had been a pelting downpour from which he'd done his inadequate best to shelter Marta, but now it settled into a slow, steady soft rain that brought a refreshing coolness to this hot, dry land.

The hard rain had exposed those who'd lain beneath the other mounds of sand. Ed gasped to see Veronica washed free of sand. She couldn't be dead too. But her stillness, the lack of any sign of breathing, told him otherwise.

Others just as still now lay exposed, and the rain, while freeing them from the sand, revived none of them. He refused to believe they had all suffocated beneath that mantle of sand. That Marta had.

Continuing to stroke Marta's hair and face while murmuring words of endearment and pleas for her to return to consciousness—to life—he noted in his peripheral vision Jerome's sudden reappearance, Lore at his side. He looked up and saw Jerome give Lore a shove and Lore sprint toward Renni and Winter.

Ed knew he should do something to help them, but how could he leave Marta? He watched Lore barrel into Renni, knocking her into Winter so that both of them fell backward with Lore on top of them. Ed wouldn't be able to reach them in time even if he abandoned Marta. Jerome stomped toward the three—victims and attacker—without casting so much as a glance toward Ed.

A shadow fell over him. Ed looked up. Kyla stood just behind him. "I'll take care of Marta," she said.

"You go distract Jerome so he won't see what I'm doing."

He didn't question her order but eased Marta back onto the now wet and soggy ground. He hesitated just long enough to see Kyla bend over Marta and reach down to place her hand on Marta's forehead. As he ran toward Jerome, he heard Kyla say," Take life from me as I take death from you."

Ed's steps slowed. He turned to look at Kyla and Marta, saw Marta's eyelids flicker. He caught his breath as her eyes opened and she looked up into Kyla's face. Kyla smiled at her, then glanced at him. "Don't waste time," she ordered. "Go!"

This time he obeyed.

Marta shook her head, feeling as though she'd been awakened suddenly from a very long and deep sleep that still clouded her mind. She couldn't seem to recall where she was, why she'd been sleeping, or why Kyla had awakened her.

Kyla was speaking to her, but the words were indistinct, and the few she caught didn't make sense.

Kyla caught hold of her arms and raised her to a sitting position and supporting her there. "Marta, I need you to listen to me. You have to concentrate. I don't have much time."

Marta nodded, finding it easier to understand now that she was sitting up. But then she looked around. She thought she remembered lying on hot, dry sand, but around her the ground was wet and water pooled in many places. Her soaked clothing stuck uncomfortably to her body. Rain was falling, not a hard rain but steady. She wasn't cold; the air was warm. Somewhere nearby a voice sang a stirring melody.

Veronica lay sprawled on the ground not far from her. Marta stared. The girl didn't seem to be breathing. Her mouth was partway open, her eyes were closed, and no movement was visible.

"Veronica?" Marta managed a hoarse whisper. "Dead?"

"I'll take care of Veronica. Don't worry about her. Just listen to me and don't look around. Look at me."

Thinking more clearly now, Marta felt certain that Veronica was dead. What else did Kyla not want her to see? "Ed?" she asked. "Where?"

"Ed is all right. Now *listen*." To emphasize her words, Kyla gave her a shake. "I must tell you something. I've talked to Claid."

"Claid!" That got Marta's full attention. "Where?"

"That doesn't matter. He gave me a job to do. But I have to talk to you before I do it."

"I'm listening."

"I'm going to do what I can, what Claid told me to do, but it won't be enough to defeat Jerome. It's going to be up to you and Ed and Veronica to defeat him. And to do that, you have to have Claid's help because Jerome's power comes from an evil Dire Lord. You can't defeat him on your own, but you can pull the Community together and use their all their talents to bind him. Trille's water power has slowed him down. Winter is doing his part. But you have to be the center, the director, and the inspiration."

"I don't know that I can do that," Marta said, shaking her head. "You're the leader of the Community. It is your job."

"It was my job, but I failed at it. Now it is yours. I won't be here to lead them much longer."

"Why?"

"Don't ask questions. Just listen," Kyla said.

"We've all been working at cross purposes. Each member of the Community has a gift, and if put together correctly like pieces of a puzzle, the combined gifts will overpower Jerome at a critical moment. You'll know when that moment comes. Don't waste it."

Marta thought bitterly of the moments Kyla had been wasting. As if she'd read her mind, Kyla said, "Don't make the mistakes I did. And don't underestimate anyone. Keep them working in harmony."

"How can I do that when you couldn't?" Marta couldn't disguise her bitterness.

"You can. Think of Dreama. She's your incentive. The daughter you want. She will be your reward."

"If Ed and I can keep her safe."

"You can. You will."

Kyla sounded so sure, so positive, that Marta had to ask, "Did Claid guarantee it?"

"*I* guarantee it. Now gather your strength and get up. Ed needs your help." Kyla straightened and helped Marta stand. She turned her to the left and pointed. Looking where Kyla indicated, Marta saw Jerome swinging Ed around in a circle by his arms as though he were a rag doll, and all the while laughing uproariously.

She ran toward them, her strength returning as she ran. Drawing near, she heard Jerome say, "How do you like the ride, Simple Eddie? Good as the ones at the County Fair back in Carey, right? Getting dizzy? Let's see if we can go a little faster. Oh, how sweet! Here's the little wife, come to watch the fun."

Oh, how she despised Jerome at that moment! How she wanted to tear him apart! But she was no match for him. Just past him she saw Lore sprawled on top of Renni, choking her. She was struggling against him, but she was losing the battle.

Marta ran in a wide arc around Jerome and launched herself at Lore. Grabbing him from behind, she caught hold of his face and poked her fingers in his eyes. With a roar of rage and pain he released his grip on Renni to tear Marta's hands from his face.

Coughing, Renni pushed Lore off her and rolled off Winter. Instead of helping Marta subdue Lore, Renni helped Winter sit up. "Draw in the sand," Renni said, her voice so hoarse Marta wondered how she got the words out.

Lore fought Marta only with his physical strength, not power. Even so, she couldn't defeat him. Worse, she heard a loud thump followed by Jerome's raucous laughter. Although she couldn't, in the midst of her battle with Lore, look to see what had happened, she knew Jerome had tossed Ed free. She could only hope he hadn't been badly injured.

Lore had her flat on the ground, pounding her into the sand, getting the sand into her eyes, blinding her. And then he jerked back, and she lifted her head, shaking the sand from her hair and face, and saw that Renni had attacked Lore from behind, pulling him away from her. As he turned on Renni, Marta sat up and gathered her strength. She had to help Renni as Renni had helped her. But first she looked for Ed.

Jerome had thrown him with a force that landed him some distance away. His unsuccessful attempts to rise showed her he'd been injured by the fall as well as being dizzied by being swung around. She wanted desperately to go to him, but she couldn't leave Renni to cope with Lore alone.

Winter was trying to follow Renni's instruction, and Renni was doing all she could to keep Lore from stopping him. Marta understood the reason Lore had to be stopped. But as she launched herself at Lore she was jerked back by her hair with such force that she screamed in pain.

"You deserve the same treatment as your dear husband," Jerome said, releasing his grasp of her hair only to grab her arms and pick her up. But before he could twirl her around as he had Ed, his arms stiffened. She glanced at Winter, saw him sketching furiously with his fingers in the damp sand.

Jerome let out a roar of fury when his hands opened and Marta dropped free. She scrambled to her feet and went back to help Renni with Lore.

Veronica sat up with the help of Kyla, who then bent and kissed her on the forehead. "Always remember that I love you," Kyla said and turned away.

Veronica watched her surrogate mother move toward someone lying near her. As Kyla bent down over that person, Veronica saw that it was Winnie.

"Take life from me as I take death from you." As Aunt Kyla spoke those words, a shiver ran through Veronica. She hadn't realized that Winnie was dead, but she saw now that the older woman lay stiff, motionless, no sign of breath, no reaction to the falling rain, no flicker of life.

But as Kyla touched her, Winnie's body relaxed. Her chest heaved. She drew in an audible breath. Another. And another. In moments Kyla was helping her sit up as she had helped Veronica.

"Take care of each other," Kyla said, addressing both Veronica and Winnie.

She circled around them and Veronica saw, lying on her other side, Gorvy Mack and just past him Professor Morence. Dead, both of them.

Kyla went to Gorvy and bent over him as she had Winnie. Veronica noted that as she reached out to touch him her hand trembled. "Take life from me as I take death from you," she said, repeating the words she'd uttered before restoring Winnie.

Like Winnie, Gorvy Mack's body relaxed and in a moment he took one shuddering breath and then another and another. This time Aunt Kyla did not help him to sit but moved on past him to Professor Morence, where she repeated the process. As life returned to the professor, Veronica was alarmed to see Aunt Kyla stagger and almost fall. Her face paled, losing almost all color. She seemed to remain on her feet only by great effort of will.

Veronica struggled to stand and, although still a bit shaky, went to Kyla, who stumbled through the wet sand toward still another corpse: that of Marchion Blandry.

"Aunt Kyla, how can you bring back life to the dead?" she asked.

Aunt Kyla shook her head. "No time to explain," she said, her voice weak, barely more than a whisper.

She bent over Marchion and repeated the mantra that had restored life to the others. "Take life from me as I take death from you."

Cold chills ran up Veronica's spine as she guessed what that meant. "No, Aunt Kyla. You can't."

But already Marchion was returning to life, and this time Kyla would have fallen had not Veronica caught and supported her.

The Honorable Wellner hurried to help Veronica support Kyla. As he reached them, Abigail's voice rang out. "Over here," she called. "Help Leah. Hurry!"

Kyla turned toward Abigail, and Veronica turned with her, Camsen Wellner assisting. Although Abigail sat some distance from them, holding Leah in her arms, Veronica could see that Leah was dead. Blood, already dried, stained her blouse and the hole where a bullet had entered was visible as a darker splotch within the dark red stain. Seeing that, Veronica guessed that Isham or one of his men had shot Leah. She hadn't died in the same way as the others, suffocated under the sand. And she'd been dead longer than any of the others.

"Aunt Kyla, don't," Veronica begged. "I know how Aunt Abigail loves her, but Aunt Leah's been shot, through the heart it looks like, and bringing her back can kill you."

"Doesn't matter." Kyla's voice was so faint that Veronica had to place her ear by Kyla's mouth to understand the words. "I have to do this."

"I won't let you" Veronica declared. "Honorable Wellner, don't let her go there."

Camsen Wellner stopped, still supporting Kyla but not letting her move forward.

"Ondin would want this." Kyla gasped out the words. "Your duty ... as a priest ... you must ... in his name."

"What about the Power-Giver, Aunt Kyla?" Veronica implored, shocked that Kyla would invoke Ondin. "He wouldn't want this."

"Not his choice."

This was all wrong. But Wellner was moving forward again, helping Kyla toward Abigail and Leah. Veronica dropped Kyla's arm and moved to stand in front of her. "I won't let you do this," she said.

Kyla didn't answer, just gave Camsen Wellner a pleading look.

"I think you'd better let her do it," he said. "If it's the will of the gods—"

"It's not the will of the gods," Veronica burst out. "She doesn't even believe in your gods. You can't let her do it. It will kill her." Tears fell though she tried to hold them back.

Kyla shook her head weakly. "Claid," she said. "I promised."

"You promised Claid? The Dire Lord Claid?" Veronica could not accept what Kyla said. "He wouldn't want you to die, I know."

"You don't know anything," Kyla said more forcefully, gathering strength with obvious effort. "You don't know Claid. I do, and I trust him." To Camsen Wellner, priest of Ondin, she said, "Help me."

"In Ondin's name, I will," he said, and, ignoring Veronica, he lifted Kyla into his arms and carried her to Abigail and Leah.

Veronica ran after him, tugging at him, trying to hold him back. Still weak, not fully recovered from her own resurrection, unable to use her power, she could not stop him. When they halted before Abigail, Veronica burst into tears. "Aunt Abigail, you can't let her do this," she said. "She'll die."

But Abigail said, "I can't live without Leah."

Kyla reached out and rested her hand on Leah's head. Her lips moved, and though no sound came out, Veronica knew the words she repeated. "Take life from me as I take death from you."

Moments—or an eternity—passed.

Leah took a breath. A bullet erupted from her chest and the wound closed behind it.. Abigail let out a cry of joy. Kyla crumpled to the ground.

Veronica fell beside her, weeping. Camsen Wellner placed a hand on her shoulder. "I'm sorry, Veronica," he said. "I think I was spared from being buried with the others to help Lady Kyla complete this work."

Shrugging off his hand, placing her hands on Kyla, Veronica tried desperately to summon her power to heal. It failed her.

"Aunt Abigail, heal Aunt Kyla now," She begged.

Perhaps Abigail tried. Veronica didn't know. She only knew that Kyla gasped, coughed, and then lay still, no longer breathing.

CHAPTER TWENTY-TWO
HOPE

Ed sat up as soon as his head stopped spinning enough to permit the required movement. He couldn't yet stand, and the arm and wrist he'd landed on hurt terribly. One or both were broken, he was certain. His immediate reaction was rage mixed with humiliation. It had been a long time since he'd been called "Simple Eddy," a longer time since he'd thought of himself that way. Jerome thought him a fool, and being thought a fool made him act like a fool. He'd wanted to help Marta, but he'd only made matters worse.

He finally dared raise his head and turn to see what was happening to Marta. He saw Jerome grab Marta by her hair, then grasp her arms and lift her. Understanding that Jerome's intention was to swing her around as he had been swung and possibly toss her either toward him or in the opposite direction, he lowered his head again, unable to watch. Instead he stared at the damp ground around him. The young woman, Trille, had sung and the rain had come. She'd now stopped singing and the thirsty ground was soaking up the water. Soon, Ed guessed, it would be as dry as before, no longer his land but Jerome's.

To calm himself he closed his eyes and pictured this world as it had been when it was his "special place." He pictured the grassy meadow with its riot of wild flowers, the brook with fish filling its sparkling waters, the apple tree in bloom beside it. It had been so lovely, and—

And it can be again, said a voice in his head. Not the Power-Giver, but the other voice, the one he recognized as Claid's. Claid, the Dire Lord, whom Marta had declared the real Power-Giver, the source of the power that flowed through the Power-Giver, he who had been the Mage Alair, to Kyla and Marta and all those who received his gifts. Whom Claid chose to receive his gifts.

He'd chosen Ed, had spoken to Ed, as he never had to Marta. That counted for a lot. It had convinced Ed that he wasn't Simple Eddy. Not simple at all. Highly gifted, Marta had declared.

Marta was right, the voice spoke again. *You were and still are.*

Ed opened his eyes. Had he dreamed the voice? Nothing had changed. He still sat on wet sand. The streambed nearby was still empty and dry.

No! It wasn't filled with sparkling water as he remembered it, but a trickle of muddy water flowed over the pebbles that filled its center. A trickle that widened as he stared at it. It brought him hope, enough to let him turn and look at Jerome and Marta.

Marta was no longer in Jerome's clutches. She was free! Jerome stood still, glaring at her and at Renni. They had subdued Lore and were sitting on him so he could not rise. Winter was sketching madly in the sand.

Marta looked toward Ed and grinned. He smiled back at her and with his good hand waved toward the brook, though from where she was sitting she wouldn't see the water running through it.

He looked down at the ground around him and saw green sprouts poking up from the wet sand. Yes!

The land was not as dead as he—as they all had thought. He could bring it back.

Marta enjoyed the moment of calm, a moment for taking stock of where they were and what they needed to do. As soon as Jerome was immobilized, all the fight had gone out of Lore. Renni could handle him by herself. She rose and went to Ed. He must be hurt, or by now he would have come to her.

As she stood, Winter said, "Miss Marta, I can't hold him much longer. The sand is drying, and I can't keep the drawing intact."

She sighed. The moment of calm was already past.

A voice spoke in her mind. Hoping it was Claid, she was disappointed when she recognized the sender as Professor Morence.

My power has come back, and I rather suspect that all who had been felled by the evil one have also regained at least some of their power. It might be good to alert everyone to be ready to act in concert, each according to his or her abilities. If you agree, I can send a message to them to that effect. Please nod if you agree or shake your head if you don't. I can see that from where I'm standing.

She nodded without turning around. His suggestion couldn't have come at a better time.

In seconds came his next sending: *I've delivered the message. They await your signal. Nod again when you are ready.*

Professor Morence's message only added to Veronica's despair. Act? In concert? Even if they could act all together, they weren't ready to do so. Her power hadn't returned, and in her present frame of mind she couldn't imagine that it ever would.

Aunt Kyla was dead. Nothing else mattered. Jerome would destroy them all, and Veronica didn't care. If Aunt Abigail hadn't insisted on her bringing Leah back to life, Aunt Kyla could have been saved. Veronica loved Aunt Leah, but Aunt Kyla was her rock, her anchor.

Oh, sure, she'd rebelled sometimes when she thought Aunt Kyla was being too strict, and occasionally she'd even complained to Aunt Leah about it, but down deep she knew, even before Aunt Leah defended Aunt Kyla, that Aunt Kyla was right. Even when she'd been angry about something Aunt Kyla had said or done, she'd never questioned adoptive aunt's love for her, and she'd always known that Aunt Kyla wanted what was best for her.

She rose from beside Kyla's still form and looked for Marta and Ed. She spotted Ed sitting off by himself some distance from where Marta and Renni were struggling with Lore. He cradled one arm in a way that suggested he'd hurt it. But the thing that amazed her was that around him the sand was tinged with green. Even as she stared, the green spread out further. He must be healing his land!

Ed was bringing life back to a dead land. Maybe Aunt Kyla could be brought back. Surely she could! It was up to her to find the way.

She headed toward Ed, her confidence resurging and with it, her power. She'd heal his arm. She could do that now.

Jerome was facing Marta, Renni, Lore, and Winter, his arms stretched toward them. He was standing absolutely still. Something or someone had again immobilized him. Unless he was pretending to be held fast as a joke and would spring free and wreak havoc when least expected.

She ran to Ed, not wanting to waste any time. He'd be needed when Jerome acted against them, and she had a strong feeling that the time for that was near. "Your arm," she said, "what's wrong with it?"

"Broken. Possibly in two places."

She knelt beside him and ran both her hands on his arm, feeling for a break in the bone. She nodded. "Upper arm and wrist. Hold real still."

She wrapped one hand around his wrist. He winced but made no sound. The other hand she placed over the break she'd detected in his upper arm.

"Should you be using your power this way?" he asked even as he felt the bones begin to knit together.

She ignored his question, gritted her teeth against the pain flowing through her hands up into her arms, and nodded at the circle of green sprouts spreading out from around him. "You've been busy," she said.

"Took my mind off the pain," he said with a grin.

She had to take *her* mind off the pain she was drawing from him. "Do you know who or what is binding Jerome?"

"No idea. He may be faking. He loves to torment us, get our hopes up and then let them down in a big way."

"I know, but I don't think he would have let Aunt Kyla raise everybody from the dead if he'd been able to stop her." Her voice caught in her throat as she added, "I'm glad she did it, but why'd it have to kill her?"

"She's dead?" Ed asked, shocked. "I didn't know."

"I think she is, but maybe not. I mean, I don't think she's breathing but I keep hoping she's just in a deep, deep trance or something."

"Or something," Ed echoed. "Let's hope."

"You saw something in your crystal before. Why can't you now?" Petros demanded, holding Dreama in his arms and rocking her gently even while he glared at Zauna.

"Because it's cracked. Why can't you understand that?"

It was the same complaint he'd heard too many times, and although he was a patient man, his patience with her was exhausted. "It was cracked when it showed you something earlier. 'They're all dead,' you said, and you still haven't told me exactly what it was you saw."

"I'm not sure any more. It couldn't have been a true picture, it had to be from the crystal being cracked."

"Zauna, we have to face whatever it was you saw. And you need to stop believing that what you saw wasn't real because the crystal ball is cracked. Look into it, please. Try."

"I can't," she insisted. "I can't bear to. What it showed was too horrible. I have to cling to the hope that it wasn't a true vision."

He sighed. He couldn't win. She would neither describe what she'd seen, which must have been horrific, nor dare to look again. He hadn't pegged her as a coward, but she simply could not and would not summon the courage to gaze into the crystal again. She preferred to clutch the bit of hope that remained—the hope that the vision had been false.

As for him, he could do nothing but hope that what she had seen was incomplete and not as dire as it had seemed to her. And hope that an answer would come soon from some other source than the cracked crystal globe.

Lore no longer struggled. Whether that was a good thing or a bad, Renni didn't know. It did give her hope that he might have come to his senses. Or that Jerome might have released his hold on him.

Winter's alarming declaration chilled her, but then she had a thought. The rain had stopped. His sketchpad might have dried out a bit. She thought it had fallen onto the ground in front of Winter, and it must be under Lore. If they were lucky, Lore's body heat might have dried it.

Winter was trying his best to shield his sand drawing now that he knew its power. *His* power, newly discovered and surely a comfort to him for the modicum of control it gave him.

"Marta, help me get Lore up." Renni hoped she wouldn't have to explain the reason for that request.

Marta understood. She grabbed his arm, Renni grabbed the other, and they raised him to a sitting position.

The sketchpad was beneath him, still wet, covered with sand, its pages wrinkled and torn from Lore's struggles. Winter retrieved it and said in a sad voice, "It's not much use. And my charcoal's wet. But I'll see if there's any page that I can use at least a part of."

He didn't sound hopeful, but he was willing to try. And really, Marta thought, what more could any of them do? What hope did any of them have?

CHAPTER TWENTY-THREE
FINAL BATTLE

Professor Morence strolled toward Veronica and Ed as though he were taking a walk in a park. When he reached them, he stared for a moment at the green shoots still sprouting around Ed. "Amazing!" he commented. Then to Veronica he said, "I'm trying not to call Jerome's attention to me. I noticed he moved his hand as I was walking here, and I fear he'll break free at any moment. We must all be ready. I would definitely draw his attention if I walked to Marta, but I hoped it would be safe to come here to you."

Veronica nodded. She understood, but she didn't agree. Once Jerome broke free, no one was safe anywhere.

"I've been taking inventory to be certain all are accounted for. Darnell Mastry, Gorvy's wife, is missing. I think she may have shape-changed and dashed off when the sandstorm began. We need her here. I've sent a mental message, but I don't know whether in her wolf form she's able to receive. We need everyone here. If there were a way to do so, I'd have Petros and Zauna brought here as well."

"They're taking care of Dreama and trying to keep her safe." Veronica spoke more sharply than she'd intended.

"I know that, but we need everyone. I feel certain of it."

"You may be right, but they'll have to do what they can from back home," Veronica said, this time intending the sharpness.

"What can I do?" Trille asked, coming up to them. "The clouds I brought rain from are gone."

"There's a little water in the streambed," Ed offered. "Can you do anything with that?"

"Not much, I'm afraid."

"But wait," Veronica said. "There's more water upstream. I don't think that water in the streambed is all from the rain." Quickly she told Trille of the pool she'd found and the dam she'd destroyed. She didn't think Jerome would have had an opportunity to rebuild it as yet.

Trille gave a big sigh of relief. "I can work with that."

Veronica glanced around, noting the positions of the various Community members. They had grouped themselves in small clusters spread out in a sort of circle, not by design she thought. Her own cluster, consisted of her, Ed, Trille, and Professor Morence, Directly opposite them on the other side of the circle Abigail huddled with Leah, holding her as though she feared Leah would be taken from her. On the curve of the circle to her right, halfway between her cluster and that of Abigail and Leah, Winter sat hunched over his sketchpad, Renni stood looking down at him, while Marta seemed to be remonstrating with Lore. To her left, Marchion and Gorvy engaged in animated conversation or perhaps argued over something. Opposite them, to Abigail's right, Camsen Wellner bent over Kyla's body and Winnie knelt beside it. Jerome stood near the middle of the circle, reminding Veronica of the children's game of "Circle 'Round the Kettle," with Jerome portraying the kettle.

The circle comparison wasn't wholly accurate though. The symmetry was marred by a gap opposite Marta's cluster. Why this mattered and why she should be noting it instead of watching Jerome, Veronica couldn't say. Ed had risen, ready to head toward Marta, when a scream followed by the howl of a wolf drew everyone's attention.

Isham dashed into view followed closely by a large wolf. "Darnell," Veronica whispered. "I'd almost forgotten about her." To Ed she said, pointing to the wolf, "That's Gorvy's wife, the shape-shifter. That's what she changes to."

Isham reached that gap in the circle that had drawn Veronica's attention, and at that point the wolf leaped on him, bringing him sprawling face down in the sand.

As if he'd been waiting for that signal, Jerome gave a roar very similar to that of the wolf. He spun around, taking in the circle of Gifted around him. "Well, now, isn't this cozy?" he shouted. "How nice of you to gather around to provide my entertainment. You've had your fun. Now mine begins."

He gazed again around the circle. "But wait! Aren't we missing some guests? Where are the fortuneteller and the cripple? And the guest of honor, the baby? You failed to invite me to her Naming-Day fete, but I won't neglect her at my victory party."

"How'd he know about Zauna and Petros?" Veronica whispered to Ed, who merely shushed her without taking his gaze from Marta. Waiting for her nod, Veronica guessed, recalling Professor Morence's sending. But so far as she knew, the professor hadn't sent any instructions as to what to do when Marta nodded. And Marta couldn't mindspeak.

She could! They needed to act before Jerome

carried out his threat to bring Zauna, Petros, and the baby here.

Too late! With a loud plunk Petros's wheeled platform, with Petros clinging to it, landed in the center of the circle, and Zauna, holding the screaming infant and adding her screams to Dreama's, landed beside him, falling onto her rump and looking terrified and thoroughly undignified. In her arms along with the baby she held her crystal ball.

That won't be much help, Veronica thought.

When Marta still did not nod, Veronica concluded that Jerome must be preventing her. Marta had never been slow to act. If anything, she could be too impulsive. Jerome must have heard some, maybe all, of Professor Morence's mindspeech.

Jerome probably didn't know that Veronica could mindspeak, but he would know as soon as she did it. She had no way to block him. So she had to act quickly and send to everyone.

Act, people. Marta's blocked, she sent. *Do whatever you can.*

That got through, she was certain. To those in her cluster she could speak directly. "Trille, there's water in the stream. Use it," she said. "Ed, keep rebuilding the land. Professor, use your power of coercion to force Lore to cooperate with us rather than with Jerome."

Trille lifted her voice in song. Veronica launched a stream of fire at Jerome. He deflected it, but it kept him from quieting Trille. Winter held a charcoal stick in his fingers; his hand moved rapidly over the torn sketchpad.

Veronica sent another stream of fire at Jerome. A second stream rushed toward him from the opposite direction. The priest of Ondin had overcome his scruples and acted!

In response to Trille's song, water rushed through the stream that had held only a trickle. It overflowed the stream banks and rose up in a waterspout. Twirling and twisting, it headed for Jerome, who was already having a hard time deflecting the two fire streams. Veronica gave a shout of triumph.

The wolf jumped off Isham, who seemed to be unconscious, and bounded toward Jerome. Zauna handed the squalling Dreama to Petros, took careful aim, and hurled her heavy crystal ball at Jerome. Under normal circumstances he could have easily deflected it, but he was so busy redirecting fire and water that he probably didn't see the missile coming.

The fire and the water didn't touch him. Zauna's crystal orb hit him squarely on the forehead. Jerome staggered, fell to his knees. Both streams of fire struck him, but so did the waterspout. Water swirled around him, putting out the flames that were licking at his clothing and flesh. Moments later he rose slowly to his feet and roared, but this time not with laughter. "You're all going to die," he shouted. "Everyone of you. And I'm going to savor every death." He swung around and pointed at Camsen Wellner. "Starting with you, fire thrower!"

"And you, water singer." He pointed at Trille, then glared at Veronica, "And you, red-haired brat, I have a very special death planned for you."

With that pronouncement, he turned and again pointed a finger at Wellner. "I'll fight fire with fire."

The wolf, which had stopped short to avoid first the flames and then the swirling funnel of water, vaulted forward and sank its teeth into Jerome's calf, jolting him so that he raised his hand and the jet of flame that flew from his finger streaked skyward, sparing his intended victim. It soon found another. Jerome's hand swung toward the wolf, and a flame shot toward it. Gorvy had broken into a run the instant he'd seen the wolf head for Jerome and had been standing next to the wolf when it launched its attack on Jerome. Gorvy dashed forward and threw himself across the back of the wolf, taking the blast of flame on his back. Despite the pain of the burns, he clung to the wolf's back, protecting her.

Veronica shot another stream of flame at Jerome. And Trille sang a stream of water that doused the flames on Gorvy's back. Veronica was doing her best to shield herself and Trille, who could not shield well, if at all, and also Ed.

Zauna, having used the only weapon she had and in so doing had quite possibly destroyed her livelihood, took Dreama from Petros and rocked the baby, trying vainly to quiet her cries. Winnie made her way to Zauna and placed her hand on Dreama, and the cries eased.

Petros, following the wolf's example, launched himself on his wheeled platform toward Jerome and careened the platform against the leg the wolf had not attacked. Jerome howled with pain and shot a blast of power at Petros that knocked him off his platform and left him lying motionless in the sand.

Winnie took a couple of steps toward Petros, hesitated, and glanced around the group. She was the nearest healer to him, and he needed help. So did Gorvy. But they were lying dangerously close to Jerome. She took two more steps. Almost there.

"You!" Jerome bellowed. "Come here and heal me."

She wanted to refuse but felt herself being forced to approach him. She tried to resist, but she couldn't shield and Jerome's power was strong despite his injuries.

"Gorvy, help me if you can," she asked as she passed him, still protecting the wolf, his shape-shifted wife.

Gorvy shook his head. He'd already tried to use his power of quenching. It had no effect on Jerome. Winnie cast a desperate glance at Veronica, who responded by shooting another stream of fire at Jerome. Despite his injuries, Jerome easily deflected the flames, sending them back at Veronica. Her shields held.

Camsen Wellner sent a stream at Jerome from the opposite direction. Jerome deflected that stream, too. The blaze rebounded and struck Wellner's raised arms. His long-sleeved priest's tunic caught fire. He threw himself on the ground and rolled in the sand to put out the flames. Abigail hurried to him, leaving Leah's side for the first time since Leah's resurrection. He sat up, groaning, and she placed her hands on his burned arms. Grimacing, she took the painful burns into herself.

Throughout this time, Winnie had been slowly moving toward Jerome, fighting against the compulsion with every step. She moved as though slogging through thick mud, but she could not stop making progress; she could only slow it by her resistance. Inevitably, she reached Jerome's side, near where Petros lay unmoving, and against her will her arms moved toward Jerome's burned arms, burns less serious than those Wellner had suffered. With a shudder Winnie fell to her knees; her unwilling hands found the deep and nasty bites the wolf had inflicted.

She'd healed the burns, but despite her hands being pressed against the wolf's bites, healing didn't come. Gorvy was suppressing her talent!

"What's wrong, woman?" Jerome bellowed. "Why aren't you healing my leg?"

"My power's exhausted," she said, hoping to keep him from suspecting Gorvy. "I've used too much."

"I'm sick of you people!" Jerome roared. "You work at cross purposes from each other, you scarcely know what you're doing, and your puny power runs out at the worst times. I'll show you what real power can do. You think you can defeat me because you've had some petty victories. I can move you around like pawns on a chessboard."

He turned toward Ed, Veronica, Trille, and the professor. "Simple Eddy, did you think I hadn't noticed your feeble attempts to heal your land? Did you think I'd allow you to do that? No, I just let you occupy yourself with the attempt to keep you busy. But enough of that."

A blast of hot wind swirled toward Ed and the others, picking up sand. It swept over the expanse of grass around Ed, withering the green shoots and covering them with sand.

"Now go join your little wifey." Ed was picked up and hurled through the air to land at Marta's feet. She bent and helped him rise. Jerome, laughing, sent both of them sailing through the air to land on Petros's wheeled platform. The platform rolled backward, stopping near Isham, who groaned, sat up, and glared at all those around him. Marta grabbed Ed's hand. If Isham still wanted to kill them, he'd have plenty of help. Squeezing Marta's hand, Ed got off the platform and to his feet, pulling Marta up with him. Without exchanging words, they stepped away from Isham and walked to where Zauna still held Dreama. Marta released Ed's hand and held out her arms. Zauna placed Dreama in them, and Ed slipped an arm around Marta's waist and drew her and the baby close.

Marta had expected Jerome to say something or to take some action against them. He might have, had not Veronica sent another powerful stream of fire at him. Instead of merely deflecting it back toward her, he caught the end of the fire stream, twisted it around, and sent it twirling around Trille, who screamed and fell to the ground in flames. Veronica, shielded and untouched by the fire, bent to help her.

"Oh, no," Jerome called to her. "You go back to your beloved aunt Kyla."

Veronica flew through the air to where Kyla's body lay and was dropped beside it with a force that sent her sprawling. Abigail, who'd completed healing Wellner, headed toward her but ran into an invisible barrier. Not expecting it, she hit it with a jolt that shook her so that she burst into tears. Leah ran to her and put her arms around her.

"How tender," Jerome said. "Such a touching sight deserves to be preserved."

Abigail and Leah froze in place. No false fountain imprisoned them—they just stood as though made of stone, unable to move a finger or even an eyelid.

"Now, let's see. Who's next?" Jerome spun around, stopped, and pointed at Camsen Wellner. "Water can put out flames," he said. "It's too bad flames can't put out water. But you can sympathize with the water girl." With that, Wellner was lifted across the circle and deposited beside the badly burned and weeping Trille.

"Have courage," the priest whispered to her. "I'll pray to Ondin on your behalf."

"You might as well," she sobbed. "The Power-Giver isn't helping us."

Jerome's loud cackle made it evident that he'd heard her lament. "Your Power-Giver is no match for me," he proclaimed loudly, so that even though only the nearest few had heard Trille's comment, everyone heard his response. "That should be obvious. Your leader, to whom he spoke, or so she claimed, lies dead. If he did not protect her, you should know he will not, cannot protect any of you."

He paused to let that declaration sink in. While he waited, letting the tension build, he bent down and picked up Zauna's crystal ball. Tossing it from hand to hand, he continued his speech. "You can see that I've rendered ineffective all the measly little magics you've been throwing at me. True, the wolf succeeded in inflicting a painful hurt on my leg. I assume you all know that she is the shape-shifted wife of this gentleman," he pointed at Gorvy, "who has been trying so hard and so unsuccessfully to suppress or even limit my power. Since his dear wife has been more successful, I have already punished her. Oh, you haven't seen what I've done, but I assure you it is most effective. First, I've taken away her ability to change back to her human form. Second, I've sealed her mouth shut. She will never bite me again. She'll find it difficult to eat with her mouth permanently closed and will eventually starve to death, but that is an unfortunate side effect of her punishment."

Gorvy stepped forward, fists clenched as though ready to do physical battle with Jerome. Darnell-wolf jumped in front of him and leaned against his legs, preventing his rash action.

"I have also done some other things that aren't obvious to you, though no doubt they will become so. I have taken Professor Morence's ability to mind-speak. He had become far too chatty." Jerome continued to toss the crystal ball idly from hand to hand.

"The lovely Trille will recover from her burns in time, though not by being healed by anyone in this company. The ability to heal has been taken away from those who had it." He stopped and looked at the crystal ball as though he had only just recalled that he'd been toying with it. "I'm afraid you've damaged your crystal further, Madame Zauna. Pity. It's quite useless now. Except for this—" Without warning he hurled the ball at Zauna, aiming directly at her head.

To everyone's amazement, she lifted her arms and caught the globe before it could strike her, thus saving herself from what would most likely have been a killing blow. Her look of triumph faded when in her hands the globe split into small fragments. Jerome would not be denied a victory over the crystal gazer.

"We near the end of this charade," Jerome's voice boomed so loud that some in the group covered their ears. That made Jerome roar with laughter. "I must, however, recognize one especially talented member of the group, as I fear his talent has been sadly unnoticed. Young Winter is a most skilled artist. Ah, but I should say, he *was* a most skilled artist. He will have just discovered that his fingers will no longer bend nor will his wrists flex. He cannot hold a brush or pencil or even a wide stick of charcoal. Pity. His drawings had a most lively quality."

Winter was still seated on the ground, his tattered sketchpad in his lap. He let out a howl of anguish. Renni, standing beside him, placed a hand on his shoulder. She could see that he had drawn, on a torn and wrinkled page, a long-bladed knife and a hand ready to grasp its hilt. The knife looked very real, almost ready to leap off the page. She reached toward it but was distracted by Jerome's voice, bellowing as usual.

"Now," he called out, "We bring today's drama to a close, and like any good play, we need a dramatic conclusion that was hinted at in Act One."

Jerome pointed at Marta. "My dear. I require your little one, but don't be too upset. You'll soon join her, along with your dear husband, Simple Eddy."

Marta blanched and tightened her grip on Dreama. Ed clasped her arm. Jerome took a couple of strides toward them, stopped, and pointed at the infant. Dreama let out a loud wail as Marta's arms dropped away from her and Ed's hand lost its grip on Marta. Dreama was drawn through the air to Jerome's waiting hands.

"Now, for the finale. The wrongs done me require a blood payment. A large one. Already your leader lies dead." He pointed to Kyla's body with Veronica standing guard beside it. "She, however, did not die by my hand but through her own folly. I regret not having had the opportunity to slit her throat and watch her life's blood pour forth. She took that pleasure from me, but I will not be deprived of the pleasure of spilling other blood, beginning with that of this little one, whom I'm sparing from growing up to be part of the Community of Gifted Hypocrites."

He glanced over his shoulder to where Lore and Renni stood and Winter huddled on the ground. "Lore, you alone will be spared, but only if you aid me now. Bring me the knife our friend Winter has so kindly provided through his newfound talent."

Lore looked down at the paper on which Winter had made the very realistic charcoal drawing of a knife. Frowning, he reached down, and as his hand covered the hand in the sketch, the knife in the drawing acquired substance and appeared in his hand. His fingers closed around the hilt. He lifted the knife, gazed at it a moment, and then walked toward Jerome, who wore a big smile.

Jerome turned back to face the majority of the group, and addressing that audience, he announced, "You see, I can be pleased and appeased. Unfortunately, it is too late for all of you. Only Lore has—"

His words ended in a scream. Lore, coming up behind him, had plunged the knife deep into Jerome's back.

Veronica gasped along with all the rest at the sight of their enemy lying face down in the sand, blood seeping from a deep wound in his back. Standing over him holding a bloody knife, Lore wore an expression of triumph mixed with awe. He seemed as astonished as everyone else by what he'd done.

No one moved. It seemed to Veronica that time had frozen.

Renni moved first. She hurried to Lore, clapped him on the back, and said, "I guess you've redeemed yourself. I'm proud of you and I'd guess everyone else is, too."

Ed dashed to the fallen monster and picked up Dreama, who fortunately had not fallen beneath Jerome but had landed beside him in the soft sand and was kicking her feet and squalling. He handed Dreama off to Marta, who took the baby into her arms and examined her closely for any injury.

As though freed from stasis, the group began chattering and moving around, offering congratulations to Lore and expressing their relief at Jerome's defeat. They checked Petros, determined that he lived, and carefully placed him on his wheeled platform. Winnie went to Petros and attempted to heal him, but her power was gone. Abigail and Leah remained locked in their embrace unable to move. Apparently the stabbing had not undone the damage Jerome had wrought.

Veronica stayed where she was, beside Kyla, and gazed intently at the fallen enemy. She saw his fingers dig into the sand, his head move. He still lived!

Others saw it, too, and spread out away from him.

"Healer," his voice croaked. "I need a healer."

For a time no one moved. Then Veronica walked over to where he lay. "Have you forgotten that you took away our powers?" she asked scornfully.

He groaned. "Water, give me water."

"Have you also forgotten that you turned this land into a barren desert?" she asked. "But don't worry, you'll bleed to death before you can die of thirst."

"Heal me," he pled again.

"How can I? You took my healing power away."

"I'll give it back."

"Fine. Do that," she said. She needed to see whether in his weakened state he had enough power left to restore what he'd taken.

Marchion came to her side. "He didn't take my power to enhance," he said. "I can lend him strength. But should we?"

"We need the abilities he took from us," Veronica said. "And he needs to free Abigail and Leah from the spell he put on them."

"Water," Jerome moaned again.

"Restore our powers and Trille may be able to sing you a bit of water. But first she needs healing, so you'll have to restore my healing power. And you'll have to free Abigail and Leah, because as deep as your wound is, I can't heal it and Trille as well. We'll probably need Winnie, too."

He groaned and tried to push himself up, but could not. Veronica doubted that he could restore the abilities he had taken. Nevertheless, she persisted. "If you want water, and you want to be healed, you have to restore the gifts you took. All of them."

"Can't," he mumbled. "No strength."

"I guess you'll just have to lie there and die then," Veronica declared.

She turned to walk away. A sudden infusion of power stopped her. He'd done it! He'd restored her power to heal. But she wanted more.

"Now free Abigail and Leah," she ordered. "And restore all the gifts you took."

"I'm dying," he said, his voice weak. His eyes closed. Blood trickled from his mouth.

Fearing he'd lose consciousness at any moment, she made a decision. She bent down and placed a hand on his back, near the wound.

"I hope you know what you're doing," Renni said, coming to her side. "It took a lot of courage for Lore to do what he did. Don't undo it."

"I don't plan to," Veronica said. "He has to be strong enough to restore our powers." She pulled her hand away and nodded at Marchion. "Feed him a bit of power."

Marchion must have done so. Jerome's eyes opened. He glared at Veronica. "Finish the healing," he said, his former imperiousness returning to his voice.

"You finish undoing the damage you did," she said.

"No. I'll heal myself. I have enough power for that."

"Maybe, but you're not a healer," Veronica said, hoping she was right.

He fell silent for a time, and she waited. She looked around the group, sent a mental question: *Have any of you gotten your abilities back?*

The lack of response gave answer enough. She continued to wait.

Lore stood nearby with the knife. "If he does heal himself, I'm ready to stab him again."

"He'd be on guard against that. You wouldn't get the chance again," Renni said.

That was true. But at least Lore remained on their side of the struggle. Veronica didn't trust him, but he had every reason to fear Jerome's wrath.

After a little while longer Jerome spoke. "Tell Trille ... sing water ... Bring me water."

Veronica smiled. He hadn't succeeded in healing himself. Not at all, so far as she could tell. She called to Trille, and when the singer came, Veronica asked, "Is your power back?"

"Yes, but ..." Trille held up her badly burned arms. Her face, too, was red and blistered. "I'm in too much pain to sing," she said.

Veronica placed her hands on the woman's arms and absorbed her pain. Tears filled her eyes. She gritted her teeth and continued the healing, moving her hands to Trille's face.

"Let me help," Winnie said, joining Veronica and placing her hands on Trille.

In moments Trille's flesh was whole and unblemished. In moments more, the blisters that had raised on Veronica's and Winnie's arms and faces also vanished. The successful healing verified the return of their power. But not all the group had had their power restored.

Veronica walked around, checking. Abigail and Leah were still immobile. Winter still could not bend his fingers. Darnell remained in her wolf form though Gorvy urged her to try to change. Gorvy had no way of testing his ability to quench power. The professor confided with some embarrassment that he could not mindspeak and that he had tested his other gift, that of coercion, and found that missing as well. Marchion could not see auras, but his gift of enhancing was back.

While Veronica made her rounds, Winnie again knelt beside Petros and placed her hands on him. As Veronica reached them, Petros awoke and managed to sit upright on his platform. He was able to report that his power, if he had ever lost it, was back. His hearing was as acute as ever, and he was able to transfer his consciousness into Marchion, quickly withdrawing it as soon as he knew the transfer had been successful.

When her inventory was completed, Veronica went to Marta and reported her findings. "I guess you're in charge now that Aunt Kyla's dead," she told Marta, choking a bit as she spoke.

"No, Veronica," Marta said. "You're doing fine. And my powers haven't come back, nor have Ed's. See what you can do about that."

Veronica went back to Jerome. "All right, Trille will sing you some water, but you must complete the restorations. Until then you'll get no more than a swallow, and you'll be healed no further."

"I can't," Jerome mumbled. "So dry. No strength."

He could be faking. "You must do something to show your good faith. Give Winter back his gift and free Abigail and Leah. Then Trille will call water."

He shook his head, rolling it back and forth in the sand.

"Then, no water," Veronica stated firmly and turned to walk away.

"Wait," Jerome said. "I'll try."

"I'll check Winter," Renni told her and left to do that. After a brief wait she returned. "His hands are back to normal. He's already trying to find another usable page in the sketchpad."

"Good," Veronica said. "But Abigail and Leah still aren't freed. And Marta needs her power back. And Ed, and Professor Morence."

"My power's gone," Jerome said, the words coming out in a hoarse whisper. "I need water. Please."

It was that "please" that convinced Veronica that he wasn't feigning thirst and weakness. Jerome would never say *please* if he weren't truly desperate. "All right. I'll get you some water. But then you must finish giving back all the gifts you took."

Trille looked at her. "Must I?" she asked. "I can. My power is back. But I don't want to give him anything."

Veronica smiled. "It's all right, Trille. You don't have to."

"You lied?" Jerome's question came out as a high-pitched squeal.

"No," Veronica answered. "I have water for you. Just a moment."

She had dropped the pack she'd brought next to Kyla. She went to it, opened it, and removed the canteen of water she'd brought with her, smiling at the thought that she could have given him the water he'd begged for at any time.

She opened the canteen and put it to his lips. He drank greedily. When he finished, she said, "Now. Complete the restoration and I'll complete the healing."

Jerome looked up at her, wary, pleading. "Do you give your word?"

"I do. I swear by the Power-Giver."

He grimaced, whether in pain, in disgust, or in defeat, and said, "I'll have to accept that or die."

"That's right," Veronica said. "But I will keep my promise."

She drew Renni away ostensibly to help her survey the group and make certain Jerome kept his word. But when they had gone a considerable distance from Jerome, Veronica whispered, "How far back can you erase memories?"

"I don't know," Renni said. "The longest back I've ever taken them is three weeks." She didn't have to add that those had been Ed's memories, that she'd deprived him of the memory of the trip to Port-of-Lords, his first sight of the child who'd become his daughter, the excitement of the Naming-Day ceremony, the horror of having his newly named child abducted by his most dangerous enemy.

"We'll feed you all the power we can. I hope it will be enough. Now let's see if Jerome has kept his word."

"It might be easier if he was asleep while I did it," Renni suggested. "That would give me better access to his memories, even very old ones."

"Hmm, I wonder ... I think I know who might be able to arrange that. Let me see whether Professor Morence has his abilities back. You check with Marta and Ed." While Renni carried out that assigned task, Veronica headed for the professor.

He smiled as she approached, and his voice in her

head said, *I believe I can mindspeak again. Let me know if you receive my words.*

Perfectly clear, Professor, she sent back. *How about your gift of coercion?*

I haven't been able to test that, he sent, his smile turning to a frown.

She stood beside him and spoke softly, judging that oral speech was safer. Jerome might be able to receive the mindspeech. "I have a way for you to test it, but it depends. Can you coerce someone into going to sleep? Jerome is already weak. Could you nudge him into a deep sleep?"

"I've never used coercion in that way." He paused, then added, "But I don't see why I couldn't."

"Good. As soon as we know that everybody's talents have been restored, I'll give you a signal—I'll nod my head twice. We'll have to hope it works."

"So you don't really intend to keep your word to him?" The professor looked relieved.

"I will do as I promised," Veronica said. "I swore by the Power-Giver. I won't break that vow."

"He'll be a danger to all of us again when he's healed," the professor pointed out as if she wouldn't have understood that. "You're risking all our lives because of a vow you shouldn't have made."

"I know what I'm doing, Professor Morence. Just do your part, please. If all goes well, we'll be safe."

"*If* it goes well," he responded, his voice laden with skepticism.

"Just do what I've asked," she snapped and walked away from him. He was treating her like a child. She might be young, but she had far more experience with power than he had. She rejoined Renni, who reported that all those she'd checked with had regained their powers. "Good. Let's try this."

She and Renni walked back to Jerome. "Well, Mr. Esterville, you've carried out your end of the agreement, so I'm ready to carry out mine."

Abigail marched up to her. "Veronica, don't you dare heal him," she said in her stern "teacher voice." You know perfectly well what a monster he is."

"Aunt Abigail, I've given my word. I even swore by the Power-Giver."

"The Power-Giver will understand. You cannot, must not heal that fiend. Let him die!" Abigail grabbed Veronica's arm and tried to pull her away.

Veronica shoved Abigail, breaking her hold.

"You obey me, you little brat," Abigail shouted, grabbing hold of her again.

Jerome groaned.

Marta ran up to them. "Abigail, let Veronica go. She's not a child anymore."

"She's acting like one," Abigail declared, tugging at Veronica.

"So are you," Veronica said.

Winnie placed a hand on Veronica and another on Abigail. Veronica felt her calming influence, but Abigail gave no sign of being affected.

"Do you want to lose Dreama again?" she demanded of Marta. "For good? Talk some sense into the child."

Leah came up behind Abigail. "Abby," she said, "calm down. Let Veronica do what she must."

Releasing Veronica, Abigail whirled to confront Leah. "Are you, even you, taking her part? Do you want to be made into a statue again?"

"No, I don't. But screaming at Veronica isn't going to help." She placed her hands on Abigail's shoulders. "Come, Abby. Trust the Power-Giver."

Veronica had never heard Leah speak much of the

Power-Giver. She had wondered whether Leah, not being gifted, even believed in him. That doubt vanished.

"Yes, Aunt Abigail, please trust the Power-Giver to take care of us."

"He hasn't been doing a very good job of that," Abigail huffed. But she let Leah guide her away from Veronica.

At last she could finish this.

Isham barreled toward them shouting, "You're all mad. All you witches! You all deserve to die!"

He must have been too frightened to do more than observe until Abigail's irrational outburst gave him courage. Clearly his madness had not abated.

Ed, Marchion, and Gorvy rushed to grab and subdue him. He fought wildly. They could hardly hold him. Veronica despaired of ever being able to carry out her plan.

Renni slipped away from Veronica. Moments later Isham fell still and silent. Though conscious, he hung limp in Ed and Gorvy's arms, while Marchion, wearing a puzzled look, helped to support him. Renni returned to Veronica's side. Veronica met her gaze and Renni mouthed the name, *Winter.*

Veronica nodded twice. "Now," she said to Jerome, "I'll heal you as I promised."

He gave a weak sigh, blinked, and his eyelids drifted shut.

"Now," Veronica whispered to Renni. Then she sent out a general call. *Everyone, send power to Renni.*

Marta, her gaze sweeping around the entire group, nodded.

Renni's eyes closed and her brow furrowed in concentration. The entire group fell silent, waiting, though they couldn't know what was going on. Probably some guessed. Looking around, Veronica saw that Ed stared intently at Renni, no doubt recalling what she'd done to his memories.

Time passed. Dreama began crying. Her cries grew louder, more insistent. How long had it been since she'd been fed? And changed? They had to end this soon. She restrained the urge to beg Renni to hurry.

At last Renni opened her eyes. "It's done," she said. "It's safe to heal him now."

The healing was the easy part. Though she was exhausted, Veronica retained enough power to complete what she had started earlier. Breathing a word of thanks to the Power-Giver, she set herself to the task, absorbed the pain and weakness, and felt health and strength flow through Jerome's body.

When she'd finished, she needed Renni's help to rise to her feet. "Let him wake now," she said to Professor Morence.

Jerome's eyes opened. He sat up, looked around. His face registered bewilderment. And fear. "Mama?" he called out in a plaintive, childish voice. "Where's my mama?"

CHAPTER TWENTY-FOUR
A MEETING OF THE GIFTED

Once again the entire Community had gathered in the small sitting room of the house that had been Kyla's and now had passed to Marta and Ed along with the leadership of the Community.

Marta relaxed in a wing chair, Dreama gurgling happily in her arms. Veronica relaxed too, as Ed, having just returned, addressed the gathering.

"I'm pleased to report that Jerome Esterville, whose memories were successfully regressed to the age of three by the very accomplished Renni Natches, has been safely delivered to his mother, the esteemed Mother Esterville. With Mother Esterville's careful guidance, as his mind catches up to his actual age, his attitudes, goals, and beliefs will be those of a decent person, not a cruel and callous one"

Renni reddened and looked embarrassed but also proud. "I guess you don't know what you can do until you're willing to try," she said.

Veronica giggled at the formality of Ed's announcement. He regarded her, his eyes twinkling. "We're happy that Veronica challenged you to try," he said to Renni.

Smiling at both girls, he continued his official report. "To those of us privileged to know Mother Esterville, this was the perfect solution to the thorny problem of what to do with our enemy. For those of you who have not had the privilege of her acquaintance, I will say that she accepted what was done to her son with complete understanding. She has added the Power-Giver to those deities to whom she has constructed altars in her attic, and she prays to him daily along with all the other provincial patron gods, as well as the great gods Dor and Dora."

Veronica snorted.

Marta said, "Don't make fun of her devotion. It is wholly sincere, and she is a good woman, perhaps the best I've ever encountered."

Ed nodded. "Mother Esterville attributes to the Power-Giver the opportunity to have a second chance to raise her son right. She promises not to neglect his training and vows that the new memories he develops will be happy ones, filled with the experience of her loving attention and patient training in ethical behavior. I'm confident that Jerome will never again be a threat to us or to anyone."

Some in the group looked doubtful, but Leah spoke up from her seat beside Abigail. "I know some of you are skeptical, but that is because you don't know Jerome's mother. If she dedicates herself to her son as in the past she's dedicated herself to serving the gods, I'm sure he'll turn out well."

"I agree," Marta put in. "Most importantly, he is no longer gifted. His power has been taken from him permanently, as have his memories of having it. So he won't miss it and with his mother's guidance, he'll lead a normal and fulfilling life without it."

Marta waited while the group applauded, then resumed speaking. "Unfortunately, we had no such satisfactory solution for Isham Tellent. We could have erased his memories of the time he spent in what had been and is again Ed's land, but that would still have left him angry and determined on vengeance. His experiences in what was then Jerome's land left him completely deranged. Whether he will ever recover his sanity we cannot know, but as long as he remains in his present state he will be confined in the Garden of Tranquility maintained by the priests of Ondin for those whose mental condition does not allow them to live in normal society. He will be well cared for there and kept calm, if necessary, with the herbal remedies employed by the keepers. We are grateful to the Honorable Camsen Wellner for arranging that care."

"What about his little boy?" Zauna asked.

"Little Bennie will be raised by his aunt and uncle," Marta replied. "The aunt is Mayzie's sister, and is quite fond of the boy. Fortunately, he's too young to have any understanding of what happened to his mother and father."

Veronica was growing impatient. She had important news to share, and Marta was dealing with everything else, though she *knew* how vital Veronica's news was. Marta droned on. She mentioned that Ed would visit his land from time to time to restore it to its former beauty. She praised Winter for the help his newly discovered talent had been in their victory over Jerome and encouraged him to continue his art studies.

"I will," he assured her with a shy smile. "And I've learned to shield. I had to in that place."

Trille rose to her feet and waited for Marta's nod, giving her permission to speak. "You and Ed will be staying here then? And leading the Community?" she asked.

"Our home is still in Sharpness," Marta said and lifted her hand, signaling for the groans that followed that statement to subside. "We've written to the people caring for our house and Ed's horses in our absence and told them that we won't be returning for some time. We'll stay until Dreama is weaned and until the Community can select another leader. That will take at least a year, possibly two."

Her announcement elicited cheers and declarations of gratitude.

Veronica bounced around in her seat, increasingly impatient. Marta looked her way. It must be time at last.

But Aunt Abigail cleared her throat and said, "I have something I'd like to say."

And Marta said, "Of course, Abigail. Go ahead."

"I want to apologize to Veronica. I behaved abominably toward her." Meeting Veronica's gaze, she said, "I'm sorry I treated you like a child and tried to prevent you from carrying out your plan. I should have trusted you. It isn't easy for me to say this, but you were right. I was the one acting like a child. I was just so afraid of Jerome."

She began to cry. Leah patted her on the shoulder. Veronica rose, went to her, and said, "We were all afraid of Jerome, Aunt Abigail." She kissed her honorary aunt on the cheek.

Still blubbering, Abigail returned her kiss.

And then, finally, Marta said, "Thank you both. And now, Veronica has some very important news to share with the group."

Veronica stood and walked to the center of the room. She turned slowly, eyeing the entire group before speaking. "After everyone else returned from Ed's land, I stayed behind to meet someone," she said. "I was directed to do so by a voice that spoke in my mind. It wasn't the Power-Giver. Five years ago Ed heard that voice, the voice of the Dire Lord called

Claid." She paused, letting the excited murmurs die away before continuing. "Ed met him in the ruined building near where you, Lore, first met Jerome."

Lore hung his head, clearly uncomfortable at being reminded of that meeting.

"Lord Claid told me that, and lots of other things," Veronica continued, deliberately tantalizing her audience with the hint of knowledge that she wasn't going to share with them.

"But here's what's important." She paused again, letting anticipation build before her great announcement. "It was Lord Claid who caught Aunt Kyla away after she created the sandstorm that smothered those of us Jerome had struck unconscious. He told her what she had to do to bring us all back to life. But she could choose whether or not to do it. He told her what the outcome would be. Because she'd lost her temper and let the sandstorm get out of hand, and therefore she was responsible for the deaths of all of us it buried, she said she owed us our lives and would gladly give hers in exchange."

Again she paused, this time not for effect but to get her emotions under control. When she could continue, she said, "Now the big news is that Aunt Kyla isn't dead. Not entirely, anyway."

That brought outcries of joy and relief and a lot of chattering. She raised her hand, calling for quiet.

"I don't mean that you'll see her alive again," she continued, and waited until the disappointed groans subsided. "At least, I don't think you will. She's in a state of suspension and can remain that way for a long time, seeming dead to anyone who sees her. I don't really understand why Lord Claid is doing this, but he swore he had a good reason. 'You'll understand some day,' he said.

"Now I'm to convey his orders to you. Kyla is to be placed in a special coffin. He's given me the directions for its construction. And she's to be taken to a place called Hillcross. It's the site of a powerful nexus. That's a point where our world and other worlds intersect. You could even reach the Dire Realms from there. It's in the mountains in Northwoods Province, just north of Inland Province, a short distance from the headwaters of the Soileau River."

Marta, who'd been apprised of all this ahead of time, while they waited for Ed's return from taking Jerome to Carey, distributed maps showing the location Veronica described.

"At Hillcross in a mountainside, there's a cave that is precisely over the nexus I told you of. That's where you're to place Aunt Kyla's coffin. Then you're to seal the cave and in front of it you're to build a shrine to Aunt Kyla—to the Lady Kyla, as Lord Claid said."

Ed interrupted to say, "That sounds like he means for her to be there, in what you called 'suspension,' for a very long time."

Veronica bit her lower lip and hesitated before answering. "I think he does expect it to be a long time. But he promised me that I'd see her alive again in my lifetime." She paused again and then added, "He did say I should expect to have an unusually long life."

Abigail frowned, looking skeptical. Some of the others just shook their heads. But Renni and Lore were both watching her intently, and Renni raised her hand. Veronica nodded permission to speak.

"Are we all—all of us—" She made a sweeping motion with her hand to encompass the roomful of people, "supposed to go on this journey?" She looked at the map Marta had given her and traced the route with her finger. "It's a long way."

"Yes, it is a long way, but you can take a train as far as Harnor, which is a port on the Soileau River, and then take a boat upstream as far as Highport, and from there it's just a short trek north to Hillcross. There's a road. Or another way would be to take the train only as far as Marquez, then rent a horse and wagon and go northeast to Pescatil in the northeastern corner of Wide Sands Province, and from there a mining road runs due east to Hillcross."

"Hillcross is what? A village?" Darnell asked. "It looks awfully isolated."

"It's small," Veronica agreed. "But it's big enough to be on the map."

"You didn't answer my question about who's to make this trip," Renni called out. "All of us?"

"No, the Lord Claid said only four should go. We'll need volunteers. Those who go should expect to be gone for several months, maybe even a year or more."

"Why can't Ed or Lore or you or someone use power to transport them there?"

"The distance is too great, and none of us with that talent has seen Hillcross and could visualize it."

The room was quiet for several minutes as they all looked at one another. Then Lore spoke. "I volunteer. I owe it to the group and to Lady Kyla to make up for what an ass I was, believing that bastard Jerome. Excuse my language."

Everyone laughed at that. Renni's hand went up. "I'll go," she said. "I'm up for some adventure. Oh, and don't worry, Veronica. Before I leave I'll teach you to milk the goat."

Again laughter rippled through the room.

"Good," Marta said. "Now we just need two more. Ed and I can't go. We have Dreama to take care of. Trille has her singing career."

"And Winter has his art classes," Veronica supplied. She made a face and added, "And I have to go to school."

"I wouldn't be much help," Petros put in from his seat on his wheeled platform.

"I wouldn't want to be away from my grandchildren that long," Winnie said.

Winter raised his hand, drawing gasps of surprise. He shook his head frantically and blushed a deep red. "I wasn't volunteering," he said. "I just ... I have something I want to ... I mean, I'd like to have taken to put in, uh, the place where her coffin will be left. It's a painting. A-a portrait of Lady Kyla. A large one. But," he added hastily, "it's painted on a canvas that can be rolled up. It wouldn't take up much room."

"That's very generous and thoughtful of you, Winter," Marta said, searching for the right words before adding, "We don't know exactly what sort of place Kyla's last resting place will be, but surely your portrait of her would be a welcome addition to it."

Murmurs of approval that followed carried an undertone of doubt until Veronica stood up. "I think that's a wonderful idea, Winter. You've shown what a gifted artist you are, and who knows? Your portrait could even hold the power that will restore Aunt Kyla to life. So thank you." She began to applaud, and others joined in.

Winter, still blushing furiously, shook his head, and said so softly that Marta suspected few heard him, "It's only a painting."

"We'll be happy to have it, whether or not it holds power," Marta assured him. "And in fact, I'll add another to it. Kyla showed me one you did secretly for her of the Mage Alair, our Power-Giver, based on her description of him. She said you and she both agreed it was to be for her alone, and no one else would know about it, but I think it would be fitting to send it as well."

"She wanted it as a reminder to her of the man he had been," Winter said, his red face paling to white. "She didn't want it seen because she didn't want people to focus on his humanity."

"I did see it once," Veronica exclaimed. "She wouldn't tell me who it was. but I suspected it was Alair. It's a powerful work."

"But if Kyla didn't want it shown ..." Marchion left his objection unfinished except for a shrug.

"Perhaps we should defer that discussion until later," Ed put in. "I personally can't see the harm in sending it. But we've gotten far from the business at hand. We still need two more volunteers."

"That's right," Marta said, bestowing a grateful smile on her husband. "Unless two more of you are willing to go, there won't be an expedition at all."

After a short silence in which the gathered members looked around at one another, Camsen Wellner stood up. "I volunteer," he said, drawing gasps of astonishment. "I've decided to withdraw from the priesthood. This experience has made me comprehend that my first obligation is to the Power-Giver."

The group burst into applause. Marta gave Veronica a questioning look, and Veronica nodded.

"So we need only one more," Marta said.

"I'll go," said Zauna. "Without my crystal ball, I have no way of earning a living here. Except—how are we to finance this trip?"

Veronica shook her head. Lord Claid hadn't mentioned the cost. And such a trip would be expensive. She should have thought of that.

Marchion Blandry stood. "I can't go. I have my business interests here. But I'm a wealthy man. I can finance the trip."

"So we have our four volunteers and the way to finance it," Veronica stated. "Now what about the paintings? Let's take a vote. I move we send them both. All in favor, raise your hands." She raised hers as she spoke.

Winter raised his, and one after another, some quickly, others hesitantly, hand after hand lifted. There were no negative votes.

"So the paintings go, and with that we've concluded our business," Marta said. "I think it's time to celebrate."

The group greeted her suggestion with cheers. Veronica cheered louder than all the rest.

THE END

Turn the page for an excerpt from
Deniably Dead
the sequel to *Bringers of Magic.*

DENIABLY DEAD

CHAPTER ONE
A ROUGH RIDE

Renni shifted about, trying to arrange herself more comfortably, a nearly impossible feat in the narrow space left to her on the wagon's rough floor boards. Not to mention having to share space with three other people and a coffin.

She kept reminding herself that she just had to get through this night. Tomorrow they would reach Marquez, where they could stay in an inn. She'd still have to share a room with Zauna and endure the older woman's loud snoring, but at least they would have separate beds. With more space between them and a soft mattress to lie on, she should find it easier to sleep.

This was the sixth night since they'd left Port-of-Lords, and sleeping grew more difficult with each night. Her companions' snores, Zauna's especially, were only part of the problem. Sleeping so close to the coffin that she often reached out in her sleep and touched its wooden side grew creepier with each passing hour. No odor issued from the coffin, for which she should have been grateful. A decaying body would give off an odor strong enough to escape from this specially built coffin. Its lid was tightly sealed, but on the top a metal faceplate hid the face from view but was pierced with many small air holes that not only let air flow in but would also allow odor to escape. No odor meant no decay, Renni figured. And so, she asked herself, was the coffin's occupant dead or alive?

She'd seen and touched the body of Kyla Cren, the former leader of the Port-of-Lords Gifted Community, before they'd placed her in the coffin. The cold flesh and corpselike pallor along with no discernible breathing all told Renni that Kyla was dead. Yet Veronica, Kyla's fourteen-year-old ward, insisted that her honorary aunt still lived, at least in some sense. Veronica had provided the specifications for making the coffin and had sworn that those specifications and the instructions for transporting Kyla's body to a place no one in their Gifted Community had heard of had been delivered to her by a Dire Lord.

Renni had begun to reconsider the wisdom of having joined three other members of the Community in volunteering to follow those instructions. They had, after all, acted on the word of a fourteen-year-old girl. A girl known to be excitable and moody. Yet at the time everyone accepted Veronica's words as true, her instructions as the mandates of a Dire Lord and not to be disregarded.

The first two nights, when they slept comfortably in inns, Renni thought the trip a lark, a marvelous adventure. Then their road took them into a desert area, stifling hot during the day, cold at night, and without inns where they could enjoy a good supper, a fortifying breakfast, and a restful sleep between. That this would occur they knew from the outset, but Renni had discovered the difference between *knowing* and *experiencing*. Now eight days into the journey, doubts grew daily and more questions crept into Renni's mind with each passing night.

If it had not been for the absence of any odor emanating from the coffin, Renni would have persuaded, or at least tried to persuade, her companions to turn back and forget this quixotic venture. She could convince Lore, she felt certain. Like her, he'd set out with the notion that they were embarking on a grand adventure. Just two years younger than her own age of twenty-five, he did not consider her in any way his superior, but at the same time, he was easily swayed by the opinion of others and would more readily defer to her judgment than that of their much older companions.

Mulling all this over instead of getting the sleep she needed, she would have tossed and turned, had there been room to do so. In her cramped space she could only grind her teeth and consider the fact that most of their journey remained in front of them. Marquez would offer them only a brief respite, even if they stretched their stay there into three or four days to get much needed rest and to allow Zauna to shop for a new crystal ball. Zauna's gift was seeing both present but distant and future events in a crystal ball, but hers had been broken, and for her this trip was above all an opportunity to find and purchase a new one as well as the only way she could make herself useful without her crystal ball.

The wealthy merchant who was generously financing their trip would not be pleased to see them return to Port-of-Lords without achieving their goal. That consideration as much as anything else kept them going. The others must have doubts just as Renni had, although they hadn't expressed those doubts to her any more than she'd expressed hers to them. Maybe it would help to discuss frankly the difficulty of the trip and the doubts about its purpose. Or maybe it would make everything worse. Renni couldn't decide.

She longed to stretch or turn over or something, but every movement made the wagon creak, and if she could turn over, she'd be face to face with Zauna, breathing in the old woman's rancid breath. She could do nothing but clench her fists and wish for morning.

Zauna let out a spectacularly loud snore that ended in an equally loud snort, followed by rustling and a mumbled, "Whassa matter?"

Renni lay quietly, not answering.

"I know you're awake," Zauna persisted maddeningly. "What's wrong?"

"Nothing," Renni said shortly. "I just woke up and I'm trying to get back to sleep."

"No, I sensed something. Is Kyla all right?"

"Oh, for—No, she's dead, or something near it, and safely sealed in her coffin. You must have been dreaming."

The wagon's floorboards creaked and from the other side of the coffin came Lore's sleepy grumble. "Can't you hens be quiet? It's the middle of the night. Save the chatter for morning."

"It was more than a dream," Zauna harrumphed. "I sensed danger. Strongly. If I had my crystal ball it would show me the danger, but without it—"

"Oh, by all the gods, woman, will you stop harping about that crystal ball and let us all go back to sleep!" Lore's patience, limited at best, had grown increasingly short the past couple of days.

"You don't have to be so cross with me. These presentiments I have may not be specific, but they are real. You'd be foolish to discount them."

"Both of you, be quiet," Renni whispered. "You'll wake Camsen. If you haven't already."

"Somebody ought to get up and check outside around the wagon," Zauna insisted.

"Do it yourself," Lore shot back. "You're the one that's worried."

"Zauna, we're out in the middle of nowhere," Renni said softly in an attempt at reasonableness. "I've been awake for some time, and I haven't heard a sound outside. I'm sure you just had a bad dream."

"No. Even if I dreamed the warning, it meant something. Something serious either is happening or will happen soon. I know it. Listen! I think I heard something just now."

"I didn't hear anything at all," Renni said, making no effort to keep her disgust from registering in her voice.

"There's no way *I* could hear anything, with you two yammering like that," Lore sounded even grumpier.

"Someone ought to go outside and check," Zauna insisted.

Renni silently cursed the woman's stubbornness. Aloud she said, "It's too dark to see anything out there. We'd just be wasting what little time we have left for sleeping."

"Well, I can't go back to sleep without knowing," Zauna declared, sitting up.

"I'll go and check," came the offer in Camsen Wellner's deep and now sleepy voice. "We're all awake, and there'll be no getting any more sleep unless we relieve Zauna's fears."

With much creaking of the wagon a shadowy figure rose, pulled open the canvas flaps and leaped down.

"Well, you've done it now, Zauna," Lore grumped. "We're all wide awake, and for what?"

Camsen's footsteps could be heard circling the wagon. They paused at the sound of snorts and a whinny.

"Oh, wonderful! Now even the horses are awake."

Camsen must have paused in his circuit to calm the horses. They settled down, and his footsteps resumed their march. If a person or an animal had come near the wagon, Camsen's stomping about would obliterate their footprints or tracks, so now they'd never know whether Zauna's dream held any real substance.

Renni might have expressed that gloomy thought, but at that moment the canvas flaps opened once more, and the gap revealed a ghostly figure illuminated by moonlight. Zauna let out a loud gasp, and Renni forced back the scream that fought to pass her lips.

A NOTE FROM THE AUTHOR

Dear Reader, I hope you've enjoyed this book, but whatever you felt about it, I ask you to consider leaving a review on Amazon and possibly on Goodreads as well. State honestly what you thought about it: parts you enjoyed, or ways in which you found it lacking. Your comments help me become a better writer, and reviews help to sell books.

I also invite you to like my Facebook Author page:
https://www.facebook.com/ERoseSabinsBooks/
and to visit my web page,
https://erosesabin.com, where if you like you can sign up to receive my newsletter.